To Astera, With Love

Amanda Ross

A New World Order:
Restoration Is Death for Us All

By Freddie Karr

The staff here at *Jonquil* conducted a poll and the consensus was clear: 2021 was trash. It was the year that gave us Lil' Freak Nick, a middle-class white rapper from the hardened streets of Saginaw, spiders with tails and the world's first (known) Vampire for President. We Americans have been through a lot this last decade with the recession and the resurgence of the culture vulture Crispin sisters. But since the universe is a bitch and is constantly urging us to hold its beer, the man taking up residence at 1600 Pennsylvania Avenue is undead.

When President Harvey Vael—native Virginian and Republican iconoclast—announced his plans to run for our nation's highest office, the nation was torn: Vael was relatively new to his office but he'd already established himself as a man with values that call back to the good ol' days before women had the vote and us black people were sold at auction to the highest bidder. Polls completed after Vael announced his candidacy, however, showed a strong following for the senator with favorability ratings in the high 50's.

For many Americans, Vael's rise in fame was easy to ignore at first. Here was another pasty-white man with a vague southern accent and a lifetime of privilege throwing his hat in the ring for president. It wasn't until the first debate that Vael dropped a bomb of the highest order: that he, and many others in the upper echelons of American society, were vampires. It was laughable at first—this Nosferatu-sounding motherfucker, a vampire? But Vael quickly showed his true fangs when his campaign manager, Cullen Johansen, filmed an Instagram story of Vael feeding on and turning another member of his campaign team. Twitter literally seemed to blow up with responses. Black Twitter responded with a collective 'what's good?' and the whites lost their damn minds.

But instead of Vael being removed from office, or from the presidential race, his momentum grew and so did his following. Vael's admission of his "true nature" was called the Awakening. Many journalists, including the undead-looking but supposedly alive Cordelia Edwards, opined about Vael's bravery to live his truth. Vael truly inspired his constituents, many of whom were actual vampires themselves. Suddenly, people across the nation from Portland, Maine to Galveston, Texas to Vancouver, Washington were having their own Awakenings. For weeks, my social feeds were flooded with videos of people coming out of the coffin.

And it wasn't just the plebs. It was celebrities, like Veni Vedi Amavi singer Masha Oakwood (though with a name like that who didn't pick up on her Carmilla-like nature before this), actor Vincent Marshall and podcaster Larkin Margerella. Even senators and journalists and thought-leaders Awakened, leaving half the country in support of their differences and the other half scared as hell.

We took this all in stride—until Vael swatted aside every one of his opponents like cheap, silver-plated dollar store crosses and ascended to the White House. He contracted a company who specialized in vampire-proofing homes (which blows my mind that this is an actual thing) to install v-glass in the West Wing.

Within his first month, the violence he only hinted at became real. He reminded people of his campaign slogan constantly: restore. He intended to restore America to its former glory, and that would be done by allowing his people to have a coffin in the room. Vampires everywhere were impassioned by his speeches and his thoughts and his endless Facebook and Instagram videos, which he recorded at all hours of the night because, *vampire*. But most importantly, they began to see people less like comrades and more like dinner. Current polling has vampire attacks sitting at a solid

30% increase over the last year. And that number is higher among another group of people who had their own #glowup this year: witches.

According to my sources, witches have always been around, having retreated underground after a little thing called the Salem Witch Trials. Their distrust of humans was well-founded, but nowhere was their acrimony more well-placed than with the vampire community, whose members actually helmed the Trials and have led every other literal and figurative witch hunt throughout America's history. Witches and vampires get along like oil and water and when either one enters into a crowd of their nemesis, they stick out like white girls with cornrows.

But since the creature in the White House is a vampire, he and his cabinet have consistently turned a blind eye to the plight of the witch community. Despite the rumors of peace talks between President Vael and the head of the Witch Council, the indomitable Oliana Murtaza, there seems to be little end in sight for the witches and their supporters who have been bitten, abused and burned at makeshift crosses at the hands of vampires.

President Vael has been in office for a year, and that means his State of the Union is imminent. Will he spend time bloviating about his (failed) foreign policy, his (egregious) treatment of the disaster and cleanup of Hurricane Jericho off the coast of his own home state, or will he finally address the Fright Night creature in the room: that his version of restoration means the desolation of humans and witches alike.

Chapter 1

Mercury wished he lived in another decade. He wished he lived in the '80s and that he was break dancing on a pad of cardboard, boom box on high and middle finger in the air, shouting "Fuck the police." Or that it was the '90s and he was in Long Beach, drinking brass monkey and listening to 'Pac. Or that he lived in Oakland in the early aughts, ghost riding and beating out to E-40.

But instead, Mercury was 21, and it was 2022. He watched the news as actor Regan Phipps lied on the Hollywood Walk of Fame, dead from a vampire bite. The hot reporter on channel 11 stood at the corner of Hollywood and Vine interviewing witnesses.

"He was accepting his star on the Walk of Fame," reported the head of the Hollywood Chamber of Commerce. "During his speech, we heard someone shout 'restore' and then they tackled Regan. His throat was ripped out before we could do anything."

Mercury's stomach turned. It'd been a few months since a vampire attack happened in Los Angeles. The last time there was an attack, two humans and ten witches —*his people*— were killed. He took a long sip of coffee then slid his jean jacket on.

He looked over his shoulder, glancing at the back of the jacket in the mirror. It bore the symbol for air, the element from which he drew his magic. Most witches wore something to signify their element, but it was usually with subtlety. To Mercury, this was cowardly bullshit. Vampires and their allies boldly displayed their distaste for witches, so why should witches be coy?

He patted his back once then turned to face his desk. Lifting his hand, he gestured toward his backpack and it floated to him. His slid it over his shoulder just as his roommate walked in.

"You believe this shit?" Oliver said, nodding at the television. He inched closer and Mercury stepped back to avoid his roommate's large belly and the overwhelming smell of stale beer and chili. "They're blaming that man for killing that shitty-ass actor but he was the one egging him on, he and all those harridans."

"Yeah, it's crazy," Mercury said. He knew better than to call his roommate out and tell him his dumb-ass opinion was factually incorrect. Oliver wasn't an avowed dhampir, someone who supported vampires. In Mercury's opinion, he was too stupid to formulate an authentic thought. He just took whatever he read on *The Vanguard* and heard on the radio as gospel. Though Oliver wasn't the sharpest tool, and he was most certainly a tool, Mercury wasn't an idiot. He may be militant, and he may have magic, but he knew there was no way he'd come out of a fight with Oliver, a grass-fed good ol' boy, with all his teeth intact.

So he kept his mouth shut and tried to ignore Oliver and his friends and their wrong opinions.

"Well, I'm gonna be late for work. Later," Mercury said. He stepped out of the room, closed the door and sighed.

His stomach was in knots and Oliver's presence wasn't exactly comforting. He took several deep breaths as he walked down the hallway toward the stairwell, a sudden pressure growing behind his right eye.

After waving to some of the business owners along the strip, he stepped into the Iron Bird, the tattoo shop his father and brother, Troian, co-owned. Mercury apprenticed under Troian and he handled client consultations and touch-ups, which was just fine by him. He was bound to the shop by birth, memorizing every tattoo that lined the walls, but being a tattoo artist wasn't his ideal career. He desired something of his own.

"What up, Merc?" Troian said. Mercury nodded at his older brother, who leaned over the midsection of a white woman with dreadlocks.

"Blessed be, Mercury," the woman said, her gapped-tooth smile infectious.

"Hey, Libra," Mercury replied. "Getting a magical boost I see. That's okay; we all know Water is the weakest element."

Libra narrowed her eyes and flicked her fingers at him; Mercury shifted to dodge the large clump of ice she lobbed at him.

"You know I'm only joking," he replied, laughing.

"You better be."

"Got any more of those cocaine brownies you were selling?" Mercury asked. He hung his backpack on the hook beside the stairs that led to his father's apartment.

Troian scoffed and adjusted his glasses. "You're not getting one anyway. Remember the last time you had one? You stayed up for three days straight and nearly failed your midterms."

"Yo, why you gotta be a buzzkill?" Mercury replied, incensed that his brother would bring up such an embarrassing fact in front of the whole shop.

Troian laughed and slipped his face mask back on. The buzz of the tattoo gun signaled to Mercury it was time to move on. He walked up the stairs to his father's apartment and stepped inside.

Atlas Amell was a creature of habit and on a Saturday morning, that habit was sitting half-naked on his windowsill sipping coffee and people watching.

"You know, you're about two years away from being that creepy old man ogling young chicks and yelling at kids to get off his lawn," Mercury teased. His father clucked his tongue.

"You know what they say, black don't crack. And witches are slower to age, too. What'll it be then . . . mage don't age?" Atlas said.

Mercury groaned and set his bag down. He walked over to his father and kissed his forehead then strode into the kitchen. Mercury smiled. It was also his father's habit to brew Mercury a latte and leave it on the counter. He picked up the mug and faced his father.

"So, how're things?"

Atlas shrugged. "I'm well and business is good. Troian is good, getting more clients for us all the time. He's so savvy with all of the social media and digital marketing shit."

Mercury sipped his coffee and pretended that his father's praise of his brother didn't sting, like always.

"And I'm just looking at the world in wonder," Mercury's father continued. "When I was your age, the only thing I had to worry about was being a black man in the mid-'80s, never mind being a witch and all the inter-magic conflict. Now, I'm watching my sons grow up in a world where they might be burned at the stake."

Mercury's stomach churned. "I heard that Oliana is planning to meet with Vael to talk about a peace treaty or something."

Atlas sighed. "Yes, I've heard that, too."

"You don't think she'll do anything? Don't you have any faith in your sister-in-law?"

"It has nothing to do with Oliana or my faith in her," Atlas shrugged on a button up shirt. He pulled out his suitcase and set it on the bed. He turned toward his closet and grabbed suits and button up shirts and pants with perfect pleats. "There are other things at play here, other factions in the Council that might work to ensure things stay as they are."

"Yeah, but she's also the head of The Witches' Council. I know she can change things."

"Mercury—"

"She's supposed to talk to him at Astera, right? Maybe you can talk to her before she meets with him."

"Mercury—"

The sound of a creaking floorboard made Atlas pause. They both looked up to see a petite Latina with Princess Leia buns and a vape pen in her hand. She took a long puff and expelled a cloud of smoke. It smelled like pineapple.

"Sloane," Atlas said. His voice was friendly but stern.

"My bad, Mr. A. There's someone here to see Merc."

"A customer?"

Sloane shrugged. "It's some tall white boy wearing a beanie even though it's like 80 degrees outside."

Atlas and Mercury looked at each other. Mercury then groaned and followed Sloane down the stairs. Leaning against the receptionist desk stood a lithe man wearing the standard hipster uniform of striped beanie, tight jeans, an ironic t-shirt and loafers.

"Ellis," Mercury said, his voice measured.

He could see Troian's distaste radiating off of him as he gazed up at Ellis. Ellis stepped toward Mercury and extended his hand, waiting for a fist bump. Mercury smiled quickly and fist bumped him, then crossed his arms over his body. "What's up?"

"Well, I was just in the neighborhood and thought I'd swing by."

Mercury scowled. His father had owned the Iron Bird for as long as Mercury could remember and in that time, Ellis had only visited a handful of times.

"In the neighborhood? You look like you got lost on your way home from Rodeo Drive," Sloane said.

Ellis glanced at her then turned back to Mercury.

"No one hangs out on Rodeo Drive anymore, honey. That's for poor people," Ellis called over his shoulder.

Sloane pursed her lips and crossed her arms.

Mercury shook his head and pulled Ellis away from the reception desk. "Ellis, you're never just in the neighborhood."

"What's that supposed to mean?" he replied, placing a hand on his chest in mock offense.

Mercury cocked his head. "Really? That's what we're doing now?"

After a few moments of silence, Mercury rolled his eyes. "You aren't exactly the kind of friend who just stops by. There's always a reason– either you need something or you want to show off."

"Well, damn. You don't have to drag me just because you're cranky today."

"Ellis," Mercury warned. It was only noon and already he was tired of the day.

"Fine. I came by to see if you wanted to roll with me to the Delta Zeta Chi party tonight."

Mercury frowned. He typically avoided frat parties. Found the frat bros to be douches and the girls to be obnoxious white girls with a fetish for black men. He'd never known Ellis to enjoy going to frat parties either.

10

"Why?"

Ellis lifted his brows.

"Because you're my friend, of course," Ellis said, though his voice wasn't as steady as Mercury thought it should be.

"I meant why go to a Delta party? You hate frat boys just as much as I do."

"Well, honestly, I was thinking about rushing this year."

Sloane scoffed. Mercury turned to the petite girl who perched on the edge of the desk, Wuthering Heights in one hand, vape pen in the other. She gestured toward Mercury, as if to say, "Who is this clown?"

"Why do you want to rush a frat?"

Ellis shrugged. "It just seems like something fun to do. Besides, there's probably going to be some hot chicks there. I know you've been on quite the hiatus since you and Renee broke up."

Mercury clenched his fists. He broke up with Renee almost a year ago. They didn't end on good terms, yet Ellis couldn't go one conversation without mentioning her.

"I think I'm okay, dude," Mercury said. Ellis crossed his arms and smirked. It was a look Mercury hated; it was hard to be annoyed with Ellis when he looked like the mischievous eleven-year-old who wanted to explore Los Angeles and play music and not the arrogant, problematic rich kid he turned into.

"Dude, c'mon. It'll be fun, and we haven't hung out in a while."

Mercury wanted to point out to Ellis that going to a party doesn't exactly qualify as hanging out, but he remained silent. After a while, Mercury nodded. Ellis smiled and fist bumped him again.

"Alright, cool. I'll meet you at your dorm at like ten?" Ellis said.

Mercury nodded again. Ellis waved goodbye to Troian and Mercury's father, who sat at the station at the far end of the shop. He walked out of the shop and slid behind the wheel of a BMW SUV.

Mercury exhaled a breath he hadn't realized he'd been holding. He turned back to his brother, who glanced up at him from the tattoo he was inking.

"I don't know why you're friends with him," Troian said.

It was a question he'd asked before. In the past, Mercury could answer with 'we have fun jamming together' or 'Ellis knows I'm a witch and he doesn't judge me.' But now, as he watched Ellis drive away in his BMW, Mercury realized that this time, he had no answer at all.

Chapter 2

Mercury sat on the steps of Graves Hall, drinking from an antique flask and playing with the hem of his jacket. It was already eleven thirty. As usual, Ellis was late.

Mercury wanted to walk to Robertitos and order the world's greasiest quesadilla, then go back to his room and try to finish the song he was writing. He heard it so clearly in his head, a recording on a constant loop. His whole body tingled at the thought of sitting at his keyboard and creating. He stood and pulled his building key out of his pocket just as Ellis started across the volleyball court toward him.

He wore the same beanie but different clothes. His shirt was a deep V-neck and his jeans were tighter than Mercury thought they should be. Mercury tossed the flask to Ellis, who caught it with one hand.

"Thanks, dude," Ellis said.

"You're late," Mercury countered.

"Can't rush perfection," Ellis replied. "I see you're sticking with that jean jacket of yours."

"Not all of us are flush enough to have a plethora of clothes to choose from. Besides, this is my statement piece."

Ellis shook his head but said nothing as they walked across the narrow pathway in the direction of Greek Row.

"So, I think your family still hates me," Ellis said. He passed the flask back to Mercury, who was unsurprised to find the bulk of the liquid drained.

Mercury shrugged. "Probably."

"Is it just because I'm white?"

Mercury scowled and looked up at Ellis. "Motherfucker, please. It's because you keep giving them reasons to hate you."

"Like what?" Ellis asked as they jaywalked across the street.

That same annoyance again. Mercury reminded himself of the good times he had with Ellis and tried to remember his less obnoxious qualities. As Ellis started walking farther ahead of him, though, Mercury was unable to recall such times.

"Like being a selfish asshole," Mercury called out.

Ellis looked back at him but didn't reply.

A block away from the party, already he could hear the bass-heavy music. *Why do frat boys love trap music so damn much?* He thought.

"I half expected you to cancel on that douchebag."

Mercury turned to see Sloane approaching him, hands tucked in the pockets of a bright yellow bomber jacket that looked straight out of 1996.

"What're you doing here?" Mercury asked.

"Got some connections at the frat I need to link up with," Sloane said. She took a long pull from her vape, this time exhaling a cloud of mint-scented smoke.

"Connections, huh?" Mercury asked.

"What? You think receptionist is my only job?" Sloane asked.

Mercury shook his head, smiling.

They walked the rest of the way to the frat house in silence, the sounds of trap music and Sloane's heels clicking against the concrete filling the night. They arrived just as they heard Migos bragging about their cooking skills. Ellis stood outside smoking a cigarette and drinking a beer.

"Took you long enough," he said.

Mercury rolled his eyes but didn't say anything about Ellis walking so far ahead of him that it seemed as if he decided to abandon him as soon as Mercury tried to speak the truth.

Sloane took another drag from her vape and aimed the smoke at Ellis, who scoffed and waved his hand in his face.

"What's she doing here?" Ellis asked. There was an edge to his voice that Mercury didn't appreciate.

"She came on her own. What's the problem?" Mercury asked.

"Yeah, you upset I interfered with your date here?" Sloane smirked.

Ellis narrowed his eyes and tossed his cigarette toward her. It landed on the ground at Sloane's feet; she stepped toward Ellis and ground it under her boot.

"Might wanna watch where you're tossing your shit, white boy."

"What're you gonna do about it?" Ellis replied, closing the gap between himself and Sloane. He clenched his fists. Sloane narrowed her eyes and reached into her jacket pocket.

"Yo, cut this shit out," Mercury urged as he placed his hands on each of their shoulders.

Sloane and Ellis stared at each other, seeing who would back down first. Finally, Ellis turned away.

"Your taste in friends has really gone downhill," he told Mercury before walking into the party without another word.

Sloane slid a petite knife back into her pocket, taking several steps toward the door before turning. She cocked her head toward the house and Mercury followed her.

The second his foot touched the foyer, his head began to ache. By the time he reached the bar at the far end of the hallway, he was nauseous. It felt like his eyes were being carved out by melon ballers and his stomach was being ravaged by disease.

"Merc, you good?" Sloane asked.

"A migraine," he breathed. He pressed on his right tear duct. "What frat is this?"

"Delta Kappa Douche," Sloane said. But Mercury didn't laugh. He couldn't. He met her gaze, but his vision had tunneled. He felt a million miles away from her and from the party. "I think you need a little pickup."

She pulled a rectangular sheet of paper from her pocket and opened it, exposing a line of white powder.

"C'mon, it'll make you feel better."

"I'm not tooting," he said.

Sloane leaned in and whispered in his ear. "It's Goody's Headache Powder, dummy. Do you think I'd really bring the good stuff to this shit show?"

He clutched the paper and tilted his head back, letting the powder slip onto his tongue and dissolve. Almost immediately his migraine began to dissipate and he felt a rush of energy. He didn't need to say anything to know that Sloane hadn't been entirely correct. The powder was Goody's, but there was something else, too. A slow smile spread across her face. She winked then pushed through the crowd and disappeared.

Mercury was left to his own devices. He sighed, knowing that he'd prefer to be in the security of his dorm room, writing music and having a beer. Again he contemplated leaving. Sloane was conducting business and likely wouldn't notice he was gone. Ellis probably wouldn't remember he'd invited Mercury at all. He'd pick up some girl, a dhampir probably, and go back to her house for the night. Despite his misgivings, he allowed the movement of the crowd to push him further into the frat house. He grabbed a beer from a large cooler and popped the top, knowing better than to dip into the neon green jungle juice. The last time he had it, he woke up outside of his dorm with a splitting headache, wearing only his Timberlands and a unicorn pool float.

He settled on a couch next to a few sorority sisters. He smiled at them without any intention of a conversation. Two of them looked up at him and returned the smile. As he sipped his beer and picked at the label, he felt their eyes on him.

"I've never seen you here before."

Mercury turned toward the blonde seated next to him. She had a cup full of jungle juice. Her shirt was low cut and she sported a black wire nose ring. Her eyes were heavily lined in black, the makeup already smudged.

"It's my first time at a . . . Delta party," he said.

She giggled. "This isn't a Delta party. It's Upsilon Gamma Nu."

He'd heard of UGN before. They were known on campus for two things: they were insufferable douchebags and many of their brothers were dhampirs. But that didn't explain why he'd felt so weird entering the house. He'd had those symptoms before, but only when he'd been around a crowd of vampires.

"Isn't this the Delta house?"

The girl nodded. "It is, but UGN always hosts parties here since it's the biggest house. And since it's rush week, they'll have a huge turnout."

"I see. Any chance these brothers are vamps?" he asked.

"Would it matter if they were?"

Mercury finished his beer and set it down on the coffee table.

"I'd prefer not to enter the lion's den if I can help it," he said. He then stood and walked away. He could hear the girls whispering to each other about him, using words like weird and hot and closed-minded. The path to the front door was blocked, so he wandered toward the patio. He passed the large kitchen, which was filled with several UGN brothers. Mercury felt that tingle again, his stomach churning and his heart fluttering in his chest. He was all but certain that several of the brothers had to be vampires, and he couldn't be more irritated. That Ellis didn't bother to make the connection or realize what it would mean if the brothers found out about Mercury's abilities felt like a slap in the face. As much as Ellis' attitude annoyed Mercury, he'd never put his friend in danger.

We aren't friends, Mercury thought. *We're just two people who know each other.*

As though sensing his unease, Sloane tapped him on the shoulder.

"You good?" she asked. He nodded, but Sloane narrowed her eyes. In the two years he'd known her, he'd never been able to hide his emotions from her. She saw through his façade, as she did with most people. It was a trait that Mercury found to be admirable and wonderful, but others, like Troian and no doubt Ellis, found it annoying. "Don't lie to me."

Mercury sighed. "This is a UGN party."

Sloane nodded. "Yeah, I hate having to deal with dhampirs, but they do pay good money for the stuff."

"Some of the brothers are vampires."

Sloane was silent but her large, brown eyes widened. She knew what being around a group of vampires meant for Mercury. Without a word, Sloane grabbed his hand and led him toward the front door.

"Hey, where's the fire?" said Ellis, who stood at the base of the stairs, one hand around a handle of whiskey and the other draped around a curvy grey-haired girl.

Mercury motioned to speak, but Sloane stepped toward Ellis and pushed him.

"What the fuck is she upset about?"

She pushed him again. "First of all, I've got a name, white boy. It's Sloane. Second, how the fuck can you bring your friend to a party full of dhampirs and vampires knowing what he is?"

The girl looked nervously from Mercury to Ellis.

"Uh, I should go."

"No, stay."

"But—"

"I said stay; it's fine," Ellis replied, but his grip loosened on the girl's shoulder and she crept down the last step and through the hallway without looking back.

"Goddammit. I outta call you cockblocker now," Ellis snarled.

Sloane remained unfazed. Ellis stepped down, so close to Sloane that his body pressed against hers. Mercury pulled Sloane away from Ellis, hoping to diffuse the situation. Ellis took a long sip of whiskey then extended the bottle toward Mercury.

"Just because your friend didn't change her tampon doesn't mean she should be giving me grief."

"Are you fucking kidding me?" Sloane said. She launched at Ellis, and it took all of Mercury's strength to hold her back. In any other situation, he would have used his magic and simply moved her across the room.

"Sloane, it's good. I got this," Mercury said. He did his best to avoid telling her to calm down, knowing that would only make the situation worse.

"She's, like, totally mental. Do you know she deals? Everyone's been talking about her, saying some Hispanic broad has weed and coke and Xanax on her. Dude, I can't believe your dad lets a drug-dealing skank work for him. You should—"

"Shut the fuck up," Mercury hissed. He sighed, exhausted, as he often was when it came to Ellis. Their spat had drawn the attention of a group of people, some of whom pointed and others pulled their phones out, ready to capture the next viral video. Mercury gestured for them to follow him to the dining room. The room was dominated by a long table and chairs. A guy Mercury vaguely recognized sat in the middle, flanked by two frat brothers.

Mercury turned toward Ellis. Sloane stood with her back facing the table, hands in her pockets, ready to pull her knife and fight.

"Look, did you know this was a UGN party?" Mercury asked. His voice was low.

"No," Ellis said. He pulled his beanie out of his back pocket and pulled it down over his ears.

"He's lying," Sloane said.

Mercury stepped toward Ellis and put a hand on his shoulder. In a flash, he saw Ellis walking toward the psych building, phone in one hand and cigarette in the other. He saw the curvy girl with the grey hair stop Ellis and ask him if he had plans for the weekend.

"Getting drunk somewhere with you," Ellis said. The girl giggled and told him about the party.

"It's UGN," she said. She tapped buttons on her phone and then Ellis held his hand up, a Facebook invite prominent on the screen. "They're having it at the Delta house. Bring some friends. I think you'd–"

Ellis jerked away from Mercury. "Man, what did I tell you about doing your shit on me?"

Mercury noted that he didn't say 'magic,' still aware enough to know what that word could mean around the wrong person.

"I wouldn't have to do it if you didn't lie to me. What the fuck were you thinking?"

Ellis shoved his hands in his pockets and looked away. His silence said it all.

"This isn't the kind of thing you do to a friend," Sloane said. Ellis shot a withering look at her and Mercury wished he had the power of telepathy like his mother to will Sloane to be quiet.

"What do you know? You've only known Mercury for like two seconds. I've been friends with him since–"

"Well, if you were really his friend, then you would know that bringing a . . ." Sloane dropped her voice. "Bringing him to this type of party could be dangerous."

"He's a grown man. I figured he could handle it, especially since he's got powers."

Mercury narrowed his eyes. "If you think that I wouldn't get burned alive if I tried my magic in a place like this, then you're batshit crazy. And you really aren't a friend."

Ellis' green eyes darkened. His lips settled into a grim line.

"Fuck you both," he said. He turned on his heel and walked out into the crowd of people dancing to "Chun-Li".

Mercury rubbed his eyes with the heels of his hands. His headache hadn't gone away; it had only lessened, but it returned with a vengeance when he realized his current situation. Sloane put a hand on his shoulder.

"I'm sorry dude. That guy's a fuck boy, honestly," Sloane said. "I don't see how anyone could tolerate him."

Mercury nodded. He looked past her to the trio sitting at the table. Upon closer inspection, he noticed the guy in the middle was uncomfortable. His shoulders were to his ears and his eyes were wide. The two men flanking him were barrel-chested frat boys, both clad in UGN shirts and Adidas track pants. The one on the right had his arm around the guy in the middle. He was waving a cup in front of the guy's face.

"C'mon, you know you want some," the frat boy said.

His friend chuckled, and Mercury could see that he wore a gold grill across his upper teeth, the color contrasting harshly with his ruddy skin.

As Sloane lectured Mercury, telling him that he should cut Ellis out of his life because he was toxic and problematic, Mercury watched the UGN brothers pour the cup of blood all over the middleman. He whimpered but said nothing, keeping his hands between his legs. When the other brother picked up another cup from the table and tried to force it upon the man in the middle again, Mercury stepped around Sloane and approached the group.

"Didn't know UGN was in the habit of forcing humans to drink blood," Mercury said. The frat brothers looked up at him and laughed.

"We do when they're sitting like a stick in the mud at our party," the bro with the grill said. "Besides, this isn't any of your business. This is just between us and our friend here."

The one with his arm around the guy in the middle laughed and pulled him in closer. He kept his features blank, but Mercury could tell he was close to crying, which would only make the frat boys' torture worse.

"Well, I don't think your 'friend' there appreciates your ugly-ass mug so close to his," Mercury said. The bro pulled his arm away from the guy in the middle and stood. He stepped toward Mercury, leading with his chest, expecting to intimidate him. Mercury folded his arms.

"You need to back the fuck off, boy," the frat bro said.

Mercury could hear Sloane shifting behind him.

"Who the fuck are you calling 'boy,' asshole?" Mercury said. The frat bro closed the distance between them and swung. Mercury dodged the swing then brought his fist around. It connected with the bro's jaw, and Mercury leaned into his magic, using it to send the bro back against the wall. The other frat bro stood, eyes wide, and rushed toward Mercury, head down, ready to barrel into him. Mercury stepped to the side and so did Sloane.

"Duro," Mercury said. The one-word spell kept the frat bro stuck in his position, head down. Seconds later he rammed into the wall, then collapsed onto the floor.

Mercury turned toward Sloane, who had gotten so used to his magic that she simply sucked on her vape and clicked the power button. He was thankful there was no one else in the room. Mercury walked back to the guy seated at the table, who still sat timidly in the same position. Mercury extended a hand to help him up when the dining room door crashed open.

"Griffin! Griffin, what the fuck?"

A woman with a mass of natural curls rushed past him to the guy at the table.

"Why'd you run off? Who's this? What's on your face? Is that—ew, is that blood?" The girl sniffed at Griffin's face and pulled him up. Her gaze shifted from Sloane to Mercury. Her dark eyes narrowed.

"What did you do to my brother?"

"We didn't—"

"Nothing, it was . . ."

Mercury gestured to the frat bro slumped against the wall, unconscious.

"Yeah, right," the girl said. "You're disgusting, throwing blood on some poor guy who's too defenseless to—"

"Joelle, Joelle, it's fine. It wasn't him. He stopped them from messin' with me," Griffin said. "And I'm neither poor nor defenseless." He stepped out of his sister's grasp and held his hand out to Mercury.

"Thank you for your help."

Mercury nodded and shook Griffin's hand. Without provocation, moments from Griffin's life flashed before his eyes. At eight, he tried and failed at softball. When he was eleven, his glasses were broken by a pasty-faced ginger. He won his school's science award at fourteen. Joelle and Griffin's parents were killed in a car crash when they were seventeen, leaving them in their grandparents' care. He received a scholarship to Georgia Tech for Civil Engineering the same year.

Mercury pulled his hand back quicker than he realized he should have. Griffin looked at him quizzically, but Mercury could see he wasn't wondering what was wrong with Mercury, but what was wrong with him.

"No problem at all, man. I'm Mercury, and this is Sloane," Mercury replied. He turned and gestured toward Sloane who flashed a peace sign to the siblings.

"I'm Griffin. This is my sister, Joelle," he said.

Joelle looked from Griffin to Mercury. When she was satisfied and sure that Mercury had not bullied her brother, she smiled and extended a hand.

Mercury's heart thumped in his chest. Her smile was radiant. *Damn, she's beautiful.*

"Thank you for helping my brother," Joelle said.

Mercury nodded. He tried to speak but words escaped him. Sloane stepped beside him, the arm of her canary yellow jacket touching his.

"Don't sweat it," Sloane said. "What brings you two to a UGN party, anyway?"

"We transferred from Georgia Tech. It's our first semester here. We wanted to meet new people, and what better way to do that than a party?" Griffin said.

A whistling sound cut through the air. He looked up at the group, confused. No one but Griffin seemed to know what the whistle meant. His cheeks grew red and his eyes wide. He looked down, his raven-colored dreads falling in front of his face.

"UGN brothers, to the balcony, now. That includes you, too, maggots," rang a voice over the loudspeaker.

"Maggots?" Joelle asked.

"It's what they call the pledges," Griffin said.

"Who'd ever want to pledge a place like this?" Joelle asked.

They each motioned their response. Sloane shrugged, Mercury nodded and Griffin winced.

"Grif Whittaker, get your ass to the balcony, ASAP."

Joelle's eyes narrowed. "Grif?" she questioned.

He shrugged and turned away. She grabbed his collar.

"What the hell?" she asked, puzzled. "Why would you want to join those douchebags?"

"They were just hazing me."

"By making you drink blood?" Mercury said.

"You don't know–"

"I could smell the blood," Mercury said. "It smelled like blood and whiskey." Mercury's stomach churned at the thought.

"Last chance, Grif."

Griffin turned to walk away.

"Griffin, don't go," Joelle pleaded.

"Yeah, dude, they'll just put you through hell. Why don't you hang here with us?" Mercury said. He put his hand on Griffin's shoulder. Griffin pulled away.

"I appreciate you helping earlier, but you don't even know me," he turned toward the balcony.

"Griffin, wait!" Joelle shouted. She chased after him, her Reeboks squeaking on the linoleum.

"Well, we should probably go," Sloane said as the two brothers on the ground started to stir. Mercury grabbed Sloane's wrist and walked her out of the room and back into the den of the party.

"He's getting in way over his head," Mercury said.

"Who cares? You don't even know him. I bet he'll be fine."

Mercury side-eyed her. She shrugged but dipped her head low.

"Well, cast a spell or something to get him to stop," she said.

"It doesn't work like that," he replied.

Mercury pulled her through the crowd toward the balcony. Despite her protestations, she didn't resist him. They stepped outside just as they cut the music.

"Well then, how does it work?" Sloane whispered.

"It works by me not being in a house full of leeches who'll want to kill me if I use my craft," he replied.

The girl with the black nose ring turned and shushed him. Sloane lifted her hand to flip her off, but Mercury grabbed her hand and guided it down. He smiled tightly and nodded at the girl, who rolled her eyes and turned back toward the front.

A white man stepped to the front of the crowd. He looked like every other SoCal frat boy—all muscles up top with no regard for training the legs. Hair shaved close on the sides, with the center swooped over in a severe comb-over. Stubble, a throwback Von Dutch shirt, and a shit-eating grin. To Mercury, it was clear: here was the leader of this pack of frat boys, ready to haze the shit out of the unsuspecting freshmen. He had to figure out how to get Griffin out of there.

As Mercury plotted his next move, the frat leader addressed the adoring crowd. He lifted his hands and the whispers and giggles stopped instantly. The only sounds Mercury could hear were the wind and Sloane shifting from boot heel to boot heel.

"Tonight is the night we separate the wheat from the chaff, the night we find out whose loyalty is unwavering and whose weakness will poison the whole group."

Mercury rolled his eyes. *Is he for real?* He thought. *Surely they can't be buying his surfer-accented attempt at gravitas.*

Some people clapped; others whooped. Sloane scoffed and Mercury was relieved that he wasn't the only one who found this situation to be ridiculous.

The frat leader turned away from the group and faced the UGN brothers and pledges, who sat on their knees facing the crowd, their hands clasped behind their backs. Though Mercury didn't know him very well, he could tell Griffin was nervous. Joelle stood just in front of the group, arms crossed, staring her brother down and mentally urging him to stand.

"As you know, this has been rush week for our maggots here, and let me tell you, it's been hell."

The UGN brothers laughed and fist bumped. Mercury could see the sharp edges of their fangs, and his stomach sank even lower; his head pounded even more. "But, we're not done. Tonight is the last night, the final test to see if these maggots are UGN material."

He pulled a knife from his pocket; the rest of the UGN brothers followed suit.

"Aww, shit," Sloane whispered. Mercury looked at her, and her eyes met his. She knew like he knew that this situation had escalated, and it was very likely that a person or persons would be turned or killed.

The frat leader ran his knife across the palm of his hands then walked over to one of the pledges, a pimple-faced kid with spiked hair. Without a word, the frat leader pressed his cut palm to the kid's face. The kid squirmed, but the frat leader overpowered him. After he was satisfied that enough blood had made it into the kid's mouth, he grabbed a handful of hair and pulled his head to the side. He sank his teeth into the kid's neck. The kid whimpered, then stiffened.

After several minutes, he pulled away and the kid fell to the ground.

The frat leader turned to the crowd, his lips and chin covered in blood. His pupils were dilated, making him look more like a shark than a human. Gone was the California ease; here stood a predator with strength and senses that rivaled Mercury's own. A vampire was strongest just after feeding. Where he normally felt uneasy around them, Mercury was terrified of them in the hour after they fed.

Mercury's stomach churned as the crowd lifted their drinks and cheered when the kid stood, now a vampire. The frat leader gestured to the rest of the brothers and one by one they each cut their hand and shoved it in the face of the pledge that knelt before him. The brother who stood behind Griffin was particularly rough, grabbing a handful of his locks in the process. Joelle shot out of the crowd, running toward her brother. The frat leader stepped in front of her.

"Whoa, no ladies allowed," he said.

Joelle shoved him. "Get the fuck out of my way. That's my brother."

He scoffed. The crowd laughed.

"And you think that's my problem?"

"I said get out of my way, douche. You're not going to turn my brother."

"I'm not, but Cameron is." He gestured to the frat boy who stood behind Griffin. He was still smearing his hand across Griffin's face, the blood mixing with tears and snot.

"Your brother made the choice to rush all on his own."

"I don't give a shit! Look at him; he's crying," Joelle said. Mercury winced, knowing that Joelle's attempt at helping was likely hurting Griffin's chance to make any friends at school, or to be known as anything other than the crying UGN pledge.

Joelle tried to push past the frat boy again, but he pushed her to the ground. She fell backwards, landing on her tailbone and hands with a thud.

Mercury clenched his hands, his power surging through him. He shoved through the crowd, stepping on feet and pushing people to the side. He heard Sloane calling his name behind him, but all he could think about was laying the frat leader out.

"Stop this," Mercury urged through gritted teeth.

He giggled. "Oh, please. I didn't realize Grif was such a pussy, that his sister and her boy had to save him."

Boy. That word again, so simple but so full of hate. He whispered a spell and Cameron, the frat boy assaulting Griffin, drew back and screamed. Mercury watched as he gripped the hand he'd cut, clutching it in his other hand as the blood spurted out of his body.

The frat leader looked from Cameron to Mercury then narrowed his eyes. "Witch," he spat.

The crowd gasped. Some of them started booing, others stepped forward as if to join the inevitable fight.

"So what if I am? Better than being a son of a whore," Mercury quipped. That was enough to set the frat leader off. He dived toward Mercury, attempting to tackle him.

"Okuta," Mercury whispered and instantly his body was tougher and harder. Suddenly, the frat leader's body bounced off his and fell backwards. He threw a punch, which landed square on Mercury's jaw. It damaged his hand, but Mercury still felt it. He hit the frat leader in the throat and his magic reinforced the attack, sending the frat leader flying backwards. He landed against another UGN brother and a pledge, who was now rising from his forced metamorphosis.

"Fuck," Mercury said. All of the pledges except for Griffin had been turned. All of them were searching for blood. That's why the crowd had been gathered. Why they were having such a public hazing. The fledglings were always more volatile. Their hunger was more intense the first time, and Mercury knew he'd have to fight to escape the party alive.

As the frat leader stood, his fangs protruded and his pupils dilated. He and two other UGN brothers approached the crowd.

Mercury attempted to whisper another spell when a rough pair of hands grabbed him by the back of the neck. His lungs seized. Mercury bit his tongue so hard that his mouth began to taste like copper. His heart jackhammered in his chest.

Suddenly, he was free. He turned to see Sloane, who stood with her silver switchblade out. There was blood on the end, and the vampire who'd held Mercury lied on the ground, one hand clutching his back trying to quell the blood that oozed from the wound.

"Thought you could use a little help." Sloane stepped past him and to another UGN brother, whose fangs were out and whose strength no doubt surpassed her own.

"Sloane, no!" Mercury said. But he hadn't been paying attention. While his eyes were on her, another vampire snuck up behind Mercury and pulled one of his arms. A sharp pop sounded as his arm broke. The pain was white hot, his vision blurring momentarily. He screamed, the sound seeming so distant.

But this vampire was far from the only one. The new vampires invaded the crowd. They grabbed at humans and tore at the flesh of their neck to reach the blood. Some people ran; others fought the fledglings or UGN brothers who tried to make them stay.

"It's my lucky night," said the frat bro who Mercury had knocked out earlier. "It's been a whole month since I've gotten to burn a witch."

With his good arm, Mercury gestured toward him, sending him flying back in the direction of the crowd.

But when he disposed of one UGN brother, another popped up. He turned just as this one's fist connected with his cheek. Sloane jumped in just as Mercury lifted his good hand to shield his face. She slashed the vampire's cheek open, exposing a set of yellow teeth and infected gums. The vampire howled bringing its hand to its face as blood dripped down between its fingers. As it dashed through the crowd, Mercury pulled Sloane back from following it.

Astonished by the chaotic scene before him, Mercury quickly realized there were too many of them. The frat brothers were joined by dhampirs, their dedicated human stooges. Suddenly, it had escalated from a fight between Mercury and two of the UGN vampires to an all-out brawl. Bodies knocked into him, pushing him against the frat leader, who grabbed ahold of Mercury's bad arm just as Mercury started another spell.

He tightened his grip on Mercury's arm. Tears streamed down Mercury's face as the pain from his broken limb snaked up his arm. His head was pounding, his heart pumping like a piston.

Ellis launched at the frat leader, tackling him to the ground. Now free, Mercury turned to see Joelle fighting the blonde with the nose ring. Griffin angled to get to his sister, but a trio of newly turned vampires pushed him back and forth between them.

Mercury launched at the girl, pulling her away from Joelle by her hair. Joelle backed away, her face bloody. She sank to her knees and Mercury grabbed her hand to help her up.

The girl punched Mercury in the back and pain instantly shot up his spine. Mercury turned to face her.

"Fuck you, nigger witch," she spat. He pushed her and she slid back several feet. Mercury grabbed Joelle and they started toward Griffin when the girl reappeared, grabbing at Joelle's hair and pulling her back.

Joelle screamed and tried to turn away, but the girl hit Joelle in the stomach. The punch made Mercury's heartbeat quicken, his blood run warm and his belly churn with bile.

When it came to spells, Mercury normally kept his incantations short, no more than a word or two. He was more accomplished with spellcasting than Troian–something he prided himself on. By the time he was nine, he could make an entire house disappear. Now as he stood and watched these vampires and their cronies beat and maim and bite these humans, he didn't bother keeping it short. He didn't bother sparing feelings or containing the spell to where its only goal was to maim.

"I call upon Wadjet; I call upon Oya. I call upon the souls of my ancestors burned. Salt in the wounds, lead in the belly, fire burn bright. Let the fire burn away the hate, leaving only what is pure."

The blonde backed away from Joelle and screamed. Her skin cracked and bubbled. Her face contorted in pain. She ran her hands all along her body, as though she could stop the flames that burned from within.

The frat leader rushed toward her and tried to help but the second he touched her skin, he drew back in pain. Her pale skin was now crimson.

Mercury grabbed Joelle and headed toward Griffin, taking advantage of the distraction. He'd seen people burned alive, and he didn't need to see it again. With his free hand, he motioned to the side and the three frat brothers surrounding Griffin moved away.

"Thanks," Griffin said. His face was bloodied. Already his lip was swollen. He motioned for Griffin to run ahead of them. He startled when he felt a hand on his shoulder but relaxed when he noticed it was Sloane. Ellis stood behind her, his green eyes wide. His nose had been broken. One hand held it as blood seeped between his fingers.

Mercury nodded. "Let's go."

They pushed through the crowd of people, who stopped fighting and watched as the girl with the nose ring writhed and screamed. Most of them had their phones out, taking pictures or filming a video, commenting on how many likes this would get them.

"Hey! Hey! It was you that did this to Delanie!" shouted a frat brother with a mustache and snake bite piercings. Mercury pushed him but there were too many bodies behind him. He barely moved.

"Get the fuck out the way," Joelle yelled. More people turned toward them as they tried to make their way through the den of the party and the pulsing EDM. "Move."

"No, no, you're gonna pay for what you did. We're gonna kill you, witch. You and your friends."

About a second later, Griffin threw the first punch. It landed at the guy's throat but barely made an impact. Mercury knew he was a vampire after all, and it would take much more strength to make an impact. Mercury tilted his head to the side and the vampire before him shifted in the same direction.

Delanie's screams grew louder and louder in the distance until they stopped. Then there was only the sound of the EDM music.

"We gotta go," Mercury said. He grabbed Joelle and pushed Griffin forward. They ran through the house, squeezing through the grinding and rippling bodies.

He could feel the presence of the vampires drawing near as they made it to the front lawn.

"What the fuck just happened?" Sloane asked. "What did you do to that girl?"

"He killed her," Ellis said. "Burned her alive."

There was a smirk on Ellis' face, as though he was not disgusted by what Mercury had done, but proud of his ruthlessness.

"C'mon, we gotta go," Mercury grabbed Joelle's hand but she pulled away.

"What the hell? There's no way we're going with you," Joelle protested.

"We don't really have time to argue about this," Mercury said.

"I'm not arguing. We're not going with you; we don't even know you."

"Listen, girl, Mercury just saved your life, okay? You and your brother," Sloane snapped.

"Did you just call me *girl?*" Joelle said.

"Guys–" Griffin said, trying to get their attention.

As Joelle and Sloane argued, Mercury could see the swarm of people erupting from the house and backyard. The same people with their phones out before had their phones out now, snapping pictures of the group and taking video of the pack of vampires that loomed nearby.

"We don't have fucking time for this!" Sloane yelled. "They're coming after us, and it doesn't matter if you hit them or if you just told them to fuck off. Those leeches are out for blood now."

The frat leader stepped toward them but stopped abruptly.

"Why aren't they rushing at us?" Griffin asked.

Mercury didn't answer. He wasn't focused on the group, but rather on the force field he desperately tried to maintain. He was already dehydrated. His knees wobbled and his hands were clammy.

"You can't hold that force field forever, *witch,*" yelled the frat leader.

"We need to get the hell out of here," Ellis said, his voice muffled behind his hand.

"I said we're not going anywhere with you," Joelle said.

"Jo, we don't really have a choice. They saved our lives."

"By taking someone else's," she said.

"Fine, if you want to stay, that's on you. We're going," Sloane said. She grabbed Mercury by the arm and pushed him forward. "We need a car or something . . ."

Mercury kept his gaze on the vampires, but he could feel himself getting weaker. Keeping the force field up required a staggering amount of effort, and it was something he'd only ever done once.

"Alright, fine. We're coming with you," Joelle said. She swung her purse to the side and rummaged through it. She pulled a set of keys from her bag and gestured for the group to follow her.

"You'll have to bring the car around," Mercury whispered. "If I stop focusing on them, the shield comes down."

The group paused for a moment.

"I'll stay with him," Sloane said. She bent down and pulled another knife from the side of her boot.

The rest of the group dashed to Joelle's car. Sloane put a hand on Mercury's arm, as though she could lend him strength.

"C'mon, Merc. You got this," she said.

Mercury's body shook. His breath escaped in labored spurts. More dhampirs surrounded the vampires now, seemingly as anxious as the UGN brothers were to get to him.

"Look at him; he's getting weaker," said another UGN brother. They laughed, their fangs glinting in the light of the street lamps. A set of tires screeched as a red Kia Soul rolled around the corner. They pulled up next to him.

"Get the fuck in," Ellis yelled. Sloane jerked Mercury to the side. He blinked, his focus torn.

The group rushed toward the car, shouting and screaming. Someone hit the rear windshield with a rock, splintering the glass before they drove away.

Mercury took a long but labored breath as if he hadn't taken one in years.

"Your nose is bleeding," Joelle said. Mercury met her eyes in the rearview mirror. He looked out the side window, wiping the blood away and wishing he could wipe away his troubles just as easily.

Give Vampires a Chance

By Cordelia Edwards

No other group in history has been more scapegoated, maligned and hated than vampires. For ages, they were blamed for the deaths of Romania's fair maidens. If a crop failed, or if a sickness spread throughout the village, it was the vampires' fault. Never mind that these Eastern European countries were superstitious dumps full of people with rotten teeth and pierogi for brains. If something went wrong, vampires were to blame. Throughout the ages, books and movies have portrayed them as soulless and evil predators. But that couldn't be further from the truth. Vampires are hardworking. They are loyal. They are compassionate, fiscally responsible, and most importantly, they are patriots.

Even in America, the land of the free and the home of the brave, these citizens have been rejected and sold out as the boogeyman. When they tried to live their truth in the past, they were killed, driven into the countryside, into poverty-stricken areas like Indianola, Uriah, Clearlake and Chewelah. With every election, the needs of the vampire were overlooked by politicians promising change from the bureaucracy of Washington D.C. They were losing hope but since President Vael took office, Americans can finally be proud of this great nation.

Though vampires care more about America than witches and their leftist-super fans, the harridans, these citizens are still painted as monsters. "News" organizations on the left love to parrot statistics about a so-called increase in vampire crimes. They say that vampire bitings have risen from 14% to 65% since President Vael took office. They say that those who are aligned with vampires, who call themselves dhampir (a term typically used for the offspring of vampires and humans), have caused three times more riots and destruction in the wake of the election than harridans. These data points are without merit and have been debunked by us here at *The Vanguard* and other sources like Whitehouse.gov, unvaelthetruth.com, Broadbent and more.

Not only are vampire attacks on the decline, but so are unemployment numbers, medical costs and the number of homeless citizens. Do you know what numbers are going up? The amount of witch-on-vampire crimes (increased by 40% since 2016). The number of vampires losing their jobs to witches or their cronies (37%). The number of vampires finding hex bags in their cars and homes and offices (61%). Witches and harridans call for a safe place for "all," but I guess that only applies to those without fangs.

The president is flying to Sweden this week for a summit with the European Union to discuss worldwide vampire equality policies. As more and more brave citizens Awaken—there have been hundreds in Canada, Mexico, Luxembourg, Georgia, etc.—the need to establish laws protecting our most fragile patriots has never been more urgent.

Chapter 3

The crowds at Venice Beach were less active than usual on a Friday night. Mercury gestured for Joelle to park on a side street, and then the group walked to the Iron Bird. Each one of them finally felt their collective wounds. Though Mercury felt like he was seconds away from passing out, he held his head high as he cradled his arm and led the way into the shop. Troian sat in his chair, blunt in one hand and beer in the other. He had the television on, watching the State of the Union address through large, scratched vintage glasses.

"What the fuck happened to you?" he said when he glanced at Mercury. He eyed the rest of the group, his gaze going from Ellis and Sloane to Griffin and finally to Joelle. His incredulous expression instantly turned flirtatious. He set his drink down and stood, then sauntered over to the group. He held out a hand to Joelle.

"And who is this beautiful lady?" Troian asked. Mercury scowled as he saw Joelle smile and soften under Troian's gaze.

"Hey, that's my sister, creep," Griffin said.

Troian looked at him then to Mercury. He held his hands up and backed away. "Didn't mean to offend you, bruh," he said. "But you are looking a lot worse for the wear. What happened?"

Mercury turned toward the door and flipped the locks. He pulled down the shutters and turned off the neon lights advertising the shop's availability.

"Merc–"

"Vampires," Mercury said.

Troian's playful smile turned serious; his cheeks turned pale. He rubbed his beard and sighed. "Where?"

"It was a UGN party," Sloane chimed in. She walked behind the reception desk and grabbed a first aid kit. She bandaged her hand then started toward Joelle.

"The hell were you doing at a UGN party? Were you trying to get killed?" Troian asked.

Mercury looked away. Troian had always been more like a father than a brother to Mercury. He was quick to scold, but also quick to comfort.

"It was his idea," Sloane said. She nodded toward Ellis, who still clutched his nose in his right hand.

Troian rolled his eyes. "Should have known it was the white boy."

"Why's it always gotta be about race with you people?" Ellis said.

Both Mercury and Troian scoffed. "Shut your dumb ass up and sit down."

Troian gestured toward his chair and Ellis sat, his eyes never leaving Troian.

"Move your hand; let me take a look at you," Troian said. Ellis winced as he lowered his hand. Half of his face was covered in blood, some of it already crusted to his cheeks. His angular nose was swollen at the bridge, the skin already a deep purple.

"You got clocked good, El," Troian said. "Looks like someone already beat your ass for me, so I'll refrain from doing anything for that comment you made."

"How kind of you," Ellis said, his voice nasally.

Troian stared at Ellis for a moment before redirecting his attention to Mercury. "Okay, we've got to get these guys healed before those vampires get here."

"I need a little help myself first," Mercury replied, gesturing toward his arm. Troian clucked his tongue. He placed his hand on Mercury's broken arm and uttered a spell. Within seconds, the pain in Mercury's arm disappeared. He twisted his arm this way and that then heaved a sigh.

"Thank you," he said.

"Mercury, why don't you get Griffin situated in Dad's chair. I'll take care of Joelle after I'm done with this one."

Despite the pang in his chest, Mercury nodded. He walked Griffin over to his father's chair. The twin had minor scrapes on his hands, but his upper lip was split. Like Ellis, his face was caked in blood, though Mercury knew it wasn't all his.

"What are you gonna do? Doesn't Sloane have the first aid kit?" Griffin asked.

Mercury smiled. "I've got a different kind of aid for you."

He opened the top drawer of the antique vanity his father used to store his tools. There he found aloe, sage, chamomile, all the ingredients for a healing salve. He mixed the herbs and liquids in a bowl, saying his spell over them as he did so. He applied the salve to Griffin's wounds.

"It tingles," Griffin said.

"Just wait. You'll be better soon."

Within seconds the scrapes on his knuckles faded and disappeared. His lip stitched back together, leaving no scar. The only indication of his wounds was the blood caking on his face.

"You can't get rid of the blood?" Griffin asked.

Mercury gave him a sidelong glance.

"I'm a witch, not a hazmat cleaner." He tossed Griffin a pack of Wet Ones. Mercury turned to see that Troian had replaced Sloane in helping Joelle. He sat on a chair before her, one hand gently tilting her head back and the other applying the same salve Mercury had mixed for Griffin. Already Ellis was healed, and he remained in Troian's chair watching the State of the Union address. His mouth was agape and his eyes filled with wonder as he looked at Vael. Mercury's stomach turned flips.

"Friends, let me tell you about discrimination," Vael said. "For I and my vampiric kin are all too familiar with it. When I was a child, my mother never told me we were different. She told my sister and I that we could be anything we wanted to be, go anywhere we wanted to go, but her number one rule was simple: treat people as you want to be treated."

The crowd clapped. Vael smiled, his fangs pearly white and glinting. "I was nine when I first realized what I was. I was in my English class and we got a new student, who happened to be a witch. She was seated next to me and I remember thinking she was the most beautiful thing I'd ever seen. When class ended, our teacher asked us to stand up and high five each other, and so I did. When I got to this new girl, instead of high fiving, I held her hand in mine and looked her in the eyes and said, 'I believe that you and I will be friends. And so I want to share with you as you share with me.'"

Several members of Congress shared a knowing glance. Mercury's eyes narrowed; he knew where this was going.

"Instead of giving her a high five, I bit my other hand and held it up to her. As many of my vampiric cohort know, this is a common, friendly gesture in the community. I'd seen blood sharing my whole life, so when this girl screamed and pushed me away with just the power of her mind, I was gobsmacked. My teacher got involved, so did my parents. Though this ritual is performed with members of my community and indeed, other humans in the class, I was forced to stop. And because of this girl, the other vampires in class were prevented from carrying our rituals and heritage into the world with us."

Boos erupted, forcing the Speaker of the House, one of the only witches in Congress, to interrupt and quiet the room. Once Vael started talking, he looked straight into the camera. It seemed as if he was looking directly at Mercury. "Never again will vampires know the same discrimination that I have faced. Never again will my people be forced to hide in the shadows, relying solely on animal blood or resorting to going to underground blood cafes to survive. They won't have to lie about who they are or why they cannot stay in the sun. When I took this oath of office, I made it my mission to be the savior for my people, so that no witch or human or any other creature will take away their rights to live, love and be free."

Applause erupted throughout the room. Everyone stood, their faces tightly stretched into smiles over their fangs. A cold chill slid down Mercury's spine.

"Get the fuck outta here with this," Sloane said, staring at the television in disgust.

"Well, he's not entirely wrong," Ellis said.

Sloane glared at him.

"What? I'm just saying that he's not wrong–vampires are discriminated against. Like, 53% of them worry about being fired for who they are, and

75% feel that they've consistently been discriminated against by witches, specifically."

Troian, who had just been giggling with Joelle only moments before, turned to Ellis and growled. "Care to cite those facts, kid?"

Ellis scoffed. He stood, puffing out his chest, but when he spoke his voice was soft: *"The Vanguard."*

"That fascist rag? That's where you get your info from?" Sloane said. "Fuck. No wonder you're a miserable piece of—"

"Sloane, that's enough," Mercury said, once again stepping between the two.

"You're defending him? After what vampires have done to you?"

"I'm not defending him. If he actually believes that vampires are discriminated against after info from the CDC shows that's not the case, and especially after tonight, then he's an idiot. But we're here hiding out from a group of vampires. It's only a matter of time before they find us."

"But we're here because of you, bro," Ellis said.

"What?"

"Not for nothing, but we wouldn't be in this mess if you hadn't used your magic."

"And I wouldn't have had to use my magic if you hadn't tricked me into going to that party in the first place," Mercury snapped.

"You're a grown-ass man, Merc. No one forced you to go. You could have left any time, but you were so focused on that girl's tits that you couldn't bring yourself to leave." Ellis replied, gesturing to Joelle, who quickly crossed her arms.

"Hey," Griffin said. "Let's just calm—"

"Shut up," Troian said, and Griffin went silent. He opened his mouth to speak but no words came out. Joelle leapt up and grabbed her brother's shoulders.

"Oh my God, what did you do to him?" she asked.

Troian shrugged. "It's just a spell. It'll wear off."

"But why—"

"He doesn't need to get in the middle of their bullshit. They do this every time they see each other." Troian stood and poured three shots of whiskey.

"Shut up, Ellis," Mercury said.

"No, it's true. And who wouldn't? I mean, she's hot as fuck. I'd be on her, if it wasn't for Delanie. Oh wait, that's right. You killed her."

Mercury's vision went red. He rushed toward Ellis, slamming him against the wall so hard that it knocked Troian's tattoo license from the wall. The frame hit the floor, glass shattering.

"Fuck you," Mercury shouted.

Ellis grimaced and tried to push Mercury away, but his grip was too strong.

"You could have dealt with those frat douches any other way. You could have cursed them or set up your force field earlier than you did. You wanted to show off, and now they're after all of us because of you."

Just as Mercury considered ripping Ellis apart, he heard shouting in the distance. The sound of car windows breaking and alarms trilling through the air, the sound of people screaming, grew closer and closer. The rest of them wouldn't be able to hear it yet, but he knew Troian could. He let go of Ellis and turned away. Ellis shoulder checked him on his way out the parlor door.

"Where are you going?" Joelle called after him.

Ellis turned toward them. "Anything is better than staying here. Besides, those douches are only after Mercury, not me."

He let the door slam behind him, not waiting for a response.

"Oh no, stop, don't go," Troian said, his tone nonchalant.

"What are we going to do now?" Joelle asked. Troian had completely healed her, and once again, Mercury was taken aback by her beauty. But she wasn't directing the question to him, but to his brother, who put a hand on her shoulder. Mercury clenched his jaw and sank into his father's chair.

"Lay low until those fuckers pass," Sloane said.

"Should we run, like Ellis did?" Griffin asked, adjusting his large-circular frames as he often did.

Troian scoffed. "I wouldn't look to Ellis for guidance. He's not gonna get very far."

No one questioned what Troian said, but Mercury knew what he meant. After all, his brother had been blessed with foresight. Though it wasn't as reliable as Mercury's telekinesis, it was one of the things that made him the more valuable Amell brother in many people's eyes.

They were quiet, listening as the press interviewed President Vael. They asked about The Identity Act, the bill he signed earlier in the week, which would force witches to wear dog tags signaling that they were witches. Though several journalists questioned him, saying it smacked of pre-Holocaust policy, Vael dismissed them.

"Witches are lethal. They can kill you with just their mind. The rest of the population needs to know what they are dealing with."

As more and more journalists began to agree with President Vael, Mercury rubbed his palms, slick with sweat, against his jeans.

"What do you think they'll make us wear, Merc? Our element, or a burning stake?"

Mercury avoided his brother's gaze. He walked toward his father's liquor cabinet nestled beneath the stairs. He grabbed a bottle of brandy and a few small glasses and brought it to the reception desk, which Sloane had her heels balanced on as she read *Song of Solomon*.

"Care for one?" Mercury asked.

Sloane nodded and dog-eared her book then set it aside.

He poured one for each of them and walked it over to Joelle, Griffin and Troian. Mercury lifted the glass and though he'd normally say something witty, something to pique Joelle's interest, his mind was blank and his soul was heavy. He simply smiled, clinked his glass against the others and downed his shot. Just as Griffin set his glass down, Ellis burst through the doors, this time more badly beaten than the first.

Joelle and Griffin ran to him and helped him into Troian's chair.

"Don't you ever get tired of getting your ass beat?" Troian asked as he inspected Ellis' wounds. He had gash marks on his neck. His left arm was dislocated from its socket. His face was bloody and swollen, his left eye closed shut, and his right leg was torn to shreds. He could barely speak, his breath escaping in shallow gasps. After examining him, Troian fixed his eyes on Mercury.

"He's going to need both of us for this," he said.

Mercury nodded, feeling a tiny bit of satisfaction that his brother felt he couldn't do something on his own. He slid out of his jean jacket, which was already splattered with blood. He rolled the sleeves of his red button down shirt and grabbed a mortar and pestle.

"Is he going to be okay?" Joelle asked, her voice quivering. All of them appeared shaken up by Ellis' appearance, if not concerned for his safety as well.

"Yes, he'll be fine," Troian said. To the others, it seemed like a perfectly fine, resolute answer. But Mercury knew better. Troian's amber eyes flashed with anxiety, with worry. His intuition was in high gear.

There must be something wrong, something bad coming, Mercury thought. But he said nothing as he swiftly mixed the potion and whispered a healing spell over it.

Once complete, he handed the bowl to Troian. His brother nodded and started spreading the paste over Ellis' body. Mercury joined and they both recited their healing spell aloud: "Break turn to bone, blood turn to ash, may the power of Elegua flow through him."

Ellis grunted as the salve stuck to his skin and dried. It was burning, Mercury knew, but it would heal Ellis well enough for them to plan their next move. Mercury and Troian repeated the spell, their voices rising into a cacophony.

The swelling on Ellis' face lessoned until it disappeared. His eye opened slowly, and the popped blood vessels within disappeared. His shoulder popped as his arm returned to its socket. All of his cuts and wounds dissipated, until finally Ellis was breathing normally and stood.

"Holy shit," Griffin said. His brown eyes wide. "You guys are the real deal."

"And you didn't think that when Mercury set that thot on fire at the party?" Sloane asked.

"I just mean . . . this is incredible."

Mercury smiled, then looked at Ellis, who ducked his head and nodded. Mercury returned the gesture, his anger toward his friend subsiding.

As the group inspected Ellis' newly healed body, Troian pulled Mercury aside.

"You can't stay here."

"Okay, we'll go upstairs," Mercury said.

"No, dumbshit, I mean you can't stay here in the shop. Those vampires are obviously out there, and they probably sent one of them to follow Ellis."

Mercury blanched. "But isn't the shop cloaked? They can't get in, right?"

"They can't, but dhampirs can. And right now there's a swarm of them headed this way. Didn't you see anything when you touched Ellis?"

Mercury bristled, hating his brother's chastising.

"I don't actively try to read my friends like that."

"Well, you should have. When I did, I saw them just down the street. They were in Hazy Joe's just pulling people out through the windows and chanting 'restore.'"

"God, I hate that word," Mercury said.

"Well, it's going to get a whole lot worse if you don't leave."

"But how can I protect them all? I tried my force field and it felt like I was dying. We can't defend them all with just our magic and a few weapons."

Troian paced to the other side of the room, picking up his joint from the ashtray and lighting it. He took a long drag before handing it to Mercury.

"We'll have to Mark them then."

Mercury nearly choked on the smoke from the blunt.

"You can't be serious."

"As a heart attack. We can't defend them on our own, but with more magic, we could at least take some of them out."

Mercury sighed, fearing the outcome. He'd never Marked someone before. "I've never done this before," he said. "What if it doesn't work?"

"What if it does?" Troian said. "You can do this; you've got the skill and power. It'll give you all a head start."

"And where will we go?"

Troian was silent as he looked around the room. The twins argued with Sloane and Ellis. They thought to hide somewhere in the building until the vampires passed. Sloane and Ellis wanted to make a stand, fight their way out. Mercury noticed the anxiety in Troian's eyes, which only made himself more anxious. *I thought he wasn't scared of anything*, Mercury thought.

"Astera," Troian said, his voice so low that Mercury could barely register it.

"What?" Mercury asked.

"Astera." This time Troian leveled his gaze at him. Mercury felt his heart skip a beat.

Astera, the yearly assembly of the most powerful witches in the world. Where his father was now. But this year it was thousands of miles away, all the way in Maine.

"That's impossible," Mercury replied.

"You got a better idea?" Troian asked. "You and I both know these vampires will pursue you until either you're dead or they are."

Mercury's blood ran cold as he thought about what happened to his mother. When it was dark enough around him, he could still see the flames in his mind. He shuddered.

"How will we get there? What will we—"

The chanting was louder now. The dhampirs were less than a mile away and though the group had yet to hear, they would soon have to do something.

"Alright, we'll go."

"If you can make it there, the witches will protect you," his brother said. "Now let's get to work."

Without a second thought, Troian chose Joelle and Mercury grabbed Sloane.

"What are you doing?" Sloane demanded.

"We're Marking you."

"What does that even mean?"

"It means you'll be able to do great things," Troian said. He grabbed Joelle's right hand and stretched it out on the arm of his chair. Mercury did the same for Sloane, but grabbing her left, her dominant hand. He envisioned the perfect Mark for his friend. He began tracing the lines of a long, curved dagger. Its edge was sharp and exacting. Its blade razor thin, deadly.

"Why are they getting tattoos at a time like this?" Griffin asked.

Ellis scoffed. He'd taken to slouching in a plush chair by the front window, smoking a cigarette and scrolling through his phone.

"They're not really tattoos; they're Marks."

"Marks?"

"Magic, dumbass. They're magic."

Focused on the design emerging before him, Mercury felt Griffin's presence just over his shoulder.

"Why a knife?" he asked.

Mercury looked up at Sloane, who beamed down at her wrist.

"You'll see."

As he started the hilt of the blade, Mercury wondered what Troian was tracing on Joelle's skin.

"You guys? You've gotta look at this," Ellis said. He jumped up from his chair and strode toward them. He shoved his phone in Mercury's face and as Mercury stopped the needle, he began to watch the UGN brother's Instagram story.

The head frat brother stood down the street from the house, his back to the still raging riots.

"We're here to take vengeance on those that killed Delanie. And we know exactly where to go."

His fangs extended and his pupils dilated so large that his eyes looked black. "Iron Bird is a tattoo parlor right on Venice Beach. We know it's warded against vampires but that doesn't stop any of you from getting in. Help us avenge this sweet angel's death. Find that witch and his harridan friends and burn them to the ground."

The video snapped abruptly to a mob scene where vampires had captured several humans. Each of the creatures tore at the necks of their prey, pulling out large chunks of skin and tendon.

He heard Troian's needle stop. He looked up to see Joelle sitting straight up, admiring the flames coiled around her right wrist.

"Wow, this is beautiful," she said.

Troian smirked. "Give it a go," he replied. He held out his hand with his palm flexed, showing her how to use her new power.

She followed suit and a stream of flames shot from her hand. "Wicked," she said. A smile spread across her face.

Mercury finished Sloane's Mark seconds later. She sat up and ran a hand over the silver dagger on her wrist. Mercury held his hand palm up and clenched his fist. The dagger slid silently from her wrist and into her hand.

"Now you always have a weapon," Mercury said. Sloane kissed his cheek and hopped off the chair. "Ellis, your turn."

"No way, man. I don't want any of your juju on me or in me."

Mercury raised a brow. "Would you just get over here?"

"Without this magic, you're probably gonna die." Troian added, as he cleaned his needle.

"Fuck you," Ellis said. He slid into Mercury's chair anyway. "What are you doing to me?"

Mercury thought for a moment, then lifted Ellis' left hand and placed it face down.

He brought the needle to his friend's hand and began tracing his second Mark.

"Griffin, you've been chosen," Troian said. Mercury heard the teen laugh nervously as he sat down.

"Nowhere too painful, okay? I pass out at the mention of pain."

Mercury shook his head as he focused on the interlocking symbols of Ellis' tattoo. The chanting was louder now.

"Do you guys hear that?" Joelle asked.

"It's the UGN bros. They're coming for us," Ellis said. He held up his phone, and Joelle and Sloane watched in horror as the frat douche urged his followers to kill them.

"You'd better hurry up with those tattoos," Sloane warned.

Mercury lost focus in the spell he carved into his friend's hand. It was only when he heard the first bang on the bulletproof front door that he realized his surroundings again.

He threw up his force field and traced the Mark on Ellis' hand from memory.

"Hurry up, Troian," Mercury said.

He could hear Troian's needle speed up, similar to his. *Just two more sections*, Mercury thought. He felt his energy waning. His nose bled. His hands cramped. But when the tattoo was finished, it was like a lock sliding into place.

He turned back to Ellis, weakening his shield temporarily. The brunette examined his hand, the various shades of green coalescing into symbols that looked like leaves.

"What can I do with it?" he asked.

"I made you an Earth hand," Mercury said. "You've now got to think beyond yourself with this. You've got the power to poison . . . and the power to heal."

Ellis grimaced. "Are you serious?"

Mercury didn't respond. He stood and faced the window, strengthening his force field as best he could. *Troian would be so much better at this*, Mercury thought. The mob sneered at him and jeered through the window.

"I hope you like your witches burned extra crispy," said the one with the bat. "Because we're gonna burn that black witch there low and slow."

Mercury clenched his fists. His anger simmered in his belly, and it was all he could do not to send a spell toward the crowd. But they weren't ready to fight. They needed to be ready.

"Troian, I hope you're almost done there," he said. He could hear the strain in his own voice. But his brother didn't respond. Just as Mercury was about to break, he heard the buzz of the needle stop.

"All done, kid," Troian said.

Mercury turned slightly from the mob outside. Their bats slammed against the windows. Though there were no cracks yet, Mercury wondered how much longer they would hold.

"What is it?" Griffin asked. He held up his left hand and examined the new tattoo, a series of interlocking glyphs. Mercury's eyes widened.

"You gave him transmutation?" he asked.

Troian nodded. "He's gonna need it."

"What's transmutation?" Joelle asked.

"It's the ability to turn objects into other objects," Griffin said. "Like batman in the dark knight or the green lantern in–"

"Okay, nerd. Look, Mercury, what's the play here? These tattoos are great but they mean fuck all if we don't have a plan," Ellis interjected.

Mercury looked to his brother, as he so often did.

"We fight our way out," Mercury said.

"And then what? Where will we go?"

"We're going to Astera," he replied. He didn't give them time to respond. He dropped his force field and rushed toward the front doors. They sprung open just as Mercury stepped before them. He thrust his hands up and unleashed a windfall, knocking the group back.

He sensed the rest of the group near him. Joelle held her right hand up and fire burst forth. The vampires screamed as the flames licked their bodies. Sloane, who had already been practicing with her tattoo in the shop, was slashing and hacking with her ever-sharp knife. Ellis worked through the crowd, wrapping his hands around throats and arms and faces, injecting poison deep into their veins.

Only Griffin stayed behind, hiding in the confines of the shop.

"Griffin, come on!" Joelle yelled. He shook his head and hid behind the desk. Joelle ran to him and grabbed his arm.

"Just leave him; he's dead weight!" Ellis yelled.

"Shut the fuck up," Mercury yelled. He moved through the crowd and as he and Sloane held the group off, Troian rushed toward Joelle and Griffin.

Mercury heard him telling Griffin about the tattoo, about how powerful he was, about how he could really make a difference.

Seconds later, Griffin stood beside Mercury.

Mercury turned toward him and nodded.

As a barrel-chested man aimed for him, Griffin lifted a hand and transformed his bat into a snake. The man screamed as it coiled around his hand and began to squeeze.

More and more vampires and dhampirs appeared. The dhampirs were easy to dispose of. The vampires, having just fed, were stronger. One punched Mercury in the ear, knocking him to the ground. Mercury stood swiftly and narrowly avoided a boot heel to his face. He fought through the pain, through the ringing in his ears.

"There's too many of them," Joelle exclaimed.

"You just need to get to a car," Troian said.

Mercury turned toward his brother, alarmed. *Shouldn't he have said we?*

They were on the brink. They were getting tired, their punches barely landing and their forms sloppy. Mercury cast a spell to dull the effects of the blows, but it was hardly effective. The UGN brothers were out for blood, and it seemed his spells were no match for them.

He stood face-to-face with the brother who filmed the video. His name was Conner.

"It must be my birthday," he said. "I've wanted to burn a witch forever."

He grabbed Mercury's throat and pulled him up. Mercury held his hands out and unleashed a windfall, but it only shifted them both. The vampire's fangs dropped and he pulled Mercury down toward him.

Sloane buried her knife into Conner's shoulder blade. He dropped Mercury and back handed her so hard that she fell to her knees. He kneed her in the face before Mercury lifted a hand and sent him through the broken window. Conner crumpled against a parked car, and the sound of the car alarm worsened the ringing in Mercury's ears. Mercury helped Sloane up but she stumbled, her mouth bloody.

"Ellis!" Mercury yelled. He turned and hesitated at first, then dashed toward them. "Heal her."

Ellis scowled as he placed a hand on Sloane's cheek. Her blood dried and her wounds healed. She grabbed her knife and without a word turned to a dhampir and buried her knife in its gut.

"We gotta move toward the cars; we're just getting bottlenecked in here," Ellis yelled. "I'll create a diversion." Troian ran toward the back of the building and returned with his father's spell book in his hands. Mercury's heart leapt. His father's magic was far more advanced than theirs. Could Troian make those spells work?

His brother stood on top of the reception desk and held a hand out. He recited a spell that Mercury had heard only once: "In Wadjet's name, I call upon the wind in the air and the fire in my belly. Bring forth the light, bring forth the fire, bring forth the fury. Cleanse these beings and scorch the earth."

The room filled with light and a booming sound filled Mercury's ears. He was knocked back into one of the tattoo chairs, his vision slowly fading.

Mercury awoke minutes later and stood, his legs shaking. His equilibrium was off, his head pulsating. His vision twisted. He saw people moving in front of him but he couldn't remember who they were. He moved forward then paused. He lurched, bent over and threw up on his Timberlands. He held out a hand and tried to reach for something to stabilize himself.

Around him echoed screams and shouts, someone crying. He stood still and closed his eyes.

"Aviavar," he whispered, and immediately felt his body healing. Though it only took the edge off, now he could make out the scene before him.

Troian's spell had caused an explosion strong enough to knock people over and break all of the windows, but not so strong that it disturbed the foundation of the building. Some of the vampires and dhampirs lied on the ground, some dead, some unconscious. Ellis was healing Joelle. Sloane stood by the door, knife in hand. Griffin sat on the stairs, hands gripping the bannister, eyes wide. But where was Troian?

"Troian?" Mercury called. He searched the tiny shop but his brother was nowhere to be found. "Sloane, where's Troian?" Mercury asked. She turned toward him and shrugged. She also had thrown up; traces of it clung to her shirt. Mercury stepped outside.

Troian had awoken before the rest of them. He was already in the streets, fighting a group of vampires. Mercury held his hand out and flung a dhampir that loomed just behind his brother. He crashed against a car and slid to the ground. He hit and flung his way through the crowd until he reached his brother.

"You've gotta go," Troian said, his voice echoing through Mercury's ears in a conversation only he could hear.

"There's too many of them for us to fight through; we'd never make it," Mercury thought. He looked up to see Sloane jumping on the back of a vampire as he nearly bit Griffin. The boy extended his hands and the fire hydrant beside the vampire turned into a dog, big and imposing. It growled and leapt at the vampire just as Sloane jumped onto the hood of a car.

Joelle emerged from the building, a stream of fire emerging from her hand.

"If you don't go, you'll all die; you know that," Troian said.

Mercury whispered the same spell that killed Delanie as he faced off with two other UGN brothers. They screamed as their bodies burned from the inside out.

"But what about you?" Mercury said. He pushed another dhampir away, then grabbed a pale man with a Swastika shirt and brought his head to his knee, breaking his nose.

The man whaled as Mercury dropped him to the ground.

"I'll fight them off to give you a head start," Troian said. Before Mercury could reply, his brother ran toward the Iron Bird where Conner and a trio of dhampirs were beating the Sandersons, the harridan couple who owned the bakery next door.

"No, let me just put up my force field!" Mercury yelled. But it was to no use. Troian was already in the fray.

Sloane had slid inside the car and hotwired it. As the engine roared to life, she honked the horn and Joelle and Griffin slid inside. Ellis emerged from the Iron Bird with a large duffle bag in his hands and slid into the passenger seat.

"Merc, bring your ass!" he yelled.

Mercury's leg was caught in a rope just has he stepped forward. He fell on his face, his teeth biting into his tongue. He tasted the coppery taste of blood as a vampire dragged him toward the stores on the other side of the road.

He whispered a spell but knew it wouldn't do any good. This was Haspal rope, meant to render a witch powerless. The same rope they used for his mother.

"Troian," he thought. His brother turned from the UGN brothers and bolted toward him. Mercury felt the slack on the rope loosen as the vampire holding it was knocked aside. Troian undid the knot and pulled Mercury to his feet.

"You've gotta go," he said. He looked at Mercury, his hazel eyes glistening.

"But what about you?" Mercury said as he pulled open the car door.

"Get to the car. I'll follow you to Astera if I can. Now go." Troian slammed the door behind Mercury.

"No, wait!"

Sloane sped off, wheels screeching on the pavement.

"We can't leave him; you have to go back!" Mercury screamed.

"If we go back, we're dead; you know that," Ellis said.

"If it was your brother, you'd be going back in a heartbeat!" Mercury spat. He turned around in his seat. The crowd converged in on itself.

"How come no one is following us?" Joelle asked.

"I don't know. But we have to go back for him."

"Mercury, Troian would want you to keep going." Sloane said, her dark eyes meeting his in the rearview mirror.

A tear slid down Mercury's cheek. He leaned against the door panel and wrapped his arms around himself. He was cold, and somehow hungry but nauseous at the thought of food. "I'm sorry, Mercury," Griffin said.

Mercury nodded and turned his body toward the window. He watched as they merged onto the freeway and into LA traffic, unsure of what lay ahead.

Chapter 4

They drove in silence, without conversation or the radio. After an hour, Sloane stopped to get gas, thinking they were far enough away to avoid being spotted. They pulled their cash and put up enough money for a full tank. Joelle slid behind the wheel, and Ellis and Sloane joined Mercury in the backseat. They'd grabbed waters and sodas and snacks and though Sloane offered him Ginger Ale and a bag of chili cheese Fritos, his go-to snack, Mercury declined.

His mind was a swirl of fear and worries. *How can I get them to safety without Troian? How can I keep them safe?*

Tears kept streaming down his cheeks, but he remained quiet, tucked into his corner. *Maybe if I stay here,* he thought, *then none of this is real. We didn't go to a frat party, or fight vampires, or abandon my brother and the tattoo shop my father built.*

When he heard Sloane whimper beside him, he knew he couldn't stay in his illusion.

"What's wrong?" Joelle asked.

Griffin turned in his seat.

Sloane was on Facebook, the start of a Facebook Live video flickering on her screen. Likes and angry faces and other reactions danced across the screen.

Conner stood in front of the Iron Bird, a torch in his hand.

"Gentleman, let's have some fun," he said. He turned and threw the torch against the cracked front windows. The building immediately went up in flames. Cheers arose in the crowd, and the camera person panned the phone up and to the left, where the crowd gathered. The camera focused back on the shop, and Mercury's insides crawled as he saw his father's home, his legacy, up in flames.

"We got one!" someone shouted. The camera turned.

Conner had his arms around Troian, who stood with Haspal rope tied around his hands. He had been severely beaten and was almost unrecognizable: his left eye was closed, his lips swollen and already turning purple. A patch of his dreads had been removed from the right side.

"No," Mercury whispered.

"I'll turn this off; let me just–" Sloane fumbled with the phone, but Mercury snatched it out of her hands.

"This is a message to any witch or harridan who thinks about helping Mercury Amell and his band of miscreants: Ellis Hall, Sloane Salvanera, Joelle and Griffin Whittaker."

"How do they know who we are?" Griffin asked.

"It's called the internet, dummy," Ellis said. But his voice lacked its usual bite.

"If you help these filthy humans, then your fate will be just like his."

Conner kissed the side of Troian's cheek. Suddenly, a noose was thrown around his neck and Troian was lifted off the ground. The camera panned toward the building, where the noose had been hung across an eve. Sloane screamed as Ellis gasped. Joelle jerked the car to the side of the road and cut the ignition. Mercury nearly dropped the phone, but Sloane grabbed it from his hands and held it in her lap.

Mercury sobbed as he watched his brother, his protector, his best friend, being kicked. As he tried frantically to pull the rope from around his neck, his eyes grew wide and his mouth hung open.

Minutes later, his legs twitched one last time, then swung in the Santa Ana breeze. One of his legs hit the side of the building and caught fire.

Mercury pushed the phone out of Sloane's hand and swung the door open. He jumped out of the car and fell to his knees and began to wretch. The sound from the Facebook video stopped and suddenly they all surrounded Mercury, each with their hand on his arm or shoulder.

"Mercury," Sloane whimpered. He looked up at her, her eyes glassy and her mascara streaming down her face in jagged streaks. He could hear Ellis shouting to himself.

Mercury couldn't move. He sat stock still, the image of his brother's legs flailing in the wind nestled just behind his eyes. As his friends cussed and shouted and sobbed behind him, Mercury struggled to catch his breath. As Ellis kicked at the tires, Mercury's limbs went numb. He didn't want to move. Moving meant time would have to keep going, that he'd have to put one foot in front of the other, get in the car and travel miles away from Troian's body.

His brother wouldn't even get a proper burial. This Mercury knew. The vampires would burn his brother's body to the bones, then collect them and mount them in their expensive homes or on the dashboards of their expensive cars. They'd tell stories of their conquest, omitting the part about Troian leveling half their crew with one spell. They'd say they caught the witch from the tattoo parlor, beat him and burned him, all in the name of their God. In the name of Lilith, their patron saint.

His father. He had to tell his father.

But he never kept his phone on him at Astera. He locked up in his room to avoid 'worldly' distractions and just live in the moment. If he had his spell books or his crystals or his ink, Mercury could try to communicate with his dad. He'd find a spell for astral projection, or he'd try to project his thoughts to his father with a crystal as a conduit. But all he had on him was his switchblade, the tattoos that boosted his natural powers, and the ring that had been his mother's: gold, carved with runes, and a sphalerite stone the color of honey. He never knew what the runes meant or what the stone was for.

His throat was dry, and his eyes were stinging and cloudy from the tears. He stood, feeling thousands of pinpricks in his legs from squatting for so long. The others stopped their mourning and looked at him. Sadness covered their faces and all but Ellis clung to each other. They were lost.

Mercury closed his eyes and took a deep breath, trying to silence his racing thoughts. He pictured himself in a wheat field, the sun on his face, the wind rustling through the wheat. He imagined the feel of the plant in his fingers, so much like hair. He thought of the warmth of the sun, the smell of spring. Then he felt the wind whipping around him and coursing through him, filling him with intention and strength.

"Let's go," Mercury said as he opened his eyes. He grabbed the keys from Sloane and slid into the driver's seat. The others were still, stunned.

"Are you okay to drive?" Joelle asked. She peered through the open passenger window, her eyes wide and full of concern. Even through his pain, Mercury still thought she was impossibly beautiful.

"Yes. I've got this. We've got to keep moving; I don't think those frat douches are going to leave us alone any time soon."

After a slight pause, Joelle nodded and slid into the passenger seat.

Everyone else followed suit. Ellis sat behind Mercury, his knees banging the back of his seat as he struggled to get comfortable. Sloane slid in beside him, and Griffin last. Just as he closed the door, Mercury sped off, away from Los Angeles and toward Astera, hopefully to safety.

Of Men and Magic:
What to Expect at Astera

By Freddie Karr

Spring is here, and you already know what to expect: seasonal allergies, rosé ingested by the gallon, and a string of holidays co-opted by the Christians (that's right—your celebration of Jesus' resurrection is actually a celebration of the goddess Ostara who represents rebirth and fertility, hence the eggs. You didn't really think those had anything to do with the resurrection of a zombie carpenter, did you).

But spring is a magical time, and for witches, it serves as an opportunity to officially welcome the new year with Astera, a gathering of all of witchkind. This week-long celebration has been a tradition in the witch community for over 500 years with mentions of the ceremony found in old books and scrolls. Astera begins with a channeling of energy, where witches call their quarters, one of the four elements that give them power, and culminates with a large festival welcoming the Vernal Equinox when day and night share equal time. Each year witches the world over sojourn to a place of spiritual energy. Sometimes that place is Thrihnukagigur. Or Fingal's Cave. Or the Bavarian Alps. This time, Astera will be held in the valley surrounding Mt. Katahdin.

While most Asteras serve as a chance for witches to harness their element's energy and generally make mischief, this year is different. Not only is this the first year in recorded history that the head of The Witches' Council has been a woman, but according to the rumor mills of Twitter, email, and our very own comment threads, this Astera will be punctuated by a meeting between the unscrupulous dead man in the White House and Oliana Murtaza, the beautiful and enigmatic head of The Witches' Council. Though Vael has made no mention of meeting with witches, I spoke to a source close to Councilwoman Murtaza, who says that Vael was the first to reach out.

"Oliana was surprised that Vael bothered to call. The magic community has been virtually under siege since he took office. Not only are they losing their jobs and their friends and family, but some of them are losing their lives in the most brutal ways. So when Vael called and suggested starting peace agreements, she jumped at the chance."

When asked if hosting the treaties during Astera was intentional, my source scoffed at me.

"Obviously it was intentional," the source said. "Astera is one of the most powerful times of the year for witches. Oliana is a Fire Hand, and she'll be able to harness her element to its fullest extent and use that power to influence President Vael. And, in the wake of the riots, it's now or never."

Of course, my source is talking about the recent riots in the City of Angels, where over eighty people, mostly humans, were killed. They started in Westwood, near the UCLA campus, where hundreds of young adult vampires were loosed on the city after drinking beer and listening to trap music. One of our own correspondents, Kezziah Greene, was killed in the riots. Though we send healing energy to his family, we know that expressions of love and light are nothing without action. That's why we're hoping that Councilwoman Murtaza reaches some kind of agreement with Vael and his cabinet so that witches, harridans, and any other group opposed to this new world order can rest easy knowing they'll survive the night. As always, your faithful correspondents at *Jonquil* will be reporting from the scene keeping you up to date on the parties, parades and the political gains that happen this Astera.

Chapter 5

Mercury drove until he spotted the sun peer over the glittering towers of Las Vegas. The car was on its last legs–they needed gas but were too leery to stop. Their faces were all over Facebook and Twitter, the vampires organizing an active bounty for them. The head UGN brother, their leader, Conner McGrady, was a senior and from a family wealthier than Ellis'. He was already using some of his parent's money, saying he'd pay $15,000 for the lot of them to be rounded up. Mercury was almost insulted by the number, knowing that the bounty averaged only $3,000 for each of them, but knew it would be enough to keep people on the hunt for them. It also turned out that Delanie, the blonde with the nose ring that he'd killed, had been Conner's girlfriend. Once Mercury discovered this, he understood Conner's reactions more–and he knew that he'd never stop gunning for them unless one or both of them were dead. After he passed the strip, he pulled the car into an alleyway and cut the ignition.

Everyone in the car was asleep, had been for the last two hours, leaving Mercury alone to his thoughts. Alone to his grieving.

One of his cousins stumbled across the video of Troian and recognized him. She texted Mercury and called him several times, but Mercury couldn't bring himself to face her. But now there was nothing else to do. He slid out of the car and closed the door behind him slowly, careful not to wake Joelle, who was curled up into a ball in the front seat.

Mercury dialed the number and stared at the phone. *I'll bet it's gonna go to voicemail*, he thought. *No way she still has her phone after all* . . .

"Mercury?" her voice sounded high and chirpy, like a bird.

"Faegan," he sighed.

"Oh, Mercury, is it true?" she moaned. He could hear birds chirping and dogs barking on her end and thought she must have been on a walk.

"Yes," he whispered.

"What happened?"

Mercury hesitated before he spoke. "Vampires attacked me at a party. I went back to the Iron Bird to hide, but there were too many of them. Troian tried to help, tried to get me and my friends away. And he . . . they . . ."

"Shhh, shhh, it's okay," Faegan soothed.

Mercury tried to control the ragged breaths and the tears rolling down his cheeks.

"Where are you now? Have you spoken to your father?"

"I'm . . . not in LA," Mercury said. "And I haven't spoken to him. Telepathy was Troian's gift, not mine."

"Right," Faegan whimpered.

"Does he know?" Mercury asked, but, of course, this was a foolish thing to wonder. His father was a powerful mage, and Faegan had a big mouth.

"Yes."

"How—"

"Mom put a spell on him to help him grieve; he was inconsolable when it happened. He wanted her to send an envoy to come collect you—"

Mercury's heart leapt.

"But she refused. She said that Astera is sacrosanct, that it can't be broken for the sake of one witch, even if it is her nephew. She said it's for the greater good, her peace treaties and all that."

Mercury scoffed. "So I'm on my own then?"

"Where are you headed?"

He narrowed his eyes when she didn't answer, and he was loathe to tell her about his real plan, lest she spill the beans. If Oliana didn't want witches going out, she was not likely to accept a witch and his magic-tinged friends coming in.

"Canada, probably," he lied. The rear door opened and Ellis slid out, rubbing the sleep from his eyes. He nodded at Mercury then lit a cigarette.

"Look, I gotta go, Faegan. Please tell Dad I'm safe."

"Mercury, I'm so sorry. I love you, and may the Goddess keep you."

With that his cousin hung up, and Mercury slid the phone into his pocket.

"Morning," he said to Ellis.

"Yo," he replied.

Mercury nodded toward the pack of cigarettes. Ellis slid one out and lit it, then handed it to Mercury. Mercury inhaled. The smoke was sharp and hot on his lungs. He definitely needed it.

"How are you holding up?" Ellis asked.

Mercury shrugged. "I don't feel anything. I'm not sad or mad. I'm just . . . a void. And that scares the hell out of me."

Ellis put a hand on Mercury's shoulder. "I don't think there's anything wrong with what you're feeling."

"My dad already knows. Cousin Faegan couldn't keep away from her phone during Astera."

Ellis smirked. He'd had a crush on his cousin since they were kids, even though she was ten years older.

"I bet he's a wreck," Ellis said. He stamped out his cigarette and lit another.

Mercury nodded. "Oliana had to spell him to keep him sedated, help him with his grief. He suggested they send an envoy out to get me, but–"

"Let me guess, Oliana put the kibosh on it?"

Mercury sighed. "Yeah. Said it was for the greater good. I just don't understand her; she's my aunt after all," Mercury gestured for another cigarette. Ellis held the pack out then handed Mercury the lighter.

"Do they know we're headed there?"

"No. I didn't tell Faegan. You know she can't keep a secret. I don't know how they'll feel about me coming to our sacred gathering with . . ."

"A bunch of humans with illegal tattoos?"

Mercury bristled. "Yeah. But, I don't know where else we can go."

Ellis shrugged. "Well, you do kind of have us all in a bind."

Mercury narrowed his eyes. He wasn't going to take Ellis' bait. They'd already had this argument, and Mercury had already explained himself. He didn't need to do it again. So he leaned against the car and smoked his cigarette.

"What'd you bring, by the way?" he asked, changing the subject.

"Oh," Ellis said. He opened the passenger door. Mercury could hear Joelle and Griffin talking in hushed tones, probably afraid to wake up Sloane. Ellis slid the brown duffle bag from the backseat and slammed the door. Sloane yelled "what the fuck" and sat up.

"Here." Ellis handed the bag to Mercury.

He unzipped it and his eyes welled with tears. Inside were several spell books, a molocate, several herb jars, his father's Black Label Bourbon, and a framed photo of Mercury's family.

"How . . ." Mercury began. He cleared his throat.

"I knew you'd need them," Ellis said, and he looked Mercury directly in the eyes. It was the most sincere look Mercury had ever seen his friend give. He set the bag on the ground and hugged Ellis. Ellis was seemingly stunned at the gesture, but returned it eventually.

Sloane emerged from the car, her hair sticking out at odd ends from her ponytail. Her makeup was smudged and the edge of her skirt was hiked up.

"Thanks for slamming the door, asshole," she said to Ellis, breaking up the brotherly moment. She turned to Mercury and hugged him. "How are you feeling?"

Mercury couldn't help the irritation he felt at the question, which he knew would be asked of him so many more times during the trip.

"Well, considering that my brother was lynched and burned, I'm just peachy," he snapped. Sloane gasped and Ellis' eyes grew wide. He had not meant to sound so harsh. "I'm sorry. I didn't mean . . ."

"It's okay," Sloane said. She smiled tightly and dug her hands into her jacket pockets. "So, what's the plan?"

"We should probably talk about it with the others," Mercury said. He opened the driver's side door as Sloane grabbed Ellis' pack of cigarettes and lighter.

"You both are gonna owe me a new pack by the time this is done," he whined.

"Good morning," Mercury said.

Joelle leaned back in the passenger seat, her feet up on the dashboard. Griffin leaned in and adjusted his glasses.

"Hey," he said.

Joelle smiled.

"We should probably talk about next steps," Mercury said. "You hungry?"

"Hell yeah," Sloane shouted in the distance.

"I guess," Joelle shrugged.

Griffin nodded.

An hour later they found themselves seated in a 50's style diner. They tried their best to look inconspicuous, though being a group of mostly black kids proved to be difficult. Sloane took point.

"We have to change our look."

"Why?" Griffin asked.

"There's a reason why in all those mysteries those white girls are cutting and dying their hair. We can't be obvious. We need to get a new car," she said. "And probably new clothes."

They'd cleaned the car top to bottom, removing the plates and slipping them into the duffle bag.

"How are we going to pay for it?" Griffin asked concerned. "We've already spent what little we did have."

"Good question, Griffin." Ellis looked directly at Mercury.

As everyone else started looking around at each other, Mercury intervened. "I've got it covered."

They found a nearby Target and grabbed new clothes and supplies. Mercury hated to part with his jacket, but he knew it would be conspicuous. He gave it to Ellis, who handed it to the first homeless man he saw. Mercury picked up a new jacket, a dark green suede bomber, black jeans, grey shirt and black combat boots. He knew that they couldn't stand out. Both girls slid into jeans and boots, and where Sloane grabbed a black leather jacket with studs on the lapel, Joelle chose a long army coat. Both Griffin and Ellis were subdued—each in blue jeans, Griffin in converse and Ellis in Nike high tops. But Ellis didn't forgo his trademark beanie despite the group's protestations. They grabbed sunglasses, underwear, socks, deodorant and water. Each of them grabbed some form of backpack or bag. They entered the store separately, paid for their items with cards that Mercury glamoured with different names, and avoided the security cameras, just like Sloane taught them.

Now back at the diner, they sat in the booth. Sloane's normally high ponytail was now a long fishtail braid snaking down her left shoulder.

"Well, I guess there's no point in a diet," she said. "Time for cheese fries and a burger."

"How could you eat at a time like this?" Joelle's voice wavered.

"This isn't the first time I've had someone I love get killed, or that I've had to get out of pocket," Sloane replied.

Joelle folded her arms and looked away.

When their waitress arrived, an elderly black woman with a wide smile and a gap between her front teeth, Mercury was relieved. He hoped she hadn't been on Facebook or heard anything about the events in LA.

"What can I get you all this morning?"

"Coffee all around?" Mercury asked of the group. They nodded. "And I'll take eggs benedict, please."

"Short stack, please, ma'am," said Griffin.

"Lox and cream cheese, everything bagel," said Ellis.

"Cheese burger, medium well, and a side of cheese fries," said Sloane. She looked at Joelle, who'd been seemingly examining her menu. She looked up at the waitress, who smiled softly.

"I'll have the same as her," Joelle said.

"Yeah girl, fuck that diet," Sloane fist bumped Joelle.

The waitress chuckled and announced she'd be back with the coffee.

Mercury crossed his arms and glanced around the table. Gone was the high they'd all felt after they pilfered their new clothes and kicks. Now they were back to being scared. Back to paranoia. Griffin kept his head down, staring at the chipping vinyl of the table.

This is my fault, Mercury thought. Ellis was right. And suddenly he was tired. The thought of pressing on, of even eating, seemed like too much effort.

The waitress, whose name was Ethyl, set five cups of coffee down, interrupting Mercury's thoughts. Then she slowly poured coffee into each cup and set the pot down. Before she left, she patted Mercury's hand. He spotted a faded symbol of water tattooed on the back of her hand. Mercury looked up at her, eyes wide, but Ethyl just smiled widely as if to tell him everything would be alright. Mercury nodded and wiped the tears at the edge of his eyes.

Immediately, Sloane grabbed four hazelnut creamer pods and dumped them into her coffee.

"Dude, do you want a little coffee with your creamer?" Ellis said. She looked at him from the corner of her eye.

"I can already tell that, as sweet as Ethyl is, that coffee is sludge. Drinking it black isn't a good idea."

Ellis shrugged and raised the cup to his lips. He set the cup on the table just as fast, his face wrinkled in on itself.

"I told you," she smirked. She grabbed a pod of vanilla and set it in front of him. He grabbed it quickly.

"So, how's everyone doing?" Mercury asked.

"I mean, we're hundreds of miles away from our families, our faces are plastered over social, this tattoo itches so much I want to rip my skin off, and death by vampire is a reality now. So, I guess you'd say I'm peachy," Joelle said.

A pang reverberated through Mercury's body. "Well, I guess aside from that . . ." he started.

"Why are we even going to this Astera place, anyway? Why can't we just go off the grid in a forest somewhere? They can't even go out in the day, right?" Griffin asked.

Mercury sighed. He looked up at Sloane who offered him a reassuring smile.

"Have any of you actually seen a vampire before last night?" Mercury asked. Ellis, Griffin and Joelle looked at each other. Joelle shook her head.

"Forget what you've read about them. Most of those things aren't true."

"What things?" Joelle asked just as Ethyl brought their food. She set their plates down in front of them and winked at Mercury as she left.

"Well, they can see their reflection. Garlic doesn't work. They don't need to be invited in; they can just come and go as they please."

"What about silver? And isn't the sun supposed to be, like, hella deadly?" Ellis asked around bits of his bagel.

Mercury took a swig of his coffee then steepled his fingers. "They don't burst into flames if that's what you're asking. They just get sunburned easily, very easily. And silver—I've never seen them react to silver or even crosses."

"So why'd you give me a silver blade?" Sloane asked, holding up her arm.

"Because cutting anything with a knife will harm it, and because it looks badass."

Sloane smirked.

"That's all well and good, but why do we have to go all the way to this Astera place? What even is it?" Joelle asked.

"It's an annual gathering of all of witchkind. My aunt, Oliana, she's the head of The Witches' Council."

"Sick flex, bro," Ellis said.

Mercury rolled his eyes. "The point is, she'll be there. My dad is there, too. They can help us, maybe cloak us from the vampires or even help us fight them. Make no mistake—that's what we'll have to do—we'll have to fight."

Joelle whimpered. Griffin put his arm around her.

Mercury looked down at his full plate. Suddenly, he wasn't hungry anymore. He pushed his plate away as his stomach churned.

"I'm sorry. None of this—none of this was supposed to happen."

"You can say that again," Ellis said.

"Dick," Sloane replied. She punched him in the arm, leaving a greasy stain on the side of his bomber jacket.

Ellis scoffed and scooted away from her, picking up a napkin to wipe the grease.

Seconds later, Ethyl dropped their check. Mercury picked it up, surprised to find it zeroed out. He looked across the diner to the kitchen, where Ethyl stood next to a burly man and a petite woman with two ruby red double buns on the side of her head. They each held their hands up and waved. The man, who was the cook, was a Fire Hand. The petite waitress, an Air Hand. He pulled out his wallet and left a large tip on the table anyway. They each slid out of the booth and walked out of the diner.

"Blessed be," Mercury whispered as he passed Ethyl, who was already on her way to her next table.

"May the Gods keep you," she replied, patting his shoulder.

They stepped into the late afternoon sun. They needed to find a car now, so they walked along the strip, sunglasses on, in search of a dealership. Mercury walked behind the group, his eyes searching the streets for the group of vampires on their tail. Ellis fell back to walk beside him.

"You know there's a chance they might not help us, right?" Ellis asked. Mercury clenched his jaw.

"Maybe, maybe not. All I know is that we find my dad and we find Aunt Oliana as soon as we get to Mt. Katahdin. We'll talk to Aunt Oliana. She'll know what to do." *Or at least I hope she does.*

HBIC:
Oliana Murtaza on What It's Like Being the First Female Head of The Witches' Council

By Freddie Karr

There's something about a woman like Councilwoman Oliana Murtaza. A woman who walks into a room with her Gucci purse first, whose shoes are so red on the bottom they look purposefully dipped in the blood of her enemies. A woman who had to watch her own sister burn at the stake, who fought pearly-white tooth and expertly manicured nail to end discrimination against witches in the Bay Area, where she was born and raised. Now, she serves as the head of The Witches' Council, the governing body of witches the world over. Councilwoman Murtaza is the first of her kind—the first black woman to serve on the Council and the first woman to sit at its head. We met on a sunny spring day at a bistro near Central Park. Clad in a designer gown, her natural hair spilling down her back, Councilwoman Murtaza is every bit a fashion icon as she is one of the most powerful women in the world.

This HBIC came from humble beginnings. She was one of two children born to a teacher and a nurse. She and her sister, Kessia, spent their nights and weekends catching the BART to San Francisco. There they got a taste of the activism and fight for social justice that she'd join years later.

"I remember being entranced by the people who'd march through the streets or meet in the Haight or at Dolores Park. They weren't just protesting for witches, but for people of color, for women, for the LGBTQ community. It blew my mind because at the time, I must have been about 15 or 16. I wasn't exposed to the things they were speaking out against."

She and her sister felt free in all aspects of their lives save one–their magic.

"We were taught to be proud of who we were, of the fact that we wielded magic, but we were also told to be careful not to tell people about our abilities or use magic in public."

The councilwoman and her sister were confused by this edict–didn't they live in a diverse neighborhood in a diverse town in what's considered one of the most diverse parts of the country?

Their parents simply played the age old "because we said so card." It wasn't until she and her sister were in college that they realized how dangerous it was to reveal themselves to strangers.

"Sampson, my boyfriend, was killed in an altercation with two police officers. They were vampires. He never had a chance, really, not with them. That was the day that I learned two things–one, that caution is necessary but silence can be deadly. And two, that I was pregnant."

Councilwoman Murtaza gave birth to her first and only daughter, Faegan, in the summer of 1997. Though she graduated college with honors, she still struggled to find work as a single mother. She moved to Los Angeles with her sister and daughter. There they became more ingrained in the activist scene. They met members of The Witches' Council, including Atlas Amell, who would eventually become Councilwoman Murtaza's brother-in-law and right hand man.

"Atlas introduced us to a core group of people who worked for the Council, both on the main council and clerks, marketers and event coordinators. I learned that the council is both an organization created for the betterment of witches, but that it's also a business–and as a graduate of Stanford School of Business, I had a lot of ideas on how to make it better."

The councilwoman set her sights on a council seat, but it took her nearly seven years to secure one. When she did, she was surprised to learn that she was the first of her kind.

"The Council was founded in 1497, in Spain. Despite one of the founders being a woman, the fact that it took over five hundred years to appoint a woman, and a black woman at that, is archaic. One of my missions when I joined the council was to put an end to those ancient ways of thinking."

In her first one hundred days as a council member, Councilwoman Murtaza pushed to end laws that officially banned witches from disclosing their abilities, to end a law that prohibited witches from marrying non-witches, and addressed discrimination against women and people of color in the magic community at large.

"Most people took a look at me and thought–oh, she's just a pretty woman. And yes, I am pretty. I am gorgeous. But I'm also smart, I'm tough as nails, I don't suffer fools. I don't have patience for discrimination and harassment especially among witchkind. We cannot have the gall to speak out for our fair treatment when we are modeling the same behavior as humans, and as vampires."

It was her moxie and sticktoitiveness that pushed Councilwoman Murtaza into the spotlight. She became a sensation both online and off, and served as the grand marshal for more than a few Pride parades. So it came as no surprise when, in 2015, her name was put into the ring when Malcolm Knotting, the Council's longest serving head, announced his retirement. Many people, including her sister, who was also a council member, and her brother-in-law, thought Councilwoman Murtaza was a shoe in.

But when Icelandic member Olafur Pierson was appointed head of The Witches' Council in 2015, the witching world collectively gagged. Councilman Pierson was experienced, to be sure, but his politics were tired. He believed in the old-school ways, and his critics pulled no punches in slamming him for it.

"Pierson was a very old soul trapped in the body of a middle-aged white man. He was affable enough, but there were many people, myself included, who felt that he would take us backwards. And we were right."

In 2020, a vampire ran for President and won. Vampires and witches have been mortal enemies since the dawn of time. During the Spanish Inquisition, they sided with the Catholics and vehemently threw witches under the horse and buggy and rolled over them twice. Vampires simply needed blood to survive; there was no joy in the act of biting or drinking blood. They were deficient; they were atoning.

Witches, on the other hand, had a special place in hell–the Bible said to burn them, and for good reason. They were playing God, vampires argued, and it didn't take long for this verbiage to spread faster than the Black Death.

When most council members wanted to speak out against the increased violence committed against witches, Councilman Pierson refused. He believed the best way to handle the vampire insurgence was to tuck tail and go underground. Blend in. Be regular degular schmegular citizens. After a massacre of witches at the Appalachian National Scenic Trail mere weeks into 2021, witches were fed up.

The Council began plotting to remove Pierson from his post in a toss his shit out the window and change the locks sort of way. Councilwoman Murtaza once again had her hat thrown in the ring. Again, her hopes were dashed when the council voted her sister in her stead. Tragedy would soon strike again, as Kessia was murdered just days after the votes were cast.

"Finding out that Kessia died was agony. It felt like a piece of me was lost, like a limb had been severed. Even now, I still get that feeling–phantom limb syndrome–where I feel like she's not really gone. And moments later, I realize she is and my world shatters all over again."

But there is no rest or grief allowed for the weary–not only did she have to continue to raise her daughter, but she now had to assume the position of the most powerful witch in the world.

"I went to Kessia's funeral and I had just enough time to hug my parents, Atlas, my nephews and my daughter. Then I had to board a flight to the Council office in New York, where I would take up residence. Right away, I had to have a hand in appointing two other council members. Then there was the business of vampire-on-witch violence."

Since Vael started his term, there have been talks of enacting a peace treaty or some legislation to address the violence against witches. Despite Councilwoman Murtaza's efforts, she had not heard from President Vael or his administration–until January 2022. Vael was gearing up for his first State of the Union, and Councilwoman Murtaza for her first Astera as head of the Council. They spoke on the phone for two hours, and the councilwoman noted that Vael seemed as eager to strike a truce as she.

"He knows that this violence isn't just wrong; it's bad PR. All over the world, people are waking up to the violent nature of vampires and it was only a matter of time before that began to hurt his chances of re-election in 2024. After all, it wasn't just vampires who voted for him. Humans did, too. And his war between us, like the Sharks vs The Jets, would only end in more bloodshed if nothing was done."

They set an appointment to meet and discuss a peace treaty on March 20th, during Astera. The councilwoman advises me and all of witchkind to be cautiously optimistic, but to live our lives without the fear of violence. After all, she says, "What good is being a witch if you aren't having a little fun?"

Chapter 6

The car's heater blew out half an hour outside of Las Vegas. Mercury crossed his arms against the cold. He felt the chill all the way to the bone, clenching his teeth to keep them from chattering.

It had been sunny when they left Las Vegas, but the clouds set in as they crossed the Utah state line. Barren trees lined the streets, looking like skeletal sentinels guarding the narrow two-lane highway. Ellis sped down the road, using the middle lane as a suggestion rather than a guideline.

They passed a sign that read "Sulpherdale pop. 1,200" and Mercury's heart leapt.

Just a little further, Mercury thought.

"So, what's this hotel again?" Sloane asked as she leaned into the front seat.

"It's a safe house, run by my Tia Santo," Mercury replied. "There are plenty of rooms, hot showers, lots of food. This'll be a great place to lay low for a few days. Santo's an Earth Hand, so she's got this beautiful garden area that she keeps blooming all year. Plus, the house is completely warded against vampires."

No one spoke.

Mercury's stomach spoke instead.

However, he pushed forward, telling the group about Santo, about how they'd be safe there. He wondered if they believed him, even if he believed himself.

He told them about a time he'd visited Santo when he and Troian were children. He remembered the persimmon tree outside of the motel, right next to a big, tall tree known as the Falwell Limb. When his father went to Astera, he'd leave Troian and Mercury with Santo, who Mercury remembered as being old even as a child. She'd tell them stories about the Falwell Limb, about trees like that all over the country that were morbidly named after the first witch who perished on them. The one in Santo's hometown had been called the Livingston Limb.

He'd eat persimmons until his stomach was upset while Santo told them about Rene Livingston, and Anna May Falwell, about Thaddeus Gordon, whose Limb was in Priest River, and Adepero Aduba, whose Limb was the tallest and longest in the state of Georgia.

At night, Mercury would lie in bed and wonder whether or not his own mother had been hung from a Limb named after someone else. Or if she'd been the first, and so now the tree would be known as Kessia Amell Limb.

The freeway teed off and the trees thinned out. Mercury gestured to Ellis to turn left, and as he did they heard the shriek of a peacock.

"What was that?" Griffin asked.

Ellis rolled his eyes. "It's just a peacock, you pu–"

Mercury cleared his throat. "You poor little scaredy cat."

"Don't talk to my brother that way." Joelle glared at Ellis in the rearview mirror.

"It's okay, Jo; I know how to handle privileged white boys," Griffin smirked.

Ellis chuckled. "That so, Poindexter?"

"Yeah, you cracker-ass bird."

Ellis opened his mouth to speak but Sloane's laughter tore through the silence.

"Well done, Griffin."

"We're almost there," Mercury said, hoping to change the subject.

They rode in silence for several minutes until a large, three story hotel came into view. The building seemed out of place in the area, as it was the tallest and brightest building, and the most adorned. It was painted a pale yellow and had shutters of robin's egg blue. The grounds surrounding the building were covered in gardens and lavish rose bushes.

"This is amazing." Joelle looked on in amazement as they pulled into the driveway.

"Some hideout," said Ellis and Sloane simultaneously. The two then shared a glance.

"Yes, well, it's the kind of place that's only found if one is really looking for it," Mercury added. Once the car stopped, Mercury stepped out, closing his eyes to smell the fragrant breeze. Roses, lemons, sage and rosemary filled the air and he felt a wave of relief wash over him.

A white mountain lion with green eyes emerged from the garden as Mercury pulled his backpack from the car.

Joelle breathed in sharply and stood stock still against the car. Mercury stepped toward the lion, causing Joelle to whimper.

"Merc, no," she said.

He strode slowly toward the animal, who assessed him wearily.

"Benedito, it's Mercury."

He knelt before the lion and held his hands out, palms up. The cat looked from Mercury's hands to his face and purred. It sniffed at his hand and Mercury slowly brought the other to its head. Its purr grew louder as Mercury stroked its fur.

"Guys, it's okay," Mercury reassured them. He stood and turned toward the group, who all looked at him like he was growing another head.

"This is Benedito, Santo's familiar," he said. He looked down at the lion and spoke. "Can you take me to my Tía?"

The lion turned and sauntered toward the hotel. Mercury didn't wait for the group to follow him. He followed Benedito into the vintage turnstile entrance, his stomach filling with butterflies as he inched closer to the interior of the hotel.

Santo was sitting in the parlor, a book in one hand and a glass of Tempranillo in another. She looked up at him and smiled, her large brown eyes narrowing.

"Well, if it isn't Mercury Amell," she said, her voice as deep and smooth as chocolate.

"Tía Santo." Mercury smiled.

Santo tossed her book on the table and glided toward him. Her long dress trailed on the fleur de lis-patterned carpet as she walked. She threw her arms around him and Mercury's heart skipped a beat. She smelled like sunflowers.

She pulled back from him and smiled, and to Mercury it felt like being in the warmth of the sun.

"What brings you here? Don't tell me Atlas still thinks you boys need vigilance while he's gallivanting with Oliana."

Mercury scoffed. "No, he doesn't. He left yesterday without really saying goodbye."

Santo laughed. "Sounds like Atlas. Well then, did you and Troian come for a visit?"

Mercury's heart skipped a beat at the sound of his brother's name. He stuffed his hands in his pockets and the ghost of a smile spread across his face.

"No, Troian is . . . in LA; he's looking after the shop. I'm on a road trip with some friends and I thought we'd swing by, introduce them to my favorite Tia."

Santo swatted Mercury's arm and smiled.

"You've always been a charmer, Mercury."

She followed him to the lobby where the rest of the group stood with their bags. They all seemed taken aback by the enormity of the hotel, just as Mercury himself had been. He was only six when his father first brought him and Troian, who was eleven at the time, to the hotel. Not much had changed since he first laid eyes on the hotel, whose interior was styled in the belle époque way. Dark green wallpaper covered nearly every inch of wall space, the areas that weren't were covered with gilded gold mirrors. The carpet stretched all the way up the stairs and throughout the entire building. To the left of the door sat the main desk, which was empty. Mercury frowned, as he always remembered someone sitting and waiting for guests to come in.

Santo must have followed his gaze, and she replied: "We haven't gotten many guests lately, so I've taken over a lot of the duties of the old staff. Times have been hard, but we get by."

"But the place looks so spotless, how–"

"It's called magic, dear. Helps with a multitude of sins." She then shifted her attention to the group. "So, who do we have here?"

Mercury smiled as he introduced them.

"This is Joelle and her brother, Griffin; this is Sloane and Ellis."

"It's nice to meet you," Joelle said.

"You've got a lovely place here," Griffin added.

"Yeah, too bad it's in the middle of bumfuck nowhere," Ellis groaned. Sloane elbowed him in the ribs and stepped forward, holding out a hand to Santo.

"Nice to meet you, Ms. Santo," Sloane said.

Santo lifted a brow and smirked.

"You have a lovely home."

"Why thank you, dear," Santo said. She squeezed Sloane's hand and then turned to the rest of the group. "Well, I'm looking forward to getting to know each of you. Let me get you a key to your rooms."

She stepped behind the counter and grabbed five antique keys. She then approached the staircase, her long black dress trailing behind her. Each of their rooms was on the second floor. She showed Mercury his room last, and it was the same room he always stayed in— a large corner unit with a small kitchen and garden tub. For the first time ever, he didn't have to share the large king bed with his brother.

"I can't thank you enough, Tia."

Santo smiled. "Think nothing of it. You're like the son I always wanted, well you and Troian. And besides, given the way you and your friends look, it seems like you could really use a room."

Mercury blushed. "Well, I–"

She put a hand on his shoulder. "You can tell me all about it over dinner."

Two hours later, the group sat at the long dining room table in the parlor. Santo prepared spaghetti and garlic bread. When she set the pot of pasta down in front of him, Mercury's stomach growled. He scooped a large serving of pasta onto his plate, trying to be mindful of the rest of the group and how hungry they must be. When everyone had taken a portion, Mercury dove in then stopped abruptly.

"Oh, sorry," he said to Santo. He steepled his hands. "I forgot we always start with prayer."

Santo scoffed. "No need for that anymore."

Mercury scowled briefly as Ellis and Sloane laughed. Santo had never decided not to say a prayer before. He remembered his father teasing her, insisting that a powerful witch like herself shouldn't need to look to a higher power. Santo always disagreed, saying that she felt all the more connected with God because of her power, feeling that he had endowed her with a power that was great and meant to be used to help her fellow man.

"When did you stop being the praying type?" Mercury asked. The smile that Santo had perpetually had on her face since they arrived slid off, replaced by a frown.

"When did you become one?" she spat.

"I haven't; it's just—"

She lifted a hand. "I'd think that you'd be relieved. You hated praying, even as a young child."

"I never hated praying . . . I just wanted to get to my food faster," Mercury said. He and Santo stared at each other then Santo laughed, tilting her head back. The rest of the table began to laugh and Mercury joined in.

"Oh, Mercury, how I've missed you," Santo said. She reached a hand across the table and placed her weathered hand on his. Mercury flinched. Her hand felt so cold, as though she'd just been outside shoveling snow. Santo didn't seem to catch his movement; she moved her hand away and picked up a glass of red wine.

"So, tell me, what brings you all to this Podunk town?"

Joelle and Sloane looked at each other as Griffin's gaze shifted to his plate.

"Well, dickhead here fucked up and killed a frat girl who happened to be getting dicked down by an asshole frat boy who also happens to be a vampire. Not sure if you saw anything on the news, but that turned into a riot, and even *Now This* reported on it. So here we are, fleeing the scene, especially after Troian—"

Sloane placed a hand on Ellis' shoulder and squeezed.

"What this white boy is trying to say is that we got into a fight in Los Angeles and now we're on a road trip just trying to figure it out."

Santo took a long sip from her glass of wine. "And what about Troian?"

Mercury sipped his wine as well, the mention of his brother sending a lump to his throat.

"He got beaten up pretty bad," Mercury said. "I had to heal him myself."

Santo's brows lifted. "Did you now?" That's some pretty powerful stuff—you must be exhausted."

Mercury smiled tightly and continued eating, though his appetite waned. He was thankful that Santo didn't press them about the incident in Los Angeles. She turned toward the group and asked them each about themselves and what they wanted to do in life.

"Engineering," Griffin said. "I want to fix the infrastructure."

"I want to own my own music studio and be a producer," said Joelle excitedly.

"A writer. I'm going to be the next Freddie Karr," Sloane said, holding her drink high in cheers before taking a long swig.

"And what about you, Ellis?" Santo turned to him. Ellis had barely touched the food on his plate and sat with his arms crossed. He shrugged.

"Doesn't matter," Ellis said.

"Of course, it does," she replied. She grabbed the bottle of wine and poured more into Ellis' glass.

"Well, I don't think it does. Between this shit show situation and my parents being rich . . . if I make it out alive, I'll just take over my father's business. He's in PR, runs the largest firm in all of the Golden State. I'll inherit the business and I'll help movie stars get out of sex scandals and politicians pretend their racist tweets were just a fuck up. I'll meet and marry a blonde woman who came to LA but didn't have the talent to act or the stomach to do porn. I'll have kids and the cycle will start over again."

The group sat in stunned silence. Of course, Mercury knew all of this already. He knew that part of why Ellis was so difficult involved him being filled with ennui–his choices had been taken away from him long ago.

"We always have the power to change our fate. And if you could, what would you choose?"

"A songwriter," Mercury answered for him. He sat back in his chair and held his wine glass to his chest. "Ellis always wanted to be a songwriter. He's good at it, too."

Ellis looked at Mercury, scowling, but then he nodded.

"Well, you all seem like such talented kids. You'll find your way, even if life takes you down a few odd paths," Santo assured them.

"Well, what about you? Did you always want to run a place like this? How did you meet Mercury's dad?" Sloane asked.

Santo smiled. "No, I'm afraid this is one of those odd paths I was talking about. As to how I met Atlas, well, he saved my life."

Santo stared off into the distance; her hazel eyes glazed over.

"Santo, are you okay?" Mercury asked. She shook her head and when she looked at him, he noticed the light in her eyes was gone.

"The sun is setting," she said. "I think it's time for bed now."

Griffin looked at his watch. "But it's barely six."

Santo pushed her seat back and began taking their plates.

"But I wasn't–" Sloane started.

"That's nice, dear," Santo replied. She ushered the plates into the kitchen.

"What's wrong with her?" Sloane whispered.

Mercury shrugged as Santo drifted back into the room.

"Well, let's get you all off to bed, shall we?" She turned on her heels and walked toward the grand staircase, her long black dress trailing behind her. Mercury looked at the group and then pushed his chair back.

"Come now, all of you," Santo said. This time her voice was tinged with urgency. Mercury sighed and stood to follow her to his bedroom. The rest of the group followed suit, and Sloane caught up to him.

"We're not really going to bed right now, are we?" she asked.

Mercury shook his head.

"No. We'll all just go in our rooms for a while. Once the coast is clear, we'll meet in my room," he replied.

He looked back at them to make sure they heard him. They all nodded except Ellis, who walked with his hands in his pockets and his head down. When Mercury arrived at his room, he found Santo waiting for him outside. She seemed nervous, her hands turning over and over on themselves.

"Tia, are you okay?" he asked.

"Yes, dear. I'm just tired. You've all had such a long journey. Aren't you sleepy?"

Mercury scowled and shook his head. He stepped toward her and placed his hands on her arms. He fought back a shiver because, like her hands, her arms were cold as ice. He forced himself to keep his hands steady, trying not to call attention to his growing feelings of worry.

"No, in fact I'm still hungry. Are you sure there's no reason you want to usher us to our rooms other than you wanting us to sleep?"

Santo smiled, but her eyes were large and wild.

"Oh, Mercury. I simply value my quiet time, as I am sure you all value yours. I think it's best you get some rest before setting off on your journey tomorrow morning," she replied. She leaned forward and kissed his cheek, and this time Mercury couldn't hide his surprise.

"What's wrong?" she asked.

"You're really cold. Are you getting sick, Tia?"

Santo shook her head. "Mercury, it's spring in Utah. It's not even sixty degrees outside. I'm not sick, just cold."

Mercury unlocked his door and pushed it open. "Okay. Well, good night, Tia."

Santo kissed his cheek again. She turned to leave, then stopped. "Mercury?"

"Yes?"

"Keep your door closed and locked all night."

"What—"

She turned away before Mercury could respond. He closed the door behind him but he didn't lock it, knowing that the group would be joining him at any moment. He heard Santo knock on each of the doors, asking the group to please lock behind them. Mercury faced the window and stared out into the garden and watched the darkness slowly envelop the sun's rays.

Ten minutes later, he heard a knock on the door.

"It's unlocked," Mercury called. He turned to see Joelle open the door and close it behind her.

"Where's everyone else?" he asked.

She shrugged. "Griffin said he wanted to take a shower, not sure about the other two." She tapped her hand along the tall white dresser next to the door.

"You can sit down if you want," Mercury said, gesturing to the bed.

She walked over and sat down, barely making a sound. He was impressed by her grace.

"So, what's the deal with your aunt?" she asked.

"I don't know," he replied. "Honestly, she's a bit different this time . . . more eccentric. Maybe she doesn't get enough visitors."

"Well, I can't say I mind getting sent to bed. This hotel is beautiful, and it'll be nice to actually sleep in a bed for the first time in two days."

Mercury nodded.

"So . . . any word from anyone about the riot or about Troian?" she asked, gesturing to his cellphone on the nightstand.

"No," he said. "I just spoke to my cousin when we were in Vegas. I've had it on airplane mode, and I've been too . . . freaked to go on Instagram or Twitter or anything. You?"

Joelle lied down on the bed, her jet-black curls spread out around her head like a halo.

"My grandmother called and left a voicemail on both of our phones. I called her back before dinner, letting her know I was just spending time away with Griffin and some friends for the weekend. I surfed Twitter for a minute."

"And?"

"I wouldn't recommend it. The hashtags burn the witch, kill the Air Hand and Los Angeles riots are trending right now."

Mercury's stomach churned.

"All your parents will come looking, eventually," he replied.

"What about yours? Won't yours come—"

"My mom's dead. And my dad is already at Astera. He knows about Troian, so he's likely waiting for me so he can kick my ass physically and magically."

The color drained from Joelle's face.

"I'm so sorry. I didn't realize . . . about your mom, I mean," she said. "Griffin and I know what's it's like to experience that kind of loss."

Mercury nodded. He lied down beside Joelle and sighed.

"We were walking home from the Supermercado, me, her and Troian. Dad was at the shop, working. A group of vampires started catcalling her. When one grabbed her, she let go of my hand and pushed me forward, telling Troian to hold on to me. She turned and unleashed fire on them, the flames licking their motorcycles and scorching their leather. She fought as best she could but," Mercury's voice broke. "Witch or not, she was still one woman against five vampires. They took turns feeding on her and then strung her up on a tree across from a playground."

Tears slipped down Mercury's cheeks.

"Oh my God . . ." Joelle's eyes filled with horror.

Mercury wiped at his eyes with the palm of his hand. "Troian tried to fight them, too, but they just pushed him down, pushed me down. One of them held us down as they strung our mother up and laughed."

He felt Joelle's hand stroke the side of his face, wiping at the tears. He turned and looked at her through glassy eyes. She wrapped her arms around him and his heart beat faster. He buried his face in her neck, marveling at the softness of her skin.

"Well at least you still have your dad . . . and us."

Before Mercury could respond, the door burst open and three sets of footsteps trotted into the room. Mercury turned to see Sloane, Ellis and Griffin standing there, each one wearing a different expression.

"Gross," exclaimed Griffin.

"I knew it! I fucking knew it, bro," Sloane shouted gleefully.

Ellis just smirked and seated himself at the desk. Mercury sat up.

"Hey guys," he said. Sloane giggled and puffed on her vape. Joelle rolled over onto her stomach and rested her head in her hands.

"So . . . what the fuck is up with your aunt?" Ellis said, breaking the tension. Mercury winced.

"Yeah, she's a little . . . colorful," Joelle said.

"That's one way to put it," said Ellis. "Why was she so insistent to lock us away?"

Mercury shrugged. "Honestly, I don't know. She was never like this before. In the past, Troian and I roamed around this entire hotel when we were younger. Maybe she just wants the other guests to have some quiet?"

"What other guests?" asked Griffin. "I mean . . . I haven't seen anyone else around, and there aren't any other cars outside."

"Maybe they just really keep to themselves," Mercury said, but he knew that couldn't possibly be the truth. They were likely the only guests there, so why was Santo forcing a curfew on them? The rest of the group regarded him skeptically, which made Mercury's stomach churn, his typical response to uncertainty.

"So . . . anyone want to try to sneak some booze from the bar downstairs?" Mercury tried to change the subject. When no one said anything, he stood.

"I'll go," Joelle said.

"So you guys can make out some more?" Sloane smirked around her vape pen. Mercury rolled his eyes and though he tried to hide it, he couldn't help the blush that spread on his cheeks. "I'll go, too."

"We didn't–"

Sloane scoffed taking another pull from her vape.

Ellis and Griffin didn't move. Mercury shrugged and opened the door.

The hallway was nearly pitch black, barely illuminated by the setting sun and the distant light from the downstairs lobby.

"I don't like this," Joelle said as a surge of light sprung from her hand. She held the fireball up at eye level and Mercury let her walk ahead, even though his senses were heightened enough that he could see most of the hallway with ease. Sloane followed behind them in silence, but Mercury could feel her body tense as she placed a hand on his shoulder.

They descended the stairwell and the smell of copper and dirt tinged his nostrils. He padded down the stairs, vaguely hearing movement on the other side of the building. He turned toward them and held his finger before his mouth. Sloane frowned and Joelle nodded, extinguishing the fire in her hand. The room went dark again, and it was up to Mercury to guide them.

They turned to the left and walked to the bar, which was hidden behind a set of French doors. Mercury peaked through the doors and let out a breath when he found the room empty. He rounded the bar and ran his hands over the bottles. Joelle's fire illuminated the room as Mercury grabbed a handle of rum. He slid it across the bar to Sloane, who grabbed the bottle and guzzled its contents.

"Good choice," she said.

With her free hand, Joelle grabbed the bottle and took a sip. She coughed as she lowered the bottle and slid it across the bar to Mercury. He chuckled.

"What else should we grab?" he asked. He turned back toward the liquor. A large bottle of Chivas and a globe-shaped bottle of framboise graced the top shelf. Mercury gestured and the bottles slid forward and floated down to the bar behind him.

"I still can't get used to your powers," Joelle said.

Sloane scoffed. "That parlor trick? That's nothing. Wait 'til you meet Atlas, Merc's dad. He's the big daddy of Water Hands."

Mercury bit his tongue, trying not to let Sloane's remark sting. She was right–his father was one of the most powerful witches in the world. As a Water Hand, he was highly skilled with potions, controlling liquid and blood magic. He wondered if he would ever even come close to his father's level of skill.

"Well, since my 'parlor trick' didn't impress you, Slo, I guess you're getting Evan Williams." He pulled a dusty bottle of cheap whiskey from the shelf. She muttered something under her breath and Joelle laughed, but Mercury's smile quickly faded. Below Joelle's laugh was another sound, like nails clicking across tile. He felt that feeling behind his eye again, like it was being carved out by a melon baller. His heartbeat quickened.

"We need to get back to the room," he said abruptly.

"What, why?" Sloane asked.

"Shh," he said. His unease had grown and where before he felt like he was being paranoid, he now believed he was right. They were not alone. He waited until the sound disappeared then grabbed the bottles and motioned for the women to follow him.

"Turn your light off," he said to Joelle. She started to protest, but Mercury turned to her and placed a finger in front of his mouth. "We're not alone. We need to be as inconspicuous as possible."

Joelle nodded.

He walked to the room as light but as fast as he could with Joelle and Sloane following close behind. When they reached the room, he quickly closed the door behind them and flipped the lock.

"That was quick," Ellis said. He stood and grabbed the bottle of rum from Mercury's hand.

"Merc flipped out," Sloane said. She threw herself on the bed beside Griffin.

Griffin crossed his arms and gave Mercury a sidelong glance. "What's wrong?" he asked.

"I don't think we're alone here," he replied.

"Well, obviously," Ellis said. "I'm sure Santo is roaming around."

Mercury shook his head. "No. I mean, aside from her. There are other people here, and I think they might be vampires."

"Why would Santo let vampires in her hotel? From what you've said, witches and vampires don't exactly get along, right?" Sloane asked.

"Yeah, Mercury. I'm sure it's nothing. This hotel is strange, and it's been a long time since you've been here. Just relax," Joelle reassured him, holding out the bottle of rum to him. Mercury stood stock still, listening for any other sound. But it was quiet. There was nothing else, just the sounds of the group breathing and the low hum of the desk lamp. Deciding to let his suspicions go, he nodded and accepted the bottle from Joelle.

Sloane sipped from the bottle of Chivas, while Griffin clutched the framboise in his hands. He brought the bottle up to his mouth with both hands, taking a long draw.

They sat in silence for several moments, each of them passing the bottles around amongst them. Mercury's lips started to feel numb. His limbs felt languid, and he felt if he lied down on the bed that he would simply melt into the mattress.

"We need some music," Ellis said. He turned toward the nightstand. Instead of a television, the room had a radio. Ellis flipped the dials around, wincing at the stations filled with static. Finally, he settled on a station playing "Baby I Love Your Way."

"I feel like I'm at a 70's prom," Griffin said.

Sloane giggled. She jumped up and started swaying to the music and singing along, her gravelly voice reminding Mercury of Janis Joplin.

"C'mon, dance with me," Sloane said, grabbing Griffin and pulling him up. Griffin gasped and nearly spilled the bottle of Chambord. He put his hands on her shoulders then at her waist.

"Have you never slow danced before?" she asked. Griffin shook his head and Sloane placed his hands on the smallest part of her waist. She stood on her toes to wrap her arms around his neck and swayed. She continued dancing, even when the song changed over to 'Come and Get Your Love'. Griffin couldn't keep up and quickly sat down on the bed. He drew his knees to his chin and wrapped his arms around them. Joelle rushed to his side, patting his back and whispering if he was okay.

Sloane shook her head but continued dancing and singing. She gestured to Mercury to dance and he shrugged. He stood and started dancing, copying the moves he'd seen his father do when he described *Soul Train*, which he watched as a kid.

"Damn, Merc, you've got the moves," Sloane said.

"Don't you know all black people have rhythm?" Ellis said. "It's like, in their genetic makeup or something."

Mercury shot Ellis a look but he didn't stop dancing. The languidness he'd felt before shifted into a manic energy when 'You Make Me Feel' switched on. Griffin relaxed, stretching his legs out. Joelle jumped next to Sloane and the two started bumping their hips together and laughing. Ellis swayed as he sat and drank the Chivas. Mercury gestured for the bottle of rum and it floated to him. He chugged the bottle, his head now swimming. He laughed. For the first time in several days, Mercury laughed. He lowered his shoulders and closed his eyes, letting the music fill him and nourish him.

As the radio changed to "Family Affair", a loud thump sounded just outside the room. Mercury's eyes snapped open. His stomach dropped.

"What was that?" Griffin whispered as he shot up from the bed.

Joelle switched the radio off and they listened for another sound. Another thud, this time louder. It sounded like something, or someone, being thrown against the wood framework of the door.

"What the fuck is that?" Ellis said, his voice almost a shout. Mercury looked back at him, willing him to stop.

Three sharp thuds followed, and then silence. Mercury stepped toward the door. The door knob twisted slowly, as though it were a combination lock. Joelle inhaled sharply as the door clicked and slid open.

On the other side of the door stood two people Mercury barely recognized – a man and a woman, both tall, and both vampires. The man stepped into the room and in the light Mercury recognized him as the owner of the gas station down the road, where they'd stopped earlier to get water and snacks.

"Sorry, looks like you've got the wrong room," Mercury said. "This one's already taken."

The man sneered at Mercury, no doubt sensing the power that buzzed within him. The woman stepped forward and Mercury's heart skipped a beat. She was tall and chubby, but her heart-shaped face and cat-like eyes mirrored her little sister's.

"Tia Dora," Mercury said. The last time he'd seen Santo's oldest sister, he was thirteen. She was thinner then, and a blonde. She fought with Santo over the property, over selling the Hotelario. When Santo told her no, that selling would mean one less safe place for witchkind, Dora scoffed.

"If witchkind wanted a safe space, they'd give up practicing their magic and go straight to the church."

85

Now, Dora stood before him wearing a nun's habit, her once-caramel skin a mottled gray in the lamplight.

"We knew you were here," said Dora. "We followed your stink all the way from the state line."

Mercury shuddered. "Well, as much as I'd love a reunion, we'd best be going. We're on a trip to see—"

"To see your father so he can help you escape those vampires on your tail?" the gas station owner interjected. He wore an oil-stained gray jumper with the name "Tyrell" etched on the left front pocket.

"Well, news does travel fast," said Mercury. He tried his best to keep his voice level. But inside, his stomach churned, rebelling against the alcohol. His heart beat so loud that it echoed in his ears. Mercury motioned toward the door.

"Mercury," Joelle said, her voice quivering.

"C'mon, guys; let's go," Mercury said. He took another step, standing toe to toe with Tyrell and Dora. He stared at Tyrell, willing him to stand down, to just let them leave. But when he felt the tip of a knife at his belly, Mercury knew they'd have no choice but to fight their way out.

"Now, you're just gonna sit down and not do any of your tricks," Tyrell said. He smiled, his fangs touching the edges of his bottom lip.

Mercury allowed himself to be led back into the room, knowing that he'd be boxed in between Tyrell and Dora if he stood in the hallway. As soon as he felt the back of the bed with his legs, he placed a hand on Tyrell's shoulder and pushed him away, leaning into his powers. Tyrell flew across the room and hit the nightstand. He slid down to the floor, landing in a pile of broken glass. Dora turned toward Mercury and narrowed her eyes. The electricity in the room flickered then went out.

"Mercury, what the fuck?" exclaimed Ellis.

Joelle sparked the flame in her left hand, illuminating the room in a light barely the enhancement of a candle.

"I see you've graced this human with some magic," Dora said. She walked toward the group.

"You don't touch them," Mercury warned. He flung his hand to the side, but Dora's magic was too strong. She barely shifted and when she turned to face him, she clenched her fist.

Mercury's hands flew to his neck as he gasped for air. His eyes widened and he fell back on the bed. Ellis and Griffin rushed toward him, trying to help. Mercury kicked out, his lungs burning. A tear streamed down the side of his face as thoughts of Troian and his last moments kaleidoscoped before his mind.

Dora approached Joelle and grabbed at her long curls. "Such a pretty little thing," she teased.

Joelle flung a ball of fire at Dora. Dora batted it to the side and grabbed Joelle's wrists. "Not bad work, either. But do you really think that prude aunt of yours is going to allow these abominations into Astera?"

Mercury's vision tunneled. His breath became shorter.

"What do we do? What do we do?" Griffin asked in a panic.

Mercury's head spun and his vision tunneled even more.

A scream rang out through the room and Mercury's throat opened. He sat up and breathed deeply. Sloane had buried one of her daggers into Dora's neck. Blood spurted out of the wound. Tyrell, who had been struggling to get up since falling into the mirror, crawled to Dora's side.

"Let's get the fuck out of here," Sloane said. She clenched her hand and her knives slid back into their sheaths. Mercury stood and stumbled, his body still aching from a lack of oxygen. Ellis grabbed his arm and slung it around his shoulder.

"I got you, bro," he said. Without warning he sped off and Mercury's stomach churned as they took the stairs fast. He could hear two sets of footsteps echoing behind them.

"Not so fast."

Mercury turned to see Santo standing before the front door.

"Santo?" he questioned, taking a step toward her. "What's happening?"

She held her hand up. "I'm sorry, Mercury. I can't let you leave."

"What do you mean, you can't let us leave?" he replied. He turned to see the vampires had caught up to them. Sloane had both of her knives out, and Ellis was trying desperately to touch one of the vampires to impart his poison. Griffin dodged a punch from Tyrell. He held a hand out turning the small, thin blade the vampire held in his hand into a viper. The viper hissed and slithered down Tyrell's hand, but the vampire simply grabbed the snake just behind its head and dug his fangs into it.

Santo's voice cut through the chaos. "I can't. The vampires . . . they need fresh blood. I need fresh blood," she whispered the last part, knowing that Mercury could hear her anyway.

His heart sank as his worst fears were confirmed. Santo's behavior earlier had not been because of her older age. She'd been turned.

"For how long?" he asked.

"Six years," she said. Mercury closed his eyes. Six years. That was just after the last time he and Troian had visited Santo during Astera. He'd helped her plant the roses in the front garden, had spent the evenings sleeping in a hammock outside while Benedito slept at his feet.

"Why didn't you turn us away? How could you, after everything . . . I loved you like family."

She stepped toward him and Mercury held his hands up. "I tried to save you. I told you to keep your door locked. I told the others they were not to go into the room with the locked door."

"So, what, you were just going to let them feast on my friends?"

He could hear the fight behind him, though it sounded as if only the woman was still standing. He heard Joelle yelp and he turned to see the vampire almost dig her fangs into the petite girl's throat before Sloane dug her dual knives into the vampire's back.

"They're humans," Santo said. "They're all over the place, messing up the world. It's creatures like us who are the salvation for this planet."

"And what about the fact that vampires have always been our enemy? Do you not care? If I told you that a group of them killed Troian, would that make you pause?"

He could tell that there was some part of her that didn't want to hurt anyone. But though her eyes were glassy, they were also darker than he'd ever seen them. They looked like shark eyes, soulless and predatory.

"I'm so sorry to hear about your brother. I loved him—I loved both of you like my own children. I never wanted your head to be on the chopping block." Santo paused. "If I let you go, just you, would you take your car and drive far away and forget about these people?"

"Not a chance. We came together, and we leave together."

Santo took a deep breath. "Then you will die together, too."

She held out a hand and coiled her fingers. Mercury felt pinpricks in his stomach but willed himself to stand upright. He lifted his hand toward

Santo and sent her across the room. She slid away and as Mercury attempted to run to the door, Santo was upon him. She pulled his head back and a shiver went down Mercury's spine as her fangs grazed his neck. He closed his eyes and readied himself for the pain of a bite.

However, Santo screamed as she released his neck. Mercury turned to see her wrapped in Ellis' arms. A network of black vines weaved their way up his arms as he poisoned Santo.

"Don't kill her," Mercury warned.

"Are you shitting me?" Ellis said. "She tried to kill you."

"She's my aunt, Ellis. I don't want her dead."

"You couldn't kill me even if you tried," Santo said. "Dativa."

Ellis let go of Santo and fell to his knees, screaming. The poison in Ellis' tattoo had been turned around by Santo, and now worked its way through his bloodstream. The black veins crawled up his arms and neck and as Mercury ran to him and knelt beside him, he could see them pulsating beneath the skin. Mercury summoned the pocket knife from Tyrell's overalls and wiped the blade on his shirt. He ran it across his palm and winced. He dropped his blood across Ellis' body and recited the only healing spell he could do alone.

Sloane rushed toward Santo, blade at the ready. Santo gestured toward her and Sloane stopped in her tracks. Her legs slammed together. Green vines punched through the carpet beneath her feet and crawled up her legs. Sloane yelped as the vines constricted her legs. She fell to her knees from the weight of them and cried out as the horns from the briars dug into her skin. Joelle ran to her side and tried to use her fire to burn the vines off but seconds later, her arms were being smothered by the same vines on Sloane's legs.

Griffin was the last one standing. Mercury looked up and saw his hands shaking as he stared at Santo through dirty glasses.

"There's no point in this. I assure you I'm not the only one in the area thirsting for your blood."

"We beat those vampires in LA, and we'll beat you, too," said Griffin. He closed his eyes and stretched his left hand toward Santo. She made the same motion but Griffin was quicker. He opened his eyes and grunted. Mercury looked back toward Santo and saw that her hand had turned into stone as her scream erupted throughout the room. She lifted her hand toward Griffin and Mercury seized the opportunity.

He bolted toward her, slamming her hand into the door frame. It shattered. With her free hand, she cradled her arm as blood oozed from the wound.

Griffin grabbed at the vines coiled around his sister's body. A chunk of the vine broke off in his hands. He closed his eyes for several seconds before opening his palms. An asp writhed in his hands.

Griffin tossed the snake into the air then Mercury guided it toward Santo. Before she could move, the asp dug its fangs into her hand.

Santo yelped. She slid down to the ground, her black dress bunching up against her thighs, exposing the network of dark veins in her legs.

Mercury knelt before her. Her eyes were rimmed with red. Her breath was shallow. He had hoped that now that his aunt was on her deathbed that she'd be like the old Santo, but when he looked at her now, he still saw such hate in her eyes.

"You may have killed me but mark my words– no vampire will stop until they've killed you dead."

"Well, I guess that means I won't stop either," he replied. He stood just as she fell to her side. Before he could face the group or speak, the door swung open, pushing Santo's body to the side. A group of at least ten vampires stood before him, each one looking more hillbilly than the last.

"Well, well, looks like that witch wasn't lyin'. We're going to have some good eatin' tonight," said the one who stood before Mercury. He had a long beard and even longer hair that hung in a greasy tangle down his back.

Mercury gestured and sent the leader to the side. The rest of the pack charged them. Both Joelle and Sloane barely managed to detangle themselves from the vines before being barraged by the vampires.

For the third time within a two-day period, Mercury and his friends fought their way out of a scramble. As they stood outside of the hotel, full of a group of unconscious vampires that no doubt would awaken any minute, Mercury tried to hide the blood streaming from his nose.

"Let's hope this slows them down," said Joelle. She lifted her hands and two fireballs appeared. She tossed them at the hotel and within seconds Mercury's second home was engulfed in flames. He sighed, feeling as though he'd just been punched in the gut, facing yet another harsh reality.

"What do we do now?" said Griffin.

"We keep moving," Mercury answered. "Anyone got the keys?"

He gestured to the car. They all shook their head.

"Does that mean we're stuck?" Joelle asked.

"I might be able to hot wire it," said Sloane.

"Of course, you can," Ellis said. Sloane shot him a look of disgust, but made no move toward the vehicle.

Suddenly, the front window of the hotel burst open. Mercury jumped as three vampires stood, their bodies charred from the flames. Two of them were large, burly men with matted hair and singed overalls. Mercury's heart jumped at the sight of the other vampire who stood before them.

"I told you, Mercury," said Santo. Her body was a twisted, grotesque thing, still on fire. "I can't let you go."

"What do we do?" cried Joelle.

"Run," Mercury shouted. He turned and sped into the forest, the sounds of the groups' foot falls and the crackling of the flames filling his ears, sending his senses into overdrive.

Just keep running, he thought as his lungs began to ache. *Just keep running.* It was so cold he could see his breath before him.

Mercury didn't know if the vampires were still behind them because when he allowed himself small glances back, all he saw was darkness. When he reached a clearing that lead to two paths, he stopped.

"Where are they?" Ellis said, hands on his knees and his breath escaping in spurts.

"I don't know. I haven't seen them," replied Sloane.

"Which way do we go?" asked Ellis.

"Should we stay here?" asked Joelle.

"Should we go back for the car?" asked Griffin.

Mercury tried to focus, but his head was spinning. His vision twisted and suddenly he felt his head connect with the ground. His vision went black and he heard only silence.

Hours later, Mercury sat up with a start.

Where am I? The sun was shining and he sat against a tree in the middle of a clearing.

"It's okay," said Joelle. She sat beside him, one hand resting on his thigh. "You're safe."

"What happened? Where are we?" Mercury asked.

"Nada," said Sloane, who sat with her knees against her chest across from him. "You fainted and we didn't know what to do, so we just waited."

"And the vampires?"

"No sight of them," said Ellis. He'd been leaning against Sloane's back and now stood and stretched. "We took turns watching all night."

Mercury looked from Ellis to Sloane to Griffin, who still slept on the other side of Joelle. Joelle smiled at him.

"We're just glad you're okay."

"Well, did you decide on a path?" Mercury asked.

Joelle shook her head.

"I think I know a way," Mercury said. He gestured toward Ellis, whose eyes widened at the motion.

When Ellis drew near, Mercury grabbed him by his arms and positioned him between the paths.

"You've got earth magic now. A lot of Earth Hands have the ability to pathfind."

"How the fuck do I do that?" Ellis questioned.

Mercury scoffed. "Close your eyes; clear your mind. Just try to feel it and the magic will tell you the right way to go."

Ellis inhaled and closed his eyes. He stood for several minutes, palms facing the earth, brows knitted and eyes closed.

"This way," he said. He opened his eyes and pointed to the right.

"Then that's the way we'll go," Mercury said. "Thank you."

He stepped past Ellis and started down the path, hoping it would lead to a town where they could get some supplies, some rest and something to eat without any more interruptions, at least for now.

Welcome to America

By Freddie Karr

Welcome to America, the land of the (not quite) free and the home of the (occasionally) brave. The country that gave us Frederick Douglass and Robert E. Lee. Who gave us Hollywood and the segregated South. Who gave us Brown vs. the Board of Education but who drained an entire swimming pool after Dorothy Dandridge dipped her toe into the water. Welcome to America, where you're more likely to star in a reality TV show, wear a shirt that says "suns out guns out," or be murdered by a vampire than any other country in the world.

In 2020, we appointed an undead white man with aquiline features who survives on the blood of others—literally and figuratively. In the year since Vael was elected, vampire attacks have risen exponentially. This is an undisputed fact, but after Vael's recent Lorraine Law, the CDC has been banned from studying vampires and vampire attacks.

Opponents of Vael, a mix of witches and harridans, allies of the magical community, are completely flummoxed at how a man like Vael could rise to power. "He's a monster," they say. "His policies will make people afraid to come to America for fear of getting bitten." "How can anyone be a dhampir? Can't they see the harm vampires are causing?"

When anyone says these things to me, I tell them the truth. I tell them they're right, but I also tell them it doesn't matter. It doesn't matter that Vael has ended peace treaties with Japan because of their stance on vampirism. It doesn't matter that the Hollywood-ingénue-turned-FLOTUS has a bloodlust that is well-documented—at her midsummer party, twenty sex workers were killed. It doesn't matter that his entire cabinet is filled with vampires and dhampirs who want to make it legal for employers to fire witches if their presence violates their religious liberty.

I say it doesn't matter because Vael's supporters have already determined that he's their messiah. And though he ain't shit to us sane folk, he's a lot of things to a lot of people.

To his vampiric constituents, he's God. A deity who has validated their belief that their position in life is the fault of the witch, and they, afraid of the possibility that their misfortune is due to their own actions, accept and even bolster the scapegoating. To the wealthy elites in America, Vael is the vehicle to protect and continue their accumulation of wealth at the expense of the poor, regardless of the fact that most of his base is made up of the plebs.

To the dhampir, his rhetoric reinforces their beliefs in a corrupt system that needs to be "restored". In their eyes, Vael is a comic book hero: a straight, good-looking white man who uses his powers (of blood sucking and levitation and hyperbole) to overthrow a government that tells them they have to be nice to the blacks and immigrants and gays, and that women really are equal.

To the authoritarian police-state, he's a vehicle for a sustained conflict. They get to keep their jobs if Vael keeps stoking the flames of racial tension. Bodies and blood fill the street but all they care about is their shiny witch-killing guns and their directive to 'act with extreme prejudice' when they come across a witch or their supporters.

To the batshit Evangelicals, he's Jesus reborn—a (white) man who will not suffer witches to live and who will restore America and bring her "closer to God" with his reforms on same-sex marriage, abortion and women in roles of power.

And to those white, status quo protectors, Vael is a shameful man but they'll keep on defending him. They say, "No president is perfect; what about Faulker? The man wanted to raise the minimum wage at the federal level." They are able to breathe sighs of relief and "stop worrying so much, because it's just too much, all the time," even though their lives are not the ones who have been shown time and time again to simply not matter.

Chapter 7

When the group emerged from the forest into a town that seemed even smaller than Sulphurdale, Mercury's first thought was food. They walked along the edge of the road until they reached the town's main square. The whitewashed buildings looked almost ablaze in the afternoon sun. They stepped into a cafe called Grable's and ordered five coffees and five croissants. Mercury had already glamoured the group, but the weight of this magic gave him a headache, making his movements sloppy.

The barista eyed him warily as she handed him his change.

"Shouldn't we take this stuff to go?" Ellis asked as Mercury slid into a chair.

Mercury held his head in his hands. He was still feeling the effects from the night before. His lungs hurt from the smoke and his heart ached from the death of Santo and the destruction of the hotel. He shook his head. When the barista called out their orders, Mercury made no move to get their drinks and pastries. Sloane strode across the cafe, her boot heels clicking against the wooden floor. Joelle slid across from him and placed a hand on his forearm.

"You feelin' okay?" she asked.

How can I be? Mercury sighed and nodded.

"I just really need some coffee," he said. It was probably true. He did need coffee. But he also needed sleep in an actual bed and a hot meal instead of a crusty, lukewarm croissant. Sloane slid his coffee in front of him and Mercury smiled. "Thanks."

"I got you," she replied.

He knew she meant it. They each seated themselves at the round table and began doctoring their drinks.

"What are the next steps?" Griffin said, his voice whisper-soft.

"We need a car," Sloane answered first. "And preferably some better food than these rubbery croissants."

"Is your food okay?" the barista asked. Sloane turned around and gave a thumbs up sign. When she turned back to the group, she rolled her eyes and sipped her coffee.

"We should pass through Denver next, I think," Mercury said. "Probably we'll need to stop and get some supplies."

"Definitely. We left all of our shit back at the hotel." Sloane said.

Mercury felt his heart sink again. In that moment he realized the fire had claimed his duffle bag and what little mementos of his family he had left.

"What day is it?" Joelle asked.

"Monday, I think."

"Shit," she said.

"What's wrong?" Griffin asked.

"So much has happened since Saturday."

"And I bet we're not even close to halfway there," Sloane quipped.

"There's still time, you know. If you want to do your own thing. They're mostly after me, not you."

The group was silent and Mercury's heart beat faster with each passing moment. Finally, Griffin pulled his glasses off his face and began to clean them.

"I don't know about anyone else, but I feel like I've already gone too far on this crazy train. I've got to see where it leads."

"Really?" Mercury asked.

"Well, you did save mine and my brother's lives. We kind of owe you," Joelle smiled.

"You can't get rid of me that easily," added Sloane.

Mercury looked down at his coffee cup. The only one who hadn't spoken was Ellis. Mercury was a little relieved—he'd made his feelings about the situation known multiple times. He wasn't one to change his mind so quickly.

"So, I guess we should dip out?" Ellis said. He finished his coffee in one gulp and walked out of the cafe before anyone could respond.

They walked along the backstreets, searching for the perfect car. They found one near an abandoned lot. It was a Dodge Durango, older model, with peeling green paint. Sloane leaned against it and peeped inside.

"Looks clean enough," she said. She pulled her hair out of the bun piled high on her head and used the two bobby pins to pick the lock. Mercury stood behind the car and Griffin stood in front, both watching for any sign of the owner. When she popped the lock, Sloane cracked the door and paused.

"What are you waiting for?" Ellis questioned.

"Got to see if there's an alarm, dummy," she said. When no sound erupted from the vehicle, she pulled the door open. She slid behind the driver's seat and started to hotwire the car.

"Griff, come here," Mercury said. "Ellis, watch out for anyone."

Ellis rolled his eyes but stood in front of the car.

"What's up?" Griffin said.

Mercury pointed toward the license plate. "Change it."

Griffin's eyes widened behind his glasses. "What?"

"Change the numbers. You can do it. Besides, we can't roll around with these plates—sooner or later the owner will notice the car's gone and call the police."

Griffin nodded and stood in front of the license plate. "What do I do?"

"Just think of a sequence of numbers and then . . ." Mercury held out his hand. ". . . gesture."

Griffin inhaled deeply and closed his eyes. When he opened them seconds later, the numbers on the plate changed.

"Whoa," Griffin exclaimed. He smiled at Mercury and rounded the front of the car. He repeated the action, and soon both license plates bore a different set of numbers.

The engine hummed to life, shifting their attention to Sloane.

"Get in, bitches," Sloane yelled. Mercury ease into the backseat behind her. The twins followed suit, and Mercury felt a pang in his stomach as Joelle's thigh touched his. Ellis slid into the passenger seat and slammed the door. "Aye, be careful. This beater is already fragile."

Ellis groaned.

Sloane took one last look around and pulled away from the abandoned lot and out of the town.

They drove past the sign welcoming them to Denver just as the sun set. To Mercury, it seemed like the perfect place to grab what they needed and keep moving. It was too big of a town, a place where they'd be spotted easily if they weren't careful with their glamours. Sloane turned into a large shopping center, disrupting Mercury from his thoughts.

"Where are we going?" Mercury asked.

"There's a Target here," she said. "And a few places where we can eat."

"Why don't we just grab our supplies and get back on the road?" he asked. He tried not to sound as anxious as he was.

"Because it'll be nice to get out of the car and stretch. The last food we had was some greasy hot dogs from a QT. We need something better," Joelle added.

Mercury opened his mouth to speak then thought the better of it. Maybe he was just being paranoid. His stomach began to growl as they passed a Thai food place nestled next to a rib shack. Sloane pulled the car into a space at the far end of the Target parking lot. When he got out of the car, Mercury groaned at the pressure he felt in his lower back. Being out of the car felt nice, but he still couldn't shake his unease.

"Let's make this quick at least," he said. He whispered the spell for glamouring and each of their features changed. Once done he shoved his hands in his pockets and walked toward the store. The automatic doors slid open and Mercury was met with a blast of cold air and the smell of coffee.

Wordlessly, they split up. Mercury walked to the clothing aisle first and headed straight to the clearance section. He grabbed a pair of chinos, a grey sweater with quilted sleeves and two shirts. Then he headed toward the cosmetics section. He needed deodorant, a brush. He wondered when was the last time he brushed his teeth, realizing just how much had changed in just a short amount of time. He grabbed some floss and a toothbrush, then headed to the body wash aisle. He stared at the three-tiered shelves with bottles of white and pink and yellow. He didn't know what to grab, figured it should be something nondescript. He picked a bottle at random and popped the top.

He squeezed the bottle and the smell of amber and tobacco filled the air. His eyes watered. His mind wandered. A vision of his big brother, his protector, his best friend, appeared so clearly in his mind. Since he saw the video, Mercury had tried to push down the grief. Now, as he stood alone in the middle of a Target, the fluorescent lights glaring and the masses of Middle Americans puttering through the store for things they didn't really need, the weight of his loss made his knees buckle. He dropped the bottle he held. It hit the ground with a thud and yellow liquid oozed out onto the ground. It was hard for him to stabilize himself. He took a step, but it felt like he was walking through water. He pulled his burner phone out and dialed his brother's number. It went straight to voicemail, and tears spilled down his cheeks at the sound of Troian's voice. At the beep, Mercury cleared his throat and spoke.

"I miss you. I'm so sorry this happened, and it's all my fault. I should have known better, going to a UGN party, letting them rile me up. You're gone and I don't know what to do. You were always the one who knew what to do. You were the brave one. Ellis and Joelle and Sloane and Griffin all trust me but I don't know how to lead. I don't know how to keep them safe. What if—what if I get them killed? We went to Tia Santo's—she's a vampire now and she tried to kill us. I had to kill her, and now we're in Denver and . . . I'm so scared."

Mercury pulled the phone away from his ear and stared at it as if it were a foreign object. He sniffled and ended the call. He wiped his face with the palms of his hands and turned back toward the body wash. He grabbed a bar of soap at random and strode out of the aisle. He turned left, nearly bumping into Sloane.

"Whoa, watch it, bro," said Sloane.

"Sorry," Mercury mumbled under his breath. He continued walking, not waiting for Sloane to keep up. He dug his free hand into his pockets and tried to ignore his growling stomach. When he reached the front of the store, he was surprised to find the checkout lanes mostly empty. He set his items down on the conveyor belt.

"Good evening, sir," said the clerk. She was a petite white girl with purple hair and thickly drawn black eyebrows. Her name tag read "Aimee" and as she smiled at him, Mercury could see her fangs. He tried hard to keep his expression neutral.

"Hello," he said.

"Did you find everything okay?" Aimee asked.

Mercury nodded and looked around the store. Had there been this many vampires here before? Had he just not felt their presence when he entered the store? He looked back down at Aimee, who gazed at him with a look that either meant she wanted to fuck him or kill him. Mercury smiled back at her and pretended to be occupied by the small cafe at the far end of the store.

Standing in the Juniors clothing section next to the cafe was a group of employees. One of them held a clipboard with one hand and made elaborate motions with the other. Mercury guessed she was a manager, and her three employees that stood before her were not very happy.

"I'm sorry, but there's nothing I can do," the manager said.

"That's bullshit," said one of the workers. He ran a hand through a tangled mess of blonde curls. His cheeks were red. "We haven't been written up, or warned, or done anything worth being fired."

"Yeah," said one of the other workers.

"You're only letting us go because of that asshole in the White House," said the first employee.

"That's not true," said the manager. She stepped back. "Policies here have just changed and we cannot have employees on the floor who threaten the safety of others."

"I threaten the safety of others?" questioned the second employee, a petite Asian woman with a pixie cut. "Margaret, I'm five feet even and I barely weigh a hundred pounds. How could I threaten the safety of anyone?"

"I can't disclose the reason," the manager said.

"Fuck this," the third employee said. He stepped toward the manager and twisted his fingers. "Why are you firing us?"

"Because you're witches, obviously," the manager admitted. Mercury's stomach clenched.

She looked horrified after the words left her mouth. "You . . . you all have to leave the building now. We can't have employees that—"

"We're not the ones threatening anybody's safety, you bitch," yelled the employee who'd cast the spell. "You and the rest of these vampires are the ones who bite and kill people for fun."

"I'm going to call security if you don't leave," the manager threatened. She pulled a walkie talkie from her pocket and let her finger hover over the button.

"Your total is $57.89."

Mercury shifted his attention to the clerk, who had the same smile on her face.

He nodded and dug three twenty dollar bills out of his pocket. She held the cash up to the light then typed in the amount on the register. It crashed open and she pulled a few singles and some change out of the drawers.

"Your change, sir," Aimee said. She handed him the money and slid the receipt on top.

"Thanks," Mercury said. He grabbed his bag and stood to the side, looking on as Joelle then Sloane checked out. After each of them checked out, Mercury turned and walked toward the door. When he stepped out into the night, he saw the group of witches standing to the left of the door. Two of them smoked blunts and the third one texted furiously. Mercury sighed as they walked to the van, a deep sadness once again enveloping him. Since they left LA, he'd felt hollow, like he'd been completely carved out and expected to operate without the missing pieces. He wondered if things would be different if he hadn't led the group to the tattoo parlor—would they be safe? Would Troian be alive if they'd just driven off to Lancaster or Bakersfield or Tehachapi?

They reached the van and Mercury slid into the passenger seat without a word. Griffin sat behind the wheel now, and Mercury barely heard Joelle calling out directions over the thoughts swirling in his head.

They were less than two blocks from Target when the sound of sirens brought Mercury back to the present. "Fuck," Griffin said. "What do I do?"

"Pull over, Griffin," Joelle said calmly.

"Nah, just gun it. This is a stolen vehicle; we'll all get locked up," Ellis said.

"There's no evidence of this being stolen since Griffin changed the plates. We can just use magic to get them off our backs," said Sloane. "Right, Mercury?"

Mercury blinked a few times and looked back to see everyone in the car staring at him. *I can't do this*, he thought. *I can't be the one to decide their fates.* He said nothing and just nodded, but a lump formed in his throat. Griffin pulled over to the side of the road and Mercury fought the urge to draw up his legs and coil in on himself.

He looked over at Griffin, who flinched at the sound of the door slamming.

"Change your license," Mercury whispered. He dug through the glove box and found an insurance card and vehicle registration. He handed them to Griffin, who gripped the paperwork then closed his eyes. He turned and checked everyone's glamour before checking his own.

A muscular white man with hairy arms and a thinning buzz cut tapped his flashlight on the window. He made a rolling motion with his free hand and Griffin rolled the window down slowly.

"Evenin'," the officer said. His voice was gravelly. His left cheek was puffed up from what Mercury assumed was chew.

"Hello officer," Griffin said.

"License and registration?" the officer said.

Griffin nodded and handed the paperwork to the officer. He glanced at Mercury. Mercury nodded and set his hands on his thighs, palms facing up.

The cop held on to the documents and stared down at them. He didn't speak; Mercury knew this was a tactic to make Griffin uncomfortable, to make him mess up. Beads of sweat broke out on Griffin's forehead and his legs shook.

"Did I . . . Did I do something—"

"You speak when spoken to, you hear me, boy?" the officer growled. The word sent Mercury's spine tingling. It was all he could do not to lash out. Griffin simply nodded. His legs shook even faster.

"Now, Mr. Dawkins, wanna tell me what you and your . . ." The officer looked at Mercury and narrowed his eyes. ". . . friends are doing this evening?"

"We're just running errands and now we're . . . hungry. We want to get something to eat," Griffin said.

"Errands, huh? What kind of errands?"

"Well, we–"

"I'm asking your friends now, boy. You hush," said the cop. He shined his flashlight on Joelle and Sloane, then focused it on Ellis.

"You sure are the sore thumb in this group, ain't ya?" The cop smirked.

"In more ways than one," said Ellis.

"So what are you all doing this evening?"

"Didn't you hear it when he said it?" Ellis said, nodding toward Griffin.

"I want to hear it from you."

"Well, you're shit out of luck then because I'm not talking to you."

"Excuse me?"

"We've done nothing wrong– we weren't speeding, we don't have a broken tail light and he wasn't swerving. Either you tell us why you pulled us over or we leave."

Sloane and Joelle looked at Ellis, their eyes wide. Even Mercury was surprised at his friend's bravado. He knew Ellis could be short-sided but he didn't think he'd be dumb enough to speak to a cop this way.

Though the cop seemed incensed by Ellis' response, he didn't respond. Instead, he focused his light on Mercury and reiterated his question.

"We went to Target, and now we're going to get food. We're just passing through, sir. We'll be out of Denver shortly."

"Well, I don't think you will," said the cop. Mercury turned to see another officer standing beside his window. He was a black man with a beer gut and a perfectly lined goatee.

Mercury turned to face the officer.

"You see, we got a tip that some kids in a green van were using magic. Here in Denver, we don't take too kindly to magic being used, especially after dark. We've adopted something of a sundown rule here, so I'm afraid we're going to have to take you in."

Mercury's mouth went dry and his heartbeat quickened.

"You're not serious?" Ellis questioned. Mercury heard the sound of a seat belt unbuckling and then noticed Ellis kneeling on the center console. "Did you actually see him do any magic?"

Mercury wanted to scream at Ellis to shut the hell up, tell him that he was not helping, that his bravado would only get Mercury in more trouble. But he said nothing. Realizing Ellis had a privilege that gave him an advantage, Mercury kept his eyes on the dashboard and his hands on his lap.

The second cop tapped on the door.

"Unlock the door," he said. Mercury sighed. He tried to keep his hand from shaking as he pushed open the lock. The officer pulled open the door before Mercury even brought his hand back to his lap. He grabbed Mercury's arm so hard that if he had been wearing his seatbelt, his arm likely could have been dislocated.

"Hey, wait—" Sloane began as she pulled her seatbelt off and leaned across the seat. But the officer pushed Sloane back into her seat. Ellis leapt across her and grabbed at the officer's sleeve.

"Don't you fucking touch her," Ellis spat.

"You sit back down, kid," the officer said. Mercury was incensed by the officer's usage of kid instead of boy.

"No! You cannot treat people this way—"

"Ellis," Joelle whispered.

"No, I mean really! You never saw him do any magic and you're just assuming it because he's black!"

The officer grabbed Ellis' shirt and pulled his torso through the window.

"Now listen here, kid, you want to get away from this group before it gets you in trouble, you hear me?" the officer pushed Ellis back. He fell back against the passenger seat.

Mercury heard the first officer talking to the group, warning them not to get out of the car. The second officer pulled Mercury to the rear of the van and slammed him down on the hood of the cop car. He groaned as his cheek connected with the metal, as his canines bit down hard on his tongue. The officer pulled Mercury's hands behind his back. Mercury could hear the officer fiddling with his belt, and then he felt the coldness of metal against his wrists. Instantly, he felt lightheaded. He felt like all his energy had slipped out of him. *Anti-magic handcuffs*, Mercury thought. His heartbeat quickened as he realized the cuffs likely stripped himself and his friends of their glamours, and it happened right in front of two racist police officers.

"Holy shit, Dawson, looks like we've got that LA boy who's been on the news," said the second officer. Without warning he pulled Mercury up and shoved him into the back of the police cruiser.

Dawson said one last thing to Sloane then trotted toward the cruiser. He slid behind the driver's seat and pulled out a flask from his shirt pocket.

"Boy, do you know how much of a bounty is on your head?" Dawson smirked as he pulled away from the side of the road and sped down the dimly lit highway.

"What did you tell my friends?" Mercury asked.

Dawson made eye contact with Mercury in the rearview mirror.

"I told them if they followed us, that we'd kill them all and make you watch."

Trying to hide his fear, Mercury resisted the urge to turn around and glance at his friends one last time. He instead peered out of the window, looking for some glimmer of hope.

Chapter 8

Mercury's head felt like it would burst into two. His ears throbbed and it took all of his focus to stop himself from throwing up. Even his wrists itched from the metal sitting on his skin. He'd never been stripped of his magic before. When he'd heard his mother and her friends talking about it, he hadn't been able to understand the feeling. Now, he'd give anything to make it stop.

As Officer Dawson sped down the highway, he noticed they hadn't seen a car for miles and the street lamps were nonexistent. He could barely make out the buildings or the trees or the mountains that surrounded them. The officers were quiet. There was no sound. Mercury felt as if the darkness and the attendant silence would swallow him whole.

Finally, they pulled into the parking lot of the police station. The flood lights along the building's exterior shined so brightly that Mercury squinted against them. The second officer pushed his door open and pulled Mercury out without a word. He gripped Mercury's arm and walked him inside the station. The doors opened into a small room with rows of empty desks. The light cast a sickly yellow glow across their faces as they walked through the middle of the rows of desks. Another officer sat at a desk at the far end of the room. He lifted his head briefly and made eye contact with Mercury, but his gaze shifted away just as quick. The two officers led him through the rows of desks and stopped before a large steel door. There was a key pad next to the door, and Officer Dawson typed in a six number code. Mercury watched him and as the keypad beeped and the door unlocked, Mercury repeated the numbers in his head.

529641, Mercury thought. *529641*.

They turned left and entered another door, this one leading to a bank of cells on either side of them. Most of the rooms were filled with people either sleeping or sitting on their beds with their heads in their hands. Only a few of them looked up when they spotted Mercury being led to the last cell on the left. Officer Dawson opened the doors and the second officer escorted him in. He pushed Mercury onto the bed and unlocked his handcuffs. Mercury felt his powers surge, but just barely.

"In case you're getting any ideas, these bars are coated with the same anti-magic stuff as what's on these handcuffs," the second officer said, as he held the cuffs up to Mercury's face. The cops then locked Mercury's cell door.

"Try not to get too comfortable," teased Dawson. "You'll be getting a visit from some . . . friends this evening."

Both officers laughed as they walked down the hallway. Once the door to the main room slammed shut, Mercury exhaled. He leaned against the wall and tried to calm his thoughts, hoping to keep his breath even and to stop his heart from beating out of his chest.

"Hey, over here."

Mercury looked out at the block of cells. In the dim light, he made out a man in a cell across from his.

"You get caught after sundown?" the man asked.

Mercury nodded before realizing the man likely couldn't read his expression.

"Yeah," Mercury replied.

"Me, too. That's what most of us are here for. I'm Jamie."

"Mercury."

"What's your hand?"

Before Mercury could respond, someone shushed them.

"Y'all are gonna get us all beat if you don't shut up," a woman spoke, her voice a thick Southern drawl.

"Who are you?" Mercury asked.

The woman scoffed. After several moments of silence, she replied, "Natasha."

"Natasha," Mercury said. "What's your hand?"

"Water," Natasha spoke quickly.

"You know that's the most I've heard her speak in weeks?" Jamie said.

Mercury's stomach twisted. "You've been here for weeks?"

"Oh yeah. Got popped lighting a woman's ciggie. I'm a Fire Hand."

"You two are gonna get us all beat," Natasha repeated. "Why don't you just shut up?"

"Have you gotten to make your phone call? Get a lawyer?" Mercury asked, pitching his voice lower.

There was shuffling in the cell next to him, then a new voice emerged from the darkness. "You've got a lot to learn, kid."

"Ain't no such thing as a lawyer when you're in a sundown town."

"Legally, they cannot deny you a lawyer." Mercury winced as soon as the words escaped from his lips— he sounded like Ellis. Someone scoffed.

"Legal or not, I've been here a month and haven't spoken to anyone. It's a new world order, man. With that leech in office, we're just minor inconveniences," said the person in the cell next to Mercury.

Mercury sat back against the brick wall behind him. Would his friends come for him or would he get stuck there like the others? He lied down on the bed, the metal springs digging into his back. He quelled the tears that swelled as he tried to find comfort in the darkness. But the cellblock smelled like urine and mud. He was thirsty, hungry and cold. Though the handcuffs were no longer on his wrists, his strength still waned from the coating on the bars.

He'd only ever been told about sundown towns once, from his Grannie Gwen. He was young, maybe nine or ten. His grandmother's home didn't have air conditioning, and Mercury remembered lying on the cold tile floor in the kitchen with Troian to keep cool, each of them making up shapes in the popcorn ceiling above them. Grannie told them about a town called Darien, where she and their grandfather had been shot at as they drove to Astera, which had been held on Montauk that year. She said they were lucky the officer who pulled them over was a crap shot. She said other witches had not been as lucky as them, that traveling to Astera in those times was always a gamble. When Mercury asked why they were so hated, whether it was because they were black or because of their magic, Grannie just smiled and quoted Nina Simone:

"To be young, gifted, and black, oh what a lovely precious dream."

He started at the sound of a cell door opening. He must have fallen asleep. He wiped at his eyes and stood. His lower back ached and with each step he felt a shooting pain in his legs. He grit his teeth as he walked to the cell doors and peered out. The exit door was wide open, and so were the first two cell doors. Mercury could hear whimpering and groaning and another, sharper sound. It sounded like a belt or a whip against skin. A shiver trickled down Mercury's spine. Minutes later, Mercury heard the sound of shuffling feet. He could barely make out the outline of four people.

"Next time I won't be so polite, witch," said Officer Dawson. He cackled. The sound of a cell door slamming against itself reverberated throughout the hall. The second cell was slammed shut seconds later, without a word from the police officer. The clanking sound of a belt buckle twisted Mercury's stomach.

Quiet sobs lingered in the silence.

"Are you okay?" Mercury whispered.

"Shut up," the voice replied. Mercury realized it was Natasha who was sobbing, who'd been beaten and possibly worse. He crossed his arms to keep himself from punching the walls. He lied back on the cot and stared down at the floor. Tears welled in his eyes, and this time he did not stop them from falling.

Mercury watched the sunrise through the tiny window high up in his cell. He wondered vaguely at the fact that he no longer felt hungry or thirsty. He lied in bed as the sun climbed higher in the sky, until the rays threatened to blind him. When he sat up, he was finally able to see the others in the cellblock, which was not as big as he initially thought. Instead of the twenty cells on each side he estimated last night, there were only eight total, four on each side. Natasha, who'd been in the first cell directly across from the first door, leaned against the cell doors, her platinum blonde curls tangled and stringy. Jamie was in the cell across from him, and when Mercury looked to his cell, he spotted Jamie doing push-ups.

"Good morning," Mercury said.

There was no answer. Mercury sat back on his cot and drew his knees up to his chin.

"What's so good about it?" Natasha said finally.

Mercury always thought of himself as an optimist. He liked to think he was always looking at the glass as half full. He tried to find the good in situations, but as he looked at the dingy cell and the cot that had more than one questionable stain, he couldn't find the good here.

"I don't know," Mercury said.

Suddenly, the door to the cellblock burst open.

Mercury stepped to the front of his cell and noticed Natasha flinch as two police officers walked into the cellblock. Though Mercury had not seen these two before, he could tell from the others' reactions that they were not there with good intentions. They walked slowly through the block, their eyes lingering on each cell. When they reached Mercury's cell, they stopped.

He knew they were vampires before they even opened their mouths to speak. He stepped back, but the shorter of the two pulled a keyring from his belt and opened the door.

"Looks like we've got some new blood here," he said. He was shorter than Mercury but twice as big. His gut hung well over his belt, jiggling as he approached Mercury.

"Looks that way. It's only right that we get a taste," said the other police officer, who loomed over his partner. He turned and slid the cell door closed.

Mercury's heart pumped like a piston. Suddenly, he felt like a little boy again, surrounded by vampires and unable to use his magic. He'd gotten away that time, the vampires finding more joy in watching him cry out to his mother as she was killed. He wondered if his luck would be different this time.

Back in the present, Mercury found himself pressed against the wall, his hands clammy as they rubbed against the rough stones of the cellblock.

"Don't worry. We won't take much," said the fat vampire, smiling. "This time at least."

He giggled and lunged at Mercury. Mercury dodged the vampire and slid to the other side of the wall. Again the vampire lunged for him, and again

111

Mercury dodged him. The tall vampire just stood and watched, as though enjoying seeing him try to fight back.

"Don't be afraid; we don't want to kill you," the tall vampire said softly. Their voices were soothing, but Mercury knew better. He could see how dilated their pupils were, how they were simply toying with him. Finally, the tall vampire rushed Mercury and pushed him against the wall. Mercury grunted as his head connected with the brick. Pain shot up his neck. The vampire tilted Mercury's head to the side. He could feel the fangs grazing his neck.

"Just a little taste," the vampire whispered.

There was a large thud and then the building shook. The vampire released Mercury and he and his partner rushed out of the cell, leaving the door open. Mercury stood still, his breath escaping in spurts. He approached the door but stopped just before it. He looked up at Jamie, who clutched the bars of the cell and stared at the door to the cellblock, which stood wide open. Mercury heard the sound of a scuffle. Something fell to the ground and shattered. Then there was the sound of a gunshot, and for a moment, there was silence.

"Merc?"

Mercury breathed a sigh of relief as he saw Griffin step into the cellblock.

"Over here," Mercury said. He stepped out of his cell and strode toward Griffin then stopped. He looked from Jamie to Natasha to the woman who sat in the cell beside him. He couldn't leave them to be fed on and killed.

"I need the keys," he said.

"But we really gotta go," Griffin urged.

"I can't leave them here," Mercury replied. Griffin stared at him for a moment then ducked back into the main room. Seconds later, he returned with a key ring. He tried key after key on the doors until he heard the clicking sound of the door unlocking. Natasha bounded from her cell, not bothering to look back as she ran. Griffin opened each cell door. When he reached Jamie, Mercury turned toward them. As soon as his door opened, Jamie stepped out and sighed.

"Can you feel that?" he said. Mercury nodded. Though he hadn't felt as drained behind bars as he did with the cuffs on, he still felt suffocated by whatever magic coated them. Now he felt like he could breathe a little bit more fully.

Jamie threw his arms around Mercury and squeezed him.

"Thank you," Jamie said. He pulled back and looked at Mercury.

"You're welcome." Mercury smiled at Jamie, who seemed to blink away tears.

Jamie let go and rushed out the cellblock door. Griffin brushed passed Mercury then turned.

"C'mon, Merc, we've gotta go." He walked through the cell door without another word. Mercury sighed and walked out of the cellblocks, down the long hallway, and turned into the main room. He stopped when he saw the front end of a cop car crashed into the front of the building. Glass littered the floor. The car's engine block was shoved up into the front end of the vehicle. Ellis, Joelle, Sloane and Griffin stood just outside. They all wore masks and baggy clothes. Several officers sat on the floor, each one bound and blindfolded. The two officers who arrested him the night before lied on the ground, blood puddled around them.

He slipped past the car and into the warmth of the day. The sun was high in the sky and as he inhaled the clean air, he fell to his knees and cried.

"Merc!" Sloane said. She slid her mask off and helped him up, hoisting one arm over her shoulder.

"You guys came for me," he whimpered.

"Of course, we did. You think we'd leave you there to rot?" She smiled.

They hurried through the parking lot. Mercury allowed himself to be led to their car, which was parked in the lot of Just My Type. He could see the cafe was busy—the drive through line was seven cars deep. Out front the cafe advertised their newest spring drinks—blood orange smoothies and cafe mochas with blood liquer.

"I can't believe they opened this place up across from a police station," Joelle said. "It just feels so wrong."

Mercury made eye contact with a man as he exited the cafe. He was holding a blended drink the color of crimson. Whipped crème filled the dome-shaped top of the cup. Before he could stop himself, Mercury bent over and threw up next to the car.

Sloane and Joelle stood on either side of him, rubbing his back.

When Mercury stood he wiped the edge of his mouth with this sleeve and the tears in his eyes with his other hand.

"We need to get you a toothbrush," Ellis said. Sloane scoffed and swatted Ellis' arm.

"What? He just blew chunks. Should we just let him walk around with bad breath?"

Mercury opened the car door and slid in, not bothering to jump into their argument. Joelle slid next to him and after slipping her seatbelt on, she put her arm on his shoulder.

"I'm glad you're alright," she said. Mercury could see tears welling in her large brown eyes.

"Me, too," he said, covering his mouth with one hand. "Thank you."

Joelle smiled tightly as the rest of the group slid into the car.

"Glad you're not dead," Griffin said.

"Yeah, you, too," Mercury replied. He leaned back against the seat, his body now sore from the adrenaline. Sloane began driving and within minutes, he drifted to sleep.

The Family Taking Boutique Blood Bars by Storm

When you don't have your own space, you create one for yourself. Sometimes all you can do is "make it work," and that's exactly what PlusMinus co-owners and sisters Ginger and Wren Collins have done.

The sisters have always struggled to find acceptance. Growing up they were the only vampire family living in Sausalito.

"Everyone thinks the Bay Area is so accepting," said Ginger, the younger of the two. "People couldn't handle that we were vampires. I had an easier time telling people I was a lesbian than I did saying I needed blood to survive."

The Collins family fought hard to make ends meet and find community in the confines of the liberal-leaning, Chardonnay-swilling, "I'd vote for the black president again if I could" crowd. After years of fighting, they moved across the country and settled in Marietta, a picture-perfect hamlet 20 miles outside of Atlanta. The sisters found friends and acceptance in their new home.

"It was like night and day. We were more accepted than ever before. Finally, we were able to express opinions without being judged."

The sisters attended college at Kennesaw State, where they both met their respective partners, Kline Farrell and Melinda Gwen. Farrell and

Gwen, who also serve as managers for PlusMinus, encouraged their wives to start their own business after seeing how hard it was for them to get the blood they needed while out on the town.

"Ginger would have to bring a flask filled with blood everywhere. We got kicked out of the movie theaters because some woman told the manager Ginger was drinking in front of children. We sued them and won, and we were able to put the down payment on PlusMinus with the settlement."

PlusMinus, which opened in 2020 in Atlanta's historic Old Fourth Ward, is something of an enigma. Plus, the upstairs area serves as a sun up to sun down cafe that's all sleek subway tiles, chalkboard walls, and a simple Alexa speaker system that plays the latest pop hits. It feels like a home away from home, a place to begin your weekday on a high note. Minus, on the other hand, feels like a throwback to when bars were clandestine places where the likes of the Kennedys bootlegged booze and sat in leather wingback chairs. It is open from sun down to sun up, and visitors have more than enough atmosphere and ambiance to soak up as they listen to the likes of Goldfrapp, Trevor Something and Com Truise.

The sisters make no apologies for the fact that PlusMinus is a venue primarily for vampires. With drinks like the fan favorite B-chelada and the Sang-Froid (a nitro cold brew with three pumps of blood-flavored syrup and a vanilla syrup floater), it would be hard to confuse it for any other bar. However, PlusMinus also offers a full bar, a delicious selection of pastries and finger foods, and a coffee drink menu that would make Rory Gilmore go crazy.

"We know what it's like to feel excluded, and we believe that it is possible to carve out a space for vampires without making humans feel excluded and uncomfortable," said Wren.

PlusMinus' success has set the benchmark for boutique blood bars across the country. Already bars have opened up in Tucson (El Sangre), Cheyenne (Vermillion) and Hoboken (Just Your Type). PlusMinus has become so successful that two more locations are in the works.

"We just broke ground on a location in Smyrna, near the new Braves stadium, and we're shopping for a location in College Park. Every part of the metro will have access to the blood they need to survive and a community where they can feel at home."

Of course, the success of PlusMinus and other boutique blood bars would not be possible without President Vael, a fact that Ginger, Wren and their partners know all too well.

"Without him standing by his word to do right by vampires, my wife and my sister-in-law would be hard-pressed to find the accommodations they need. His fast-tracking HB 128 really made this place possible," said Kline, who manages Plus' front of house. By now, we at *The Vanguard* are all aware of the impact of HB 128, which allowed for the commodification and sale of blood at businesses with valid licenses.

Yet still, there are those in congress pushing to restrict HB 128. Senator Oliver D'ambrosia (R- Rhode Island) is calling for the licensing renewal process to happen monthly, pending inspection and verification that the blood being sold comes from authorized vendors, and that those who are sharing blood in the confines of these bars are doing so consensually.

"The goal isn't to take away anyone's right to do business or to get access to the blood they need. The goal is to make the process safer and more transparent."

The senator is referring to the recent bust of Lyfe Blud, the now-defunct bar in San Mateo allegedly caught forcing their human employees to service their vampire customers against their will. An awful practice, to be sure, but the owners of the bar state that all their workers signed consent forms to be fed on while on the clock.

"If it's true, it's an awful way to do business," said Ginger. "But it's also possible that there are people who don't want to see vampires prosper and made false claims to end Sanford and Meryl's [Lyfe Blud's owners] prosperity."

When asked how they handle the naysayers, the harridans and the haters, Wren and Ginger looked at each other and said: "just keep on drinkin'."

△▽△▽
Chapter 9

Mercury awoke to the sound of rain against the window. There was a softer, lighter sound of voices, only he didn't immediately recognize them. When he fully came to, he realized it was the radio. It was some talk radio show, likely NPR, playing recordings of a speech by President Vael.

"Last night we received word that Allan Smitstra and Michelle Carmichael, two esteemed Supreme Court justices, passed away. While the causes of their deaths are still being investigated, Sheridan, Aimee, Geoffrey and I are keeping the Smitstras and the Carmichaels in our minds and in our hearts," said Vael.

Mercury groaned and shifted in his seat. This time Ellis was driving and Griffin was sitting in the passenger seat. Sloane sat beside him and Joelle beside her, leaning against the window. She was asleep, her tumble of hair covering her face. Sloane's long nails clicked against a small tablet.

"How long have I been out?" he asked.

Sloane looked at him and smiled. "Probably like four hours."

Mercury blinked and gazed out the window. Though the sun was setting, he could see that the terrain had changed. No longer were they surrounded by mountains. The land was now flat. Switchgrass and shrubs replaced the tall pine trees.

"Where did you get that?" he asked.

"Swiped it while you were in the slammer," Sloane replied. "Figured it'd come in handy, help us know what's going on."

Mercury could see a notes document up on the screen. It was titled "America, We Should See Other People." He recognized it as one of the articles Sloane submitted for publications around the nation. Mercury knew she was a talented writer, and he'd consoled her many times after she received the typical canned response from magazines, the stock "thank you for sharing your work but it is not right for us at this time." She was shy about her work, so he didn't say anything as she resumed her typing.

He focused back on the newscast.

"President Vael now has the advantage of stacking the Supreme Court," the newscaster said. "Now, not only will he control the Senate but depending on his picks, he could have a majority conservative court. Has there been any rumors of who he'll pick?"

"Yes, Adam. Rumors of a potential coup for two seats began as far back as January. Vael will likely choose individuals who are vampires or dhampirs, who will help advance his agenda of quote-unquote equality."

"That's a good point you bring up, Farin, because later in his speech he cited the recent massacre at a church in Bala Cynwyd. We've got a clip of that."

Mercury studied each of his friends. None of them seemed to be paying any attention to the NPR Newscast. Goosebumps rose up on his arms.

"We must now shift our thoughts to those innocents who were killed in last week's attack on St. Emmanuel in Bala Cynwyd. The perpetrators have been found to be harridans, led by a fanatical witch who seems to go by the alias Elphaba. This is not the first attack on law-abiding citizens since I took office. Witches and their sympathizers have stoked so much fear that people are unable to carry out their daily activities for fear of an attack. This violence cannot end until we know the motives of these powerful individuals. That is why I'm proposing the Identity Act. With this, we non-magical beings will be able to distinguish witches while at work, at school and in other public places. Often, these individuals carry out their magical agendas so insidiously that we are often helpless. It is the hope of this administration that we will make Americans feel safe and in control again."

Mercury unsnapped his belt buckle and reached across the center console.

"What the fuck, bro?" Ellis said.

"Turn it up."

"But Joelle's asleep–" Griffin began.

"Turn it up," Mercury urged. Griffin shrugged and turned the volume dial.

"And again that was President Vael, describing for us the new bill he has proposed on the Senate floor. Though the specifics are a bit fuzzy, what we've gleaned from the verbiage of the bill is that witches will need to wear some type of jewelry or pin or insignia that lets people know what they are."

Mercury fought the urge to punch something. Instead, he grabbed the sides of the passenger and driver's seat, his fingers digging into the faux leather.

"There's no way something like that will pass," Sloane said. She tried to sound reassuring, but Mercury knew she was just trying to make him feel better.

"You and I both know that it could," he said. "Especially if Vael gets those two leeches in office."

The guest on the show echoed Mercury's sentiments, but the host felt differently. He argued that the president would be alienating his non-vampiric base by doing something so unlawful. The guest continued to argue with the host, reminding him that Vael is a powerful man whose vampirism makes him all the more powerful.

"Yes, but I still believe that he will do right by his base and follow the rule of law. I mean, he may not be a fan of witches but he's no Hitler."

Ellis turned the radio off. "That guy's a total hack," he said.

Mercury pursed his lips and slid back into his seat. The sun had completely set and without the aid of streetlamps, the darkness enveloped them.

"Where are we?" Joelle asked. Her voice was hoarse and she seemed to be groggy from sleep.

"Close to Gothenburg," Ellis said.

Joelle didn't respond. Mercury looked over at her but he could barely make her out in the dim light.

"Are we going to stop soon? I'm hella hungry," Sloane whined.

"Think we can probably stop in Gothenberg, if there's anything there."

Ellis drove around a bend in the road, where they were met with more darkness.

"I doubt it," Griffin said. "We've been driving in the dark for the last half hour."

But Mercury saw lights on the horizon, and soon they passed a small gas station that had three out of its six pumps full. On their right was what looked to be a mill, and then they were driving through what looked to be the main part of town. They drove to the end of the road but turned around when it seemed to get more residential.

"Think I saw a motel back there," Ellis said. He pulled into the parking lot and cut the engine. It was a small, squat building with a sign that read "Gibson Motor Lodge" in fading red ink. There were a handful of cars in the lot. Mercury could see inside the office, where a rotund man with long white hair and mutton chops sat smoking a cigarette behind the desk.

"Sure you want to go in there?" Mercury asked.

"Yeah, the guy looks sleazy as fuck," Sloane said.

Ellis turned toward them and lifted a brow. "Do you have any better suggestions? I haven't seen anything else that looks like a hotel around here. And Sloane said she's hungry, and I'm tired of driving."

"We could keep going," Griffin suggested.

"Or we could sleep in the car," Ellis snapped.

"Look, it's, what? Eight o'clock?" Mercury began. "Not exactly time to pack it in. We're all hungry so . . . why don't we just head to that restaurant across the street and then we can decide what we want to do."

Ellis nodded and opened the car door. Mercury followed suit. He lifted his arms and stretched. It felt like he'd been in the car for ages. He turned to face the group and gestured toward the restaurant across the street. He paused and looked up and down the street, though he chastised himself as he crossed. The town seemed completely empty.

The restaurant was called Livingston's. The neon sign hanging above the door announcing the restaurant's name blinked off and on. Ellis opened the door and Mercury felt like he was stepping into an episode of *Cheers*. The place was all wood paneling and crooked pictures of women with Farrah Fawcett hair and men with mullets. The hostess looked no older than fifteen, and she leaned over the stand with her phone in one hand and a Pepsi in the other.

"Hello," Joelle said. "Can we get a table for five?"

The girl looked up at them through heavily lined eyes. She shrugged and gestured at the expanse of room behind her, which contained no more than twenty people.

"Thank you," Joelle said. The hostess didn't reply.

Joelle led the way to a booth at the back of the restaurant. They each squeezed in, with Sloane and Ellis and Griffin sitting across from Mercury and Joelle. After several minutes, another woman came by their table with a set of menus and a small notepad in hand.

"Evening," the woman said. Her ice-blonde hair tied back into a high, thin ponytail. She popped her gum as she set the menus down before each of them, making eye contact with Griffin as she did so. "Can I get you anything, sweet pea?"

Griffin's eyes widened. "Uh–"

"He'll take a Leinenkugel," said Ellis. "Actually, we'll just take a round of that."

The woman looked disappointed that it had been Ellis who asked for the round and not Griffin. She nodded and walked away, leaving them to scan the menus.

"Well, this is bar food if I ever saw it," said Sloane. "Chili dogs, burgers, fried chicken tenders, nachos."

"I bet you're in heaven," Mercury said. He looked up to see her smirking at him.

"You're damn right," Sloane said.

He chuckled and examined the menu.

The waitress returned with a pitcher of beer and five glasses. They each put in their order with her and Mercury, who normally kept it simple, ordered a bison burger with sharp cheddar and onion straws. Once the waitress left, Ellis began to pour each of them a drink. After he'd filled each of their cups, he lifted his glass.

"Here's to making it this far without getting killed," he said.

"And without killing each other," Sloane added. Ellis looked at her and she smirked. Mercury thought he saw something pass between them.

"Cheers," Mercury said, shifting his attention to the group. He clinked his glass against each of theirs then sipped from his beer. He winced at its taste. It reminded him of alcoholic orange juice. He set his glass down and looked out at the bar.

A group of women sat at a round table, each of them nursing a flight of beers. In the corner by the front door stood a neon jukebox. Someone had programmed it to play 'Genius of Love'. Mercury tapped his foot along with the beat. It had always been one of his favorite songs, mostly because his mother played it nonstop. She'd dance around the kitchen in their old house as she cleaned. It was the first song Mercury learned to play bass on. He remembered jamming to this song with Ellis and Troian one long ago winter break, with Ellis on drums and Troian on guitar.

Mercury lifted his head and caught Ellis' gaze. He offered Mercury a tight smile, as though the song was giving him the same memory. Mercury picked up his beer and sipped from it to keep himself from crying. They were in Nebraska, in the middle of a blue-collar bar in a blue-collar town. The last thing he needed was for them to see him with tears in his eyes. He exhaled deeply when the song rolled over to some late 70's rock tune.

The waitress returned with their food.

"Everything look good?" she asked once she'd passed out their food.

"Can we get a round of shots?" Ellis asked.

"Dude," Joelle said, brow tilted and head pitched to the side.

"What? Troian's . . . not here with us this evening, and we need to celebrate him," he replied. He didn't bother looking at Mercury, and Mercury didn't bother objecting. He couldn't remember the last time he'd gotten drunk and he wondered if it was just what he needed.

"Shots of what, darlin'? We've got a full bar."

Ellis glanced back at the bar then turned to the waitress.

"We'll take the Kraken," Ellis said. The waitress smirked and nodded. Her platinum ponytail bounced as she turned on her heel.

Mercury didn't wait to dig into his burger. He hadn't realized how hungry he was until he began to eat. It felt like his own stomach gnawed at him. He tried not to moan as he took bite after bite of the burger with its tender meat and melting cheese. Across the table, Sloane held a chicken drumstick to her mouth and tore the meat from the bone. Ellis dragged a fry through ketchup. Griffin cut up his chicken tenders with his knife and fork and dipped a piece in ranch. Beside him, Joelle picked at a plate of nachos.

"Food good?" asked the waitress as she dropped off their shots.

"Yes, thank you," Mercury said around a bit of burger.

She smiled widely. "You're welcome. You need anything else, name's Clary," she said, leaning forward to show off her cleavage.

Mercury smiled tightly and nodded. "Thank you," he said.

From the corner of his eye, he could see Joelle giving him a sidelong glance as the waitress walked away.

"Think she has a thing for black men," Joelle said.

Mercury didn't respond. His heart leapt at the thought that she might be jealous of the attention Clary gave him. He simply nodded and picked up his shot of rum.

"Here's to–" Ellis began, holding his shot up so high that the glass almost touched the light fixture.

"Let's save the toasts for some other time," Mercury said. He tossed back his shot without another word. The liquid was warm as it slid into his belly. Already he was starting to feel more relaxed.

After they finished dinner, they had another round of beer. Griffin had been the one to order this time. Mercury was halfway through his second beer when his lips began to tingle and his whole body felt languid. Griffin and Ellis traded impressions and Sloane laughed so hard that she snorted. Beneath the table, Mercury held Joelle's hand.

More people entered the bar. A group of men a little older than them shot pool in the next room, catching Sloane's eye.

"Shove out," Sloane said. She tapped Ellis' arm to get his attention.

"What gives?" he said. She continued to pat his arm until finally he groaned and glanced at Griffin, who was also staring at the men in the next room.

"Gotta scoot, Griff; Sloane wants to get out."

"Hurry up," Sloane urged.

"We're going; we're going. You get your period or something?" Ellis asked. Mercury kicked him under the table. Ellis scowled at him but continued to slide out of the booth. With her path clear, Sloane slid out of the booth and strutted toward the other room.

"Alright, dicks. Who's ready to get beaten by a girl?" Sloane said.

Ellis' eyes widened. "Oh, I've got to see this."

"Me, too," Joelle said. They both walked into the other room, leaving Mercury and Griffin to their own devices. Mercury looked over at Griffin, who now stared at his half-drunk beer.

"You good?" Mercury asked. Griffin looked up at him but didn't reply.

"Griffin, are you—"

"Yes, I'm fine, Mercury."

"Good, you had me worried," Mercury said. He grabbed the pitcher and poured what was left of the beer between his glass and Griffin's.

Griffin scoffed. "Doubtful."

"What's that supposed to mean?"

"Oh, please. I'm not dumb. I know you and my sister are feenin' for each other."

Mercury looked down at his beer. Part of him was hoping that he'd never have to talk to Griffin about his feelings for Joelle. But the other part of him was thrilled at the thought that Joelle might feel the same way about him as he did about her. He sipped on his beer to keep from smiling.

"Well, that may be true but it doesn't mean your sister—that I don't care how you feel."

Griffin rolled his eyes. "Look, you saved my life in Los Angeles, and for that I'll always be grateful. And you gave me this dope-ass power, which I'm still trying to figure out how to control. But the reality is that if I weren't here, I doubt any of you would notice."

"That's not true. Joelle . . ."

"Joelle is a good sister, but she's just as capable of being short-sighted like everyone else."

"Look, I know we don't know each other very well."

"No, we don't."

Mercury pursed his lips. "Griffin, I'm glad you're here. Joelle is glad you're here, and I'll bet Ellis and Sloane are, too."

Griffin downed the rest of his beer. He looked up at Mercury with glassy eyes.

"Ellis and Sloane? Those two are seconds away from hate-banging each other. Just face it, Merc. I'm the fifth wheel."

"You're a vital part of this team. I don't know if we'd have come as far as we have without you."

125

"Really?" Griffin said.

"Truly."

Griffin breathed deeply. "Okay."

"And if you're looking for a fling, I'm sure we can find you someone. What's your type? Personally, I'm a sucker for a great smile and natural hair," Mercury said.

Griffin exhaled, then leveled his gaze at Mercury. "My type is a man who looks like he could bench press me, but also who enjoys the works of Maya Angelou and James Baldwin."

Mercury nodded. "Lofty goals. Have you had any luck finding your knight in shining armor?"

Griffin leaned back and crossed his arms. "You're not weirded out?"

"About?"

"The fact that I'm gay."

Mercury shrugged. "We are who we are, Griffin. Why should I wish to change something that can't be changed, doesn't need to be changed?"

Griffin's eyes filled with tears. He removed his glasses and began to clean them.

"Most black men would say different. Say that I'm destroying the black race or something."

Mercury reached across the table and rested a hand on Griffin's trembling hand. In a flash, he saw a memory, one in which Griffin was pressed against a wall by an older man whose looks Griffin favored.

"It's not natural to like men. It's unholy," the man said.

"It's who I am," Griffin replied. The man slapped Griffin across the cheek.

"I thought I raised you better," the man said. He shook his head and walked away. Griffin sunk to the ground, and Mercury heard his sobs echo in the empty hallway.

Back in the here and now, Mercury saw Griffin struggling to keep those tears at bay.

"I'm sorry you've had to struggle with so much in your life," Mercury said. "But there are people who care and who want you around and who want to see you happy."

Griffin nodded and when Clary stopped by their table again, he asked for another shot.

"I'll take one, too," Mercury said. When Clary delivered the shots, they lifted their glasses and toasted.

"Here's to making it out alive," Griffin said. He threw back his head and downed the shot. Mercury followed suit. He smiled at the warmth that grew in his belly and numbed his lips. A loud crash sounded from the back room. Mercury turned. He saw Sloane and Joelle dancing on top of the pool table to Queen. Ellis and a trio of guys watched in awe as they danced together, their bodies moving in time.

"I think it's about time to dip out," Mercury said. He made eye contact with Clary, who stood on the other side of the bar on her cell phone. He mouthed the word check. She nodded and turned to the register behind her. She printed their check and dropped it off at the table.

"Quite a fun group you all are," said Clary. She nodded toward the other room.

Mercury smiled tightly. "Yeah it's . . . been awhile since we've all been out."

When Clary turned back toward the bar, Mercury grabbed a napkin and pulled it under the table. He ripped it and glamoured the strips into twenty dollar bills then set them atop the bill.

Once he stood, his vision tunneled. He started toward the back room just as the jukebox switched over to disco.

Sloane and Joelle were still dancing, their legs entwined and their arms wrapped around each other. Griffin sighed as he entered the room and leaned against the wall.

"Your sister's a good dancer," Mercury said.

"I guess," Griffin shrugged.

Sloane turned and danced low to the ground. When she stood, her hands moved to her bomber jacket zipper. She pulled the zipper down and peeled her jacket off. One of the other men whooped, and Mercury narrowed his eyes.

"Take it off! Take it off!" the men chanted.

Sloane played with the hem of her shirt. Mercury could see the lust in the men's eyes and knew their tame behavior was about to change. Before he had the chance to speak, Ellis stepped forward.

"Okay, I think that's quite the show," he said. He grabbed for Sloane's hand.

"C'mon, man, the show hasn't even begun," one of the men whined. He stepped toward Ellis, blocking off his access. Sloane and Joelle stopped dancing and stood on the pool table. Joelle turned to step off the table, but the other man held his arms up.

"I'll catch you, sweetie," he said. Joelle stepped back. Griffin shoved off the wall and stepped forward.

"I'm pretty sure it's time to go," said Griffin.

The men looked at each other and laughed.

"I don't think anyone asked you, Poindexter," one of the men quipped.

"Yeah, I'm done with this," Sloane said. "Move so I can get down."

Ellis stepped back, holding his hands up. "Damn, beautiful, you had us excited," one of the men groaned.

Mercury scoffed. The men looked over at him and sneered.

"Guess they'll just let anyone in here," said one of the men. He reached up once more to grab Joelle's hand, but again she stepped back. Sloane jumped off the table and landed with a thud. She turned and reached for Joelle's hand and helped her down. Joelle jumped down, landing with slightly less precision than Sloane. As she pulled her jacket back on, one of the men grabbed Joelle's butt.

Mercury and Griffin strode toward them, but Joelle held a hand up. She turned and grabbed the man by the throat. Mercury could see the smoke coming up from her hand. The man sputtered and his friend, who'd been about to swat at Sloane, rushed over to help. He grabbed at Joelle's free hand but she pushed him, leaving a burn mark on his shirt.

"Seems like your mom didn't teach you not to grab a lady like that," she said.

"Joelle, let him go," Mercury said. He walked over to her and put a hand on her shoulder. She turned to face him, her eyes wide and wild. "C'mon, let's go."

She turned back toward the man and released her hand.

"Let's get out of here," Mercury said to the group. He turned to the man, who was hunched over and gagging. His friend had his arms around him, trying to coach him.

"You and your witch friends better just get out of here before—"

"I trust you'll keep this incident under wraps? After all, think about what your friends would say if they found out that you got your ass handed to you by a black woman," Mercury smirked.

The man stared at Mercury for several moments before nodding and looking back down at his friend.

Mercury looked at Ellis, who nodded and put his arm around Sloane. Griffin grabbed his sister's hand and they walked out of the bar without a word. The second they stepped outside, Sloane let out a long whoop.

"Damn, what a night!" she said. She jumped and spun around, dancing to a song only she heard.

"I can't believe I just did that," Joelle said, looking down at her hands.

"It's okay—that guy was a jerk," Griffin said.

"Yeah, girl, if you didn't do something, I would have. Only I woulda slit his throat."

Sloane giggled.

"Okay, well somebody's drunk," Ellis said.

"Oh, here comes the respectability police." Sloane rolled her eyes.

"No, I just don't want you making a fool of yourself," Ellis said.

"Oh, honey, I couldn't do that even if I tried," Sloane giggled.

Ellis narrowed his eyes but kept quiet.

"I'm gonna go grab our rooms."

"I'll go with you," said Mercury. Sloane and Joelle slid onto the hood of the car. They leaned on each other and giggled. Griffin leaned against the driver's side, staring at the bar with his arms crossed.

Mercury and Ellis walked into the lobby of the hotel. They noticed the same man that had been there before, though it looked like he hadn't moved from his position. The door chimed as they walked in. The man didn't look up from the small television before him.

"Got any rooms available?" Ellis said. The man didn't respond. Ellis looked at Mercury, then turned back to the man. "Yo, you got any rooms available?"

"I heard you the first time," the man snapped. His voice was cigarette-raspy. He turned toward them and Mercury could see that one of his eyes was glazed over.

"So? Does that mean you've got rooms?"

"Would you two be needing a queen," he said looking at Ellis. He turned to Mercury. "Or a king."

Mercury clenched his fists. "No, we'd need three double rooms, please."

The man coughed and placed his hands on the counter. He rose slowly, his belly rubbing against the desk as he did so.

"I only got two left."

Mercury looked at Ellis.

"We'll take them."

The man nodded. "It's $99 a night."

Mercury pulled out a wad of cash, money he had glamoured from the napkin at the bar. The man shook his head.

"Only accept cards here."

Mercury looked at Ellis, who pulled his leather Gucci wallet out of his pocket. He slid his American Express across the counter.

"ID?" the man asked.

Ellis rolled his eyes and pulled out his ID. He tried to play cool, but Mercury could feel his friend's unease. His hand shook slightly as he set the ID on the counter. The man grabbed both cards and turned toward the register.

As they waited for the card to be run, Mercury looked at the television, where a late night show host bloviated about the unpatriotic nature of those who opposed the president's new dog tag initiative.

"These people have no desire to care for their fellow man—they simply care about their ability to use their powers, unchecked, for their own personal gain."

Mercury shook his head. Across the bottom of the screen scrolled a banner with the latest headlines. They seemed mostly to be about President Vael's choices for Supreme Court justices, the investigation into the deaths of Justices Smitstra and Carmichael, and a handful of protests happening around the country. But there was one that caught Mercury's eye. It read: "parents of missing frat party teens to speak with Jessica Robbins on *60 Minutes.*"

He felt a pang in his chest but said nothing. As the rotund hotel manager handed Ellis his cards, Mercury wondered if he should tell the group about the interview.

"Let's go," said Ellis. He exited the lobby and Mercury followed, staying silent and willing the sinking feeling in his stomach to go away. Joelle and Sloane still leaned against the windshield, but now Griffin sat on the curb, wrapping his long dreads into a high bun.

"Got our rooms," Ellis said as he waved the key cards. Sloane slid off the car and jumped up in front of him.

"Great," she said.

"But . . . we were only able to get two of them. So, some of us will have to triple up."

"Damn," Joelle said. She sat up and crossed her legs. "Well, Griffin and I don't mind sharing a bed, right?"

Griffin shrugged. "Whatever works."

"Sloane, do you want to take the other bed?"

Sloane looked from Ellis to Joelle. Mercury could tell she was hesitant.

"Sure," she said. Ellis scowled.

Sloane stood stock still for several minutes before turning back to Joelle. She eventually hooked her arm through Joelle's and they began walking to their rooms.

Their rooms were on the second floor toward the back row of rooms. Thankful that their rooms were right next to each other, Mercury watched as Ellis slid the key into the door lock. It beeped and Ellis pushed open the door. Already he was hit by the dank smell of a room that had been sitting on its own for too long. He stepped in and turned the light on. There was a small table made of particle board to the left of the door. Two queen sized beds were divided by a nightstand with a Bible resting in front of a lamp with stains on the shade. An old television set, complete with an antenna, sat across from the beds atop a dresser. Two of the dresser knobs were missing.

"What a shit show," Griffin said.

Mercury looked back at him with pursed lips. "Got a better idea? I didn't see any other hotels on this main road."

"Me neither. Look, I know it looks a bit . . . sketchy, but I'm sure it's gonna be fine." Joelle smiled. "And look, we've got joining rooms!"

She turned to the right, where their rooms were joined by a metal door with chipped paint. It was too short, leaving a gap at the bottom of the door.

131

"Well, I'm going to toss the bed and make sure there are no bugs or cum stains or, ya know, shit," said Ellis as he turned to face the beds.

Mercury walked further into the room and entered the bathroom. He turned the light on and the fluorescent tube light flickered then brightened. It was tidy, cleaned, but like the rest of the room, there was a lived in quality that Mercury found disturbing.

He turned the faucet knobs. The water sputtered out before running normally. He sighed. *Can't anything go right?* His eyes welled with tears. He looked in the mirror and was surprised at how gaunt he looked. He hadn't shaved his beard in days, and his waves were non-existent.

Mercury took several deep breaths and clung to the sides of the sink. He felt like he was crawling out of his skin. *What have I done? This is all my fault.* His breath escaped in spurts as he leaned forward and rested his head against the mirror. Just as his tears began to spill down his cheeks, he heard a knock at the door.

"Yo, you gonna stay there all night? I gotta drop a deuce," Ellis spoke through the door.

Mercury stood up and turned the faucet back on. He washed his hands then splashed water on his face. He released a long, deep exhale before opening the door. He looked at Ellis, whose smile faltered.

"Are you okay?" Ellis asked. Mercury nodded. Ellis cocked his head and stared at Mercury, his hazel eyes inquisitive.

"I'm fine," Mercury replied. "Really."

"Okay," Ellis said. He pushed past Mercury. "Well then, you got to go. Those totchos are doin' me dirty."

Mercury shook his head and walked out of the bathroom. Ellis quickly slammed the door. The sound of the bathroom fan whirring and cycling made Mercury chuckle.

He turned toward the beds. The bedding was pulled back on each bed, with one duvet cover touching the floor. The pillows laid flat on the bed. Mercury chose the one closest to the door and sunk into its softness. He kicked off his shoes then threw his legs onto the bed. It wasn't the most comfortable mattress, but compared to the jail cell and the car he'd spent the previous nights in, it was heaven.

He placed a pillow behind his head and rolled onto his side away from the light. He pulled the sheet up and over his shoulders. He felt like his world was spinning, and he didn't know if it was because of the beer and rum or because he was moments away from a panic attack.

"Just breathe" he whispered. "Breathe. It's okay. You're okay. We're all okay."

The tears came again as he repeated that mantra, one that Troian would say when he saw Mercury in the midst of anxiety.

"It's okay. You're okay. We're all okay," Mercury whispered.

"It's okay. You're okay. We're all okay," Ellis said. Mercury jumped. He hadn't realized that the fan was off and the door had opened. He flipped onto his back and found Ellis sitting on the bed beside him, cigarette in one hand. He'd taken his beanie off, exposing his russet hair that stood up at odd angles.

"Sorry," Mercury said.

Ellis scoffed. "Got nothing to apologize for."

Ellis bent over and removed his shoes. He sat up against the headboard and put his legs out, crossing his ankles. He took a long drag of his cigarette, then exhaled a cloud of smoke.

"You know, I miss him, too."

Mercury sniffled. "Really?"

Ellis nodded. "I mean, he was a real asshole when he wanted to be, but I always felt that it came from a place of just . . . wanting people to be better. Like, compassion, you know? I never felt he hated me. I even miss jamming with him. He was the one who taught me to play."

Mercury nodded. "Yeah, he taught me, too."

"Remember when you and I got into your dad's Beaujolais?" Ellis started. "I was wearing a white shirt and spilled some of the wine on me. So Troian, after cursing me out, let me borrow a shirt."

"That shit was so long on you," Mercury laughed.

"Yeah. Then your dad came home and asked what the hell I was wearing, since it was this long-ass Sean John shirt that had like a fist and stuff on it. So I said–"

"Nah, Mr. A, it's just a tall tee. Everyone's wearing them," Mercury said. The laughter bubbled up in his body, erupting along with tears that streamed down his face. Ellis laughed, too, and for several moments they sat like that, laughing.

"I never told you how sorry I was, seeing him go like that," Ellis said. He put out his cigarette and lit another.

"Yeah. I can't get it out of my mind. I see it every time I close my eyes."

"Damn."

Mercury sobbed. His breath coming out in jagged spurts. Ellis rested his free hand on his shoulder.

"Let it out, man. It's okay."

The sobs turned into wails, his sorrow echoing off of the walls.

Minutes passed. Once the tears stopped, Mercury sat up. He gestured to Ellis for a tissue from the nightstand. Ellis grabbed three and handed them to him. Mercury blew his nose then tossed the tissue on the ground.

"I'm so exhausted," Mercury said. He put his head in his hands. "I know. I think we all are. Try to get some rest. I think this bed will do you better than that beater out there," Ellis said. He leaned over and wrapped his arms around Mercury. Mercury leaned into the hug, his body relaxing.

Ellis pulled away. "Good night."

"Good night," Mercury said.

Ellis turned off the light, then put out his cigarette. He slid into his bed and drew the blankets over him. Mercury rolled back onto his side and closed his eyes, hoping the night would be kind to him.

Chapter 10

Mercury awoke to discover the windshield was broken.

It was the first thing Mercury noticed when he stepped out of the room the next morning. He'd felt groggy, his head pounding and his stomach full of acid.

"I am never drinking with you guys again," he said to the group, who were in various states of disarray. Joelle's hair was limp, the curls fallen and frizzy. Griffin's glasses were smudged and slightly crooked as though he'd fallen asleep with them on. Ellis and Sloane stood next to each other, both with hair that stood at odd angles. Her shirt was buttoned incorrectly. He had on only one sock.

Mercury was about to ask them what had happened the night before, to ask who'd been groaning at four in the morning, but his eyes landed on the car and all his questions fell from his mind. Suddenly, he was no longer hungover but alert, his naturally heightened senses working overtime.

"Yo, what the fuck?" he said. He hurried downstairs, backpack slung over his shoulder. The others followed him, shoes thudding against the metal stairs. He soon noticed the side mirrors were also broken. A jagged line was traced into the passenger side. An upside down pentagram and the word "hexe" were drawn on the hood of the car.

Mercury clenched his fists. Had it been the men at the bar the night before or had the UGN brothers finally caught up with them? A soft voice interrupted his thoughts.

"Who would do this?" Joelle asked. She tucked her palms into her sweater and crossed her arms over her chest.

"Isn't it obvious? Those dicks from the bar last night probably saw us come back here and waited until we were out of sight," Sloane said. She set her bag down on the hood of the car and rifled through it, pulling knives and box cutters from its depths.

"When the fuck did you get that stuff?" Ellis asked, picking up a pack of box cutters. Sloane looked at him but did not reply. She wrapped a box cutter at the end of her hair, coiling her jet-black tresses into a high bun. She slipped two knives into the sides of her boots.

"Seriously? We're not headed into a gang fight; you can ease up."

"A gang fight? Is that supposed to be funny?" Sloane replied.

Ellis shrugged.

She rolled her eyes and faced the group. "Well, we have a pretty good chance of finding them at that bar. We can go over there and handle it or–"

"Or we could just ditch the car and find a new one," said Griffin. He pitched his voice lower so that a group of other motel guests, who had stopped by the stairs and were surveying the situation, couldn't hear them.

"Oh, don't be such a pussy, Griffin," Sloane replied.

"Hey, you don't need to call him that," said Joelle.

Sloane scoffed. "I'm sorry; I just thought that this was something we all had to do, you know? Be prepared to kick someone's ass so we can stay alive?"

"But we don't even know they did this," Joelle said. Sloane threw her hands in the air. As the two of them argued, Mercury approached the car. He laid his hands on the top of the broken side mirror. He closed his eyes and saw a group of men huddled around the car. Two of them held bats, one of them held a crowbar. The motel attendant sat staring at the television, aware enough of the disturbance but not caring enough to alert anyone.

It was Conner who stepped onto the hood of the car and brought his bat down with a crash, instantly shattering the windshield. Two of the other UGN brothers stood at the mirrors. One of them slammed their bat into one while the other used a crowbar. They vandalized the car, all the while laughing and whooping. When they were done, one of the brothers pointed toward the motel lobby, where the large man with the overgrown white beard sat staring at them in horror.

Mercury let go of the car then turned to face the lobby.

"Mercury, what's wrong?" Joelle noticed Mercury's abrupt movement.

Mercury didn't respond. He just walked into the lobby. He didn't gasp when he saw the attendant sitting in his chair, neck bent back so far that the top of his head rested between his shoulder blades. His neck and arms were riddled with bite marks and his skin had the kind of pale that only comes with an extreme loss of blood. His mouth gaped open and already maggots twisted and writhed within. He also remained calm as he saw the family— mother, father, two children— splayed on the ground. It looked like they were in the midst of checking in when the vampires attacked them.

The father's left arm was twisted behind his back. His neck was torn and his blood had already coagulated on the tile floor. His adolescent son lied next to him on his side. His mouth and eyes were open, his eyes shifted as if he was staring at Mercury.

The mother and daughter bore the brunt of the UGN brothers' aggression. The daughter looked to be in her late teens. She lied on her back with her dress pulled up over her stomach, revealing a pair of bloody underwear. Several bruises lined her face and neck. Bite marks riddled her thighs. The mother lied on her stomach, arms clasped behind her back. Her pants were down, and her head was tilted to the right side.

"Holy shit."

Mercury turned toward Sloane, whose voice broke Mercury free of whatever stupor his vision imparted on him. She had her burner phone out recording the bodies.

"What are you doing?" he said.

"We have to show this to the world. People have to know."

Mercury tried to grab her arm but Sloane stepped back.

"These monsters posted the video of Troian's death and you want to just walk away?"

Mercury narrowed his eyes. He pushed Sloane against the desk.

"Are you fucking stupid? Don't you know that the only thing I can think about is finding those leeches and ripping their fangs out of their mouths with my bare hands?"

Sloane's eyes were fiery as a tear spilled down her cheek.

Mercury stepped back and threw his hands up.

"Do whatever you want to do," he said. "I'm getting out of here."

The bell above the door dinged as Mercury stepped back out into the sunlight. Despite the warmth, Mercury was shivering. Seconds later, Sloane stepped out of the lobby, her cheeks stained with mascara.

"Well, what's the plan?" she said, crossing her arms.

Hell if I know. "I guess we've got to find a new car."

They searched an alleyway behind the building, each of them carrying their bags. On the left was a dirty blue Impala.

"This looks okay," Mercury said.

He stepped in its direction but stopped dead in his tracks when Conner stepped from behind the vehicle, his white button-up sleeves rolled up and marbled with blood. His eyes covered with solarized shades.

"What took you so long?" Conner said. He smirked at them and Mercury's heartbeat quickened. He stepped back and nearly ran into another vampire.

"Didn't you get your ass kicked enough the last time we saw you?" Sloane said, her shoulder brushing against Mercury's.

Conner scoffed and stepped toward them. Sloane clutched her silver knives in her hands. Mercury looked to his left, where Joelle stood with a fireball at the ready. Two vampires flanked her. Ellis and Griffin stood on the other side of Sloane, where an additional three vampires stood. Two of them Mercury recognized from the party, but the other three seemed to be new—they were older, stragglers from the country roads.

"Perhaps you should take that up with your brother," Conner said. "Oh, that's right—he's dead. Burned to death with a noose around his neck, just like so many of his ancestors."

Mercury shook.

"I'd say that makes us even," Ellis said. He stepped between Mercury and Conner. "An eye for an eye—so why don't you just leave us alone?"

Conner's smile fell. His eyes narrowed and his mouth set into a harsh grimace.

"Because I don't just want to kill you—I want to feel your blood draining from your veins."

He grabbed Ellis' collar and pulled him toward him. His fangs dug into the flesh of Ellis' neck. Ellis cried out and Mercury swiped his hand to the side, moving Ellis out of Conner's grip and tossing Conner against the car's windshield.

Ellis brought his hand to his neck and the wound was healed within seconds.

Conner stood without any hesitation. "You know we have you to thank for this lovely meeting. Maybe next time you'll think twice before calling a dead man." He was smiling again, sending a shiver down Mercury's spine.

One of the other UGN vampires, a short, stocky man with large black glasses, lunged at Mercury, pinning him to the ground.

Mercury drove his hand up, his palm connecting with the vampire's nose. The vampire shouted and though blood spurted from the wound, he still continued his pursuit of Mercury's neck. The vampire punched Mercury in the temple, making his vision twist and darken. He shoved Mercury's head to the side so that his neck was exposed. Mercury saw that each of his friends had been overtaken by vampires, each one struggling against strength far greater than their own.

As Conner's fangs were about to dig into Joelle's neck, Mercury let out a guttural scream. The sound reverberated from his inner being to the outside world. The sound waves that erupted acted as a weapon, pushing everyone back and separating the vampires from the group. Two of the vampires connected with the wall, leaving bloody streaks as they slid down. The other UGN brother who'd been accosting Griffin lied at the other end of the alley, passed out in a heap of trash. Conner and two other vampires were strewn about, knocked out like the others. The UGN vampire who'd been on top of Mercury lied at the foot of the car, his body leaving an imprint in the front bumper. Blood seeped out of his mouth.

Mercury stood, his legs wobbling.

"What the fuck was that?" Griffin asked. They all looked at him in amazement.

"I don't know . . . I've never done that before," Mercury said, still shocked.

"Are your powers growing or something?" Joelle asked.

"What is this? *Charmed?*" Ellis asked. "Who cares! We've gotta get out of here before they come to."

The group sped down the alleyway, past the unconscious vampires and into the traffic of the street beyond.

They split up, each person looking for a car that looked easy to break into and hotwire. Mercury started to run but remembered where he was and realized the last thing he wanted to do was draw suspicion. He slowed to a walk even though his heart was beating out of his chest.

It was only a matter of time before the vampires regained consciousness and searched for them. He walked past a white sedan that had a passenger window rolled down. He reached for it but noticed a dog in the backseat staring up at him. He gasped and backed away.

He approached a red van next, but figured the color was too noticeable. After walking down at least five blocks, Mercury found an early 2000 Subaru. It was puke green and had a vanity plate that read "Joeb8by". He whistled, hoping the others could hear him.

He leaned against the wall next to the car and stuffed his hands in his pockets. *Hurry up*, Mercury thought. *Please hurry.*

Griffin walked over first. He already knew what to do. He looked around then lifted a hand and pointed it at the vanity plate. "Joeb8by" became "J03484T." They waited for Ellis, Joelle and Sloane to arrive. When Sloane got there, she popped open the door in less than a minute.

Without speaking they piled into the car. Sloane slid behind the wheel and peeled away. They sped out of the small town of Van Meter and onto a long stretch of road surrounded by flat, barren land on both sides.

An hour passed, and still no one spoke.

"I think we're almost there," Mercury said breaking the silence. No one responded. "I mean, we don't have a map or anything, but I think we're almost to Chicago, so—"

"How long do you think it'll take those douchebags to find us again?" Ellis said.

Mercury looked at his friend, who sat in the passenger seat. Ellis' green eyes appeared accusatory in the rear view mirror. Mercury felt a pang in his stomach. He glanced at the twins beside him. Joelle leaned on Griffin's shoulder. Griffin had his glasses off, staring at a large crack in the left glass.

"I-I don't know," Mercury said.

Ellis scoffed and looked out the window.

"I thought we already talked about this—they're not just gunning for me; it's all of us. The best way to get around this is to get to Astera, where we'll have more protection."

"Yeah, okay," Ellis said.

"Why—" Mercury started. Joelle squeezed his arm and he looked over at her. She looked tired and scared.

Mercury shifted his weight and leaned against the left window, his forehead hitting the cool glass. He couldn't believe they still blamed him for this. After all they'd been through, they all still thought it was his fault. He remembered the *60 Minutes* episode he'd seen in the motel lobby. Griffin and Joelle's grandparents and Sloane and Ellis' parents were being interviewed by Jessica Robbins, the young, red-headed version of Katie Couric.

"Just come home," Sloane's father, Esai, said. "You know we'll protect you. You don't gotta run anymore."

Ellis' father, Carrington, had a red face and clenched hands. He looked straight at the camera.

"I'm talking to the people that my son is with right now; you know who you are. My son has a future; he's going to be successful. Don't ruin his future because you got caught up in something overwhelming. Let him come home."

Mercury looked at each of his friends. He felt like he was crawling out of his skin, again.

"My son has a future," Carrington said. But not Mercury.

"You know we'll protect you," Sloane's father said. Something Mercury wasn't doing a very good job of.

He wondered what his friends would be doing if he hadn't killed Delanie. Would he have even gotten to know Joelle and Griffin? Would he still consider Ellis a friend?

For the second time in a while, Mercury felt an overwhelming sense of dread and wished he'd been granted the power to turn back time.

Freddie Karr: Undercover Witch

By Cordelia Edwards

Vampire-hater and writer for the harridan publication, *Jonquil*, Freddie Karr spoke to *Vice* this past weekend in a rare public appearance. Seeming every bit as vitriolic and unfunny as he normally is in his writing, Karr wore traditional African robes, symbolizing his ancestors (from which tribe he doesn't know) and a large, black fist overlaying a pentagram, a symbol representing all elements of magic (because co-opting a symbol is totally fine as long as they do it). When journalist Jamie Pines (another easily-offended harridan) asked what Freddie's message would be to the witches he seems so fond of protecting, he said this:

"Rise up; take back your power. You're more powerful than you realize."

Sage advice, isn't it? But those who've followed politics for these past two years and are not wholly consumed by the harridan bubble know that Karr's advice echoes the slogan and mission of President Vael. With the simple word "restore," Vael created a call to arms that encouraged people to strive for happiness, for a simpler time, and to, you guessed it, "take back their power." Karr's words are directed toward those who choose to live life under the assumption that witches and minorities, women and gays, are victims. They believe the falsehoods churned out by the caustic media that state that hate crimes against witches have increased, that they are so accepted that the police looks the other way and even takes part in the persecution.

In a recent article, Karr cited a case in which notable radio DJ Ama Deus was pulled over while driving near Hayti, North Carolina. In the officer's dash cam, one can see that there was a physical altercation. Deus was roughly pushed to the ground, tased, and had several bruises and a sprained wrist when he ended up in the Raleigh-Durham jail. The incident was brutal, to be sure, but don't forget the facts. Deus was speeding, swerving in and out of lanes, endangering the public. When he was pulled over, he cursed at the officers and when they assisted him out of his vehicle, he used his magic (Deus is a Fire Hand) and shot flames toward the officers. While he was being booked, one of the officers was treated for second degree burns. Some might call this an incident of "police brutality", another absurd harridan ploy bandied about these last few years, accusing our boys in blue of committing extra violence on blacks, Hispanics, gays, witches and the Asians. But just like one should never judge a book by its cover, one should never jump to conclusions. There's always two sides to every story and in Deus' case, it's this: Deus, a tall, Rubenesque man, was pulled over for speeding and instead of behaving and treating those officers with well-deserved respect, he cussed at them and tried to kill them using the very flames witches insisted they are dying from.

But I'm not surprised Karr ignores the truth. He, himself, is too afraid to admit his own: that he is a witch, a descendant of Tituba, the slave woman responsible for bringing witchcraft to the Americas. It was because of her that scourges of people have been killed since the 1600s, and now it's because of Karr that Americans believe that witches are the real victims.

In 1750, a group of children went missing from their homes in Philadelphia. Weeks went by until finally their corpses were found in the cellar of a known witch, Louisa Hines. When Hines confessed, she admitted that it was her coven who abducted the kids and sacrificed them in the name of Satan.

In 1867, sisters Bettina and Hattie Marshall were found dead in their Charlotte home, pentagrams drawn on their chests. In 1898, a Florida couple was killed in a pagan ritual called "Calling the Quarters". They had their eyes gouged out and their tongues removed. In 1927, a family spending the summer at their beach house in Fire Island were all murdered. The symbol for Water was painted on the walls with blood.

A group of girls were gang raped and tossed off the side of a canyon in the name of Satan in 1956. In 1960, 1972, 1984 and 1999, five girls in Lubbock went missing each year, all found arranged in the shape of a pentagram. In 2007, a school shooting took place in Des Moines. The shooter, Oliver Sweeney, confessed to being a witch with the power of necromancy. He said he killed the four victims to see if he could bring them back to life.

And last month, at St. Basil's Church in Bala Cynwyd, a group of God-fearing, praying citizens were executed in their house of worship. Seventeen people lost their lives that day because of the witches' agenda. If the folks at *Jonquil* don't want to tell the truth, then it's up to us here at *The Vanguard*. Is it true that witches have, at times, been abused in America? Yes. But it's also true that this ill-treatment ended over a hundred years ago. The same plight that affected those witches does not affect the privileged, whiny mages today. It's up to those of us with common sense to save this country from itself. It's up to us to restore it back to the days of common sense, truth, justice and accountability.

I can only hope that the likes of Freddie Karr and his victim-minded coven take note.

Chapter 11

Another town. Another diner. Another motel with chipped paint and a bathroom fan that doesn't quite work. This time Mercury shared a room with Griffin and Joelle while Ellis and Sloane shared the room right next door, not bothering to quiet their moans or stop the headboard from hitting the wall.

They each barely spoke to each other as they rolled into Cape Elizabeth.

"I've never seen the Atlantic up close," Joelle mentioned as they sat in a diner with ripped booths and sticky condiment containers. No one responded. Griffin and Sloane stared down at their plates while Ellis sat with his arms crossed, brow furrowed, scowling into the distance.

"It's not as beautiful as the Pacific, I think," Mercury said. Joelle turned toward him, her eyes glassy. She nodded. His body longed to hold hers, to kiss her and to prevent the tears that loomed on her eyelids from falling.

"No, it's not. But I guess we'll never see the Pacific again, will we?" Ellis said.

"That's not—"

Ellis shook his head. "We all know we can't ever go back to LA, despite our parents begging us to."

"What are you talking about?" A confused look spread across Joelle's face.

Mercury's stomach flipped.

"They were all on TV the other night. *60 Minutes*. They were begging us to come home despite whatever twisted shit we've gotten mixed up in. I know they'd never be able to believe the truth of what's happened, and I know that we can never go back."

"That's not true," Mercury said. But he was flailing. He could feel their eyes upon him. "Once we get to Astera, they can help. Then we can go back to school and–"

"Back to school?" Ellis said. "You're never going to get to even step foot on campus. Not after what you've . . . what we've done."

"We had to do what we had to do," Mercury said, attempting to hide his own doubt.

Ellis scoffed.

"We did; you know that. We–"

"I killed," Ellis shouted. He looked around and crossed himself, noticing the attention they were drawing. "I killed someone. We had to fight again just to steal another car so we could bullshit our way into another hotel and a diner with fake money so we could have the world's driest burger and soggy fries and a flat soda just to have something in our bellies so we can drive for hours on end to get to this magic summit where we don't even know what they're gonna do. We did all of this, and I killed someone."

Mercury stared down at his patty melt and watched as the pool of oil from the meat slowly spread, soaking a crinkle cut fry. As the group ate in silence, Mercury could feel his anger simmering beneath the surface. He was tired of Ellis' anger and resentment. After all– weren't they adults? Weren't they as capable of making their own shitty decisions as he was? He grit his teeth as Sloane and Ellis whispered in each other's ears and laughed. It wasn't enough that he blamed Mercury for his current predicament but now he was slowly stealing Sloane away from him.

As they paid for their food and left, Mercury's gut twisted as he thought about every shitty thing Ellis had ever said or done to him. Like the time he got drunk at Troian's party and punched one of his friends in the neck because he'd hooked up with Ellis' ex. Or the time Mercury walked in on him bragging about knowing that Mercury and his family were magic.

Walking back to the hotel room, Mercury thought about all the ways he could hurt his friend. He thought about Ellis' sensitive knees, his stomach ulcers, his thinning hair at the sides, which forced him to wear a beanie. *Who the fuck does he think he is?* Mercury thought.

"Who the fuck do you think you are?" Mercury's thoughts escaped from his lips. Sloane and Ellis, who walked arm in arm, both stopped and turned around.

"You good, Merc?" Sloane asked.

"I'm not talking to you," Mercury replied. "Ellis, just who the fuck do you think you are?"

Ellis scowled and dropped Sloane's arm.

"Excuse me?" he said.

Joelle put a hand on Mercury's shoulder. "C'mon, let's just—"

Mercury brushed her hand off.

"I said, just who the fuck do you think you are? You're over here acting like a victim when you're the one who killed that dhampir."

"I wouldn't have killed her if you hadn't—"

Mercury threw his hands in the air and scoffed. "Give me a fucking break. I killed Delanie and I have to live with that for the rest of my life. But you? You've had a choice this entire time. You could have easily bailed."

"Bailed?" Ellis moved toward Mercury. "How could I bail when you're the one who put a target on my back?"

"Oh, please! You could have walked away at any time and blended in with the other white boys at that party or in the city. Or you could have called your rich daddy to get you out. But you chose to stay."

"Oh, that's just how it always is with you! It's always about my race or my money or the fact that I'm not magic. Never mind that I've been your friend since goddamn pre-k and that I've never treated you different."

Mercury pushed Ellis. He stumbled back and when he regained his balance, he returned the push, barely moving Mercury out of the way.

"Guys, come on," Joelle pleaded. "We can't do this. We're all tired; let's just get back to the room."

Mercury pushed Ellis again. "Fuck you, Mercury. You think I'd choose this?"

"I think you stuck around so you could try to fuck Sloane. And it looks like you succeeded."

"Go fuck yourself, Merc," Sloane said, stepping next to Ellis. "The only reason why we're even in this position is because you had such a boner for Joelle that you had to play white knight and save her from those frat douches."

"Hey, c'mon guys, just–" Joelle began.

"Shut up. No one is talking to you. Stop trying so hard to make everything okay. Shit's not okay," Sloane spat.

Joelle stepped toward Sloane, both fists clenched.

"No you don't," Griffin intervened, grabbing his sister's shoulders and pulling her back. "Let them hash it out. They wanna fight, so be it."

Mercury felt his blood pulsing through his veins as he quickly looked around. He wanted to hit something.

"Oh, I'm sorry for giving a fuck about someone else's fate. You two and your selfish, degenerate ways . . . you'd rather screw everyone else over just to get ahead."

"Hey, man, don't talk to her that way," Ellis said. This time his chest was pressed against Mercury. The heat of his breath upset Mercury even more.

"I don't think Sloane needs anyone to speak on her behalf, least of all a piece of shit like you," Mercury said. He dug his hands into Ellis' shoulders and pushed him again. Ellis responded quickly, his fist connecting with Mercury's left cheek. The blow snapped Mercury's head to the side. Vaguely he heard Joelle and Sloane scream for them to stop, saying they were being petty, insisting they were making a scene. But Mercury didn't care. He wanted to hurt Ellis. Badly. He clenched both fists and launched at Ellis, leaning into his power when he tackled him, ensuring that his body would land extra hard on the pavement. He hit Ellis, his fist connecting with his lower lip. He felt it split beneath his fists. Ellis raised his hands in defense, but Mercury pushed them down, uttering a spell to keep them down. He hit Ellis over and over again. Because of the healing magic that pulsed just beneath his skin, Ellis' wounds started to heal almost as soon as Mercury's fist lifted.

"I guess I'm just gonna have to beat that magic out of you," Mercury said. His lifted his hand high in the air.

He smelled the burning of flesh before he realized what was happening. He yelped and looked back as Joelle gripped his arm with both hands, her flames rippling over his skin.

"Let me go," Mercury cried.

"Only if you stop this," she said.

Mercury grunted. He looked back at Ellis, whose head had rolled to the side. The sidewalk beneath him was covered in blood. Sloane knelt beside him running a hand through his hair. In that instant, all of his anger left him just as soon as it came. As Griffin and Sloane pulled Ellis to his feet, tears clouded Mercury's eyes.

"I'm . . . sorry," Mercury said.

Ellis' wounds were already healing, but his face and the front of his shirt were still covered in blood. Mercury stepped toward his friend but Sloane held out a hand, stopping him in his tracks.

"Don't. You've done enough," she said. Her chocolate brown eyes seemed to grow darker and the love and caring that Mercury normally found in them was gone.

"But I—"

"What part of don't do you not understand?" Sloane wrapped one of Ellis' arms around her. "I know Ellis can be a dick but he didn't deserve you nearly beating him to death. I could have bailed on this trip time and time again but I chose to stay with you because you're my bro, but now? I can't do this."

She turned and slowly began to walk with Ellis down the road.

"Sloane, Ellis, wait! I'm sorry!" Mercury cried out. Neither of them turned around.

Mercury sunk to his knees and wrapped his arms around himself. In all of his years of friendship with Ellis, they'd never come to blows before. Hell, Mercury couldn't ever remember yelling at him in the way he'd just done or saying the things he said. Perhaps if he'd done that sooner, if he'd been honest with his friend about the things that bother him, he wouldn't be watching him walk away with Sloane.

Sloane.

Somehow in the course of the year and a half she'd worked at the Iron Bird, she'd become a vital part of his life. She was who Mercury went to for advice or for a book recommendation or for a late night trip to get burritos and hang out on the beach. His body ached as he thought about the times they spent watching the waves crash into the beach and talked about their life at present and their dreams for the future.

"I have to go tell them I'm sorry," Mercury said without realizing it. He'd only taken three steps before Joelle grabbed his arm again.

"Merc, I don't think that's a good idea."

"Yeah, Joelle's right. You went in on them in more ways than one. Best to just let them be. They'll make their way back to the hotel and then you can hash it out," Griffin said.

Mercury sighed and looked down at his feet. Joelle wrapped her arms around him from behind.

"It's going to be okay," she said.

"I'm surprised you two are still here," Mercury replied, rubbing his head. He turned toward them. Griffin shrugged.

"It's not like you were talking about me, or saying anything that isn't true. Your approach really sucked, though," he said.

Mercury chuckled. "Yeah. I guess I need to learn to speak my mind sooner."

"You think?" Joelle asked. She smiled and slipped her hand through his. They held hands as they walked back to their room.

They each completed their nighttime rituals and as Mercury slid beneath the blankets of his bed, he was surprised when Joelle joined him. Mercury looked from her to Griffin. He lifted a brow, as if to ask if he was okay with his sister sharing his bed.

"Just go in the other room if you two are gonna get it in," Griffin said. He removed his glasses and rolled onto his side, turning his back to them.

Mercury's heart leapt as Joelle nestled onto his shoulder.

"They aren't back yet," Mercury said. Tilting his chin toward the room on the other side of the wall, where Ellis and Sloane laid claim.

"Did you expect them to be? Mercury, you were all heated and said things that were hurtful. It's just going to take them some time to get their heads right."

"This whole thing– it's all so messed up."

"Not all of it," Joelle said. She leaned up and kissed him. Her lips were soft. She smelled like mangos. Mercury fought to control himself but he could feel his sweats pulling against himself. He ran a hand through her hair. She brought her hand to his chest and leaned closer to him.

"I'd never have met you if you hadn't gone to that party. And if all of . . . if none of those things went down, we both probably would have gone our separate ways."

"No," Mercury said. "I would have gotten your number."

Joelle snorted. "How cocky of you to assume I would have given it to you."

"Not cocky, just . . . certain."

He leaned in to kiss her again, then rested his chin on top of her head.

"Good night, Mercury," Joelle said.

"Good night, beautiful," he replied. He closed his eyes and drifted to sleep.

It's okay. You're okay. We're all okay.

Mercury snapped his eyes open at the sound of a loud thud. He looked over to see Joelle and Griffin both sitting straight up.

"What's that?" Mercury whispered.

"They're at the door," Griffin said.

He looked over to the gauzy white curtains at the window. Conner stood on the other side and even from the obstructed distance, Mercury could see that he was smiling. Mercury's heartbeat quickened as the thud at the door became faster.

He jumped up as the door burst open. Conner and three of his lackeys rushed into the room. Two of them launched themselves at Griffin who had barely managed to slip his glasses on before they pulled him out of bed and tossed him onto the floor. One of them pressed his knee into Griffin's back as the other tied his hands behind his back.

"Hey, be careful with him, his glasses—" Joelle said. The one who'd knelt down on Griffin turned and slapped Joelle across the face. Mercury jumped up and threw his hand back, sending the vampire across the room and through the window.

The room fell silent.

Then Conner laughed. He was upon Mercury, pushing him against the wall and baring his fangs.

"How nice to meet you again," Conner said. "Now we finally get to talk about our unfinished business."

Mercury could barely breathe as Conner pinned him against the wall. Beyond him, Mercury spotted Joelle struggling against two vampires that were trying to pull her out of the bed. She brought her elbow down on the back of one of their necks. He screamed and jerked Joelle up by her hair. Joelle yelped and though Mercury lifted his free hand, no one moved. He scowled.

"Oh, you're probably wondering why your little parlor trick didn't work." Conner smiled. He opened the palm of the hand that rested against Mercury's neck.

Conner held a small metal chain with flecks of black on it. Mercury didn't need him to explain. It was a Thurguard, an object treated with magic-sapping power. When it touched the skin, it virtually short circuited a person's power until the object was removed.

"How did a trash heap like you talk someone into giving you a Thurguard?" Mercury quipped. Conner scoffed. "You think I asked for this? Nah, bro. I just took it. Some witch in Joliet was so willing to spread her cheeks for anyone that she didn't see me or my gang coming. Robbed her shit then drained her dry."

Mercury winced.

"Even so, that little video of me and your brother has kinda made me famous."

"Yeah, he was totally trending. Hashtag burn witch burn," said a vampire whose tanked-topped upper body was almost as large as Conner's.

Conner glared at him and the vampire went silent.

"Well, the night's young and we've got so many plans for you all," Conner said. He turned back toward his lackeys. The two that struggled with Joelle already had her hog tied and on the floor next to her brother. They moved toward Mercury as Conner placed the Thurguard around Mercury's neck. He punched Mercury in the stomach.

Mercury doubled over. He didn't fight the men as they grabbed him and pushed him onto the bed. They tied Mercury's hands behind his back and taped his mouth closed before jerking him off the bed then leading him out into the cold, dark evening.

They were on the second floor and the motel wasn't well lit. Though Mercury's enhanced senses enabled him to see almost like normal, the vampire holding him stumbled, nearly causing them to tumble down the stairs. He could hear Griffin and Joelle grunting behind him, trying desperately to speak around the duct tape on their mouths.

The vampires led them down a back alley and into a vacant lot. They found three wooden stakes awaiting their arrival. As the vampire who had gripped his elbow thrust Mercury against the wooden stake, Mercury could hear his heart beating faster. He was certain he'd throw up if he wasn't wearing a gag.

I can't believe it's going to end like this, Mercury thought. *I end just as I begin.* He looked to his left where Griffin struggled against the rope at his wrists. To his right, Joelle looked back at him with red and glassy eyes. After a few seconds, he could no longer make out her shape through the tears that clouded his eyes.

"I love you," he wanted to say. "Meeting you was the best thing that's happened to me. I'm sorry." The smell of smoke forced Mercury to turn toward the vampires standing before him. Conner stood smoking a cigarette, holding a piece of wood lit on fire.

"Any last words?" Conner said around his cigarette. Mercury groaned and twisted and jerked, trying desperately to break the rope. If only there was some way to remove the Thurguard from around his neck. If only he had more strength.

Conner lit the stack of wood at Mercury's feet. The tinder went up in flames and the smoke stung Mercury's eyes. Conner then walked over to Griffin and lit the pyre beneath him. He stood back and watched as the flames began to consume the wood. Griffin's cheap Target-brand tennis shoes began to melt. As Mercury felt the flames licking at his toes, he screamed and looked to the stars. When he heard Joelle scream, he glanced down to see that Conner had lit the fire beneath her.

Just as the flames rose and began to snake up Mercury's ankles, he heard the sound of gunshots. Mercury looked down and saw Ellis and Sloane standing at the edge of the field. Ellis held a shotgun in his hands.

"I'd suggest you get the fuck out of here unless you want holes in your asses," Ellis yelled. Sloane ran toward the fray with a dagger in one hand and a fire extinguisher in the other. She stabbed one vampire in the shoulder, then brought the extinguisher down hard against the face of another.

Conner snarled. He darted toward Sloane but stopped as a shotgun blast rang next to his ears. He cupped his ears with his hands.

"This isn't over," he shouted. "Not by a long shot."

"Looking forward to it, bruh," Sloane mocked. Conner and the other vampires hurried back across the street and into the motel parking lot. Seconds later, the sound of tires screeching against the asphalt rang through the air.

Sloane hurried over to Griffin and sprayed the extinguisher, vanquishing the flames. Next she stood before Mercury. He looked down at her as she sprayed the wood and all of Mercury's legs, which were already inflamed, with the extinguisher. Mercury felt a cooling sensation as the spray hit his legs. Then it disappeared and his legs were left aching. She moved to Joelle and sprayed the wood at her feet.

Mercury closed his eyes and leaned back against the wood, not caring about what happened around him, only able to focus on the pain in his legs. He heard a few more gunshots and the sound of running. Then he felt the ropes at his wrists loosen. Mercury lifted his hands and removed the Thurguard from this neck. His skin sizzled where it had been pressed against the chain. He peeled the duct tape off his mouth and fell off the pyre and onto his side. He screamed at the throbbing pain in his legs that seemed to worsen every second. Tears streamed down his face and he balled his left hand into a fist, pressing it between his teeth to keep himself from biting down on his tongue.

Ellis rushed over to him, his green eyes wide with concern.

"It's going to be okay, Merc. I've got you," he said. He took a deep breath and laid his hands on Mercury's legs.

Mercury cried out from the weight of Ellis' hands. Sloane grabbed Mercury's free hand. Joelle and Griffin, whose feet were in similar pain, lied on the ground beside him, groaning. Mercury looked over at them. Joelle sobbed. Griffin grit his teeth against the pain.

"I'm sorry," Mercury whispered. Joelle shook her head. She reached out and put a hand on his shoulder.

He felt Ellis' magic run through him. He felt the pain ease, but just barely. Ellis sat back and took another deep breath, his brows knitted with concentration.

"Did I do it? Did I heal you?" he asked frantically.

Mercury shook his head. "Not all the way."

Ellis motioned to place his hands on Mercury's legs, but Mercury stopped him.

"You've got to get the others. I'll be fine."

As Ellis hurried to the twins, Mercury rolled over onto his back and sat up. Gone was the feeling of being stabbed by knives. It was replaced with an intense throbbing, like a swarm of bees stinging him at the same time. He lifted himself into a crouching position but quickly fell back down. Sloane rushed to his side placing an arm around his neck.

"I got you," she said. She helped him up to a standing position, where the pain felt even worse. Mercury grit his teeth against it and began walking toward their car with Sloane's help. She opened the door and lowered him onto the passenger seat. Several minutes later, Joelle, Griffin and Ellis joined them. The twins had been completely healed, and Mercury was grateful. But he knew the amount of damage he sustained during the fire would require more magic than Ellis had.

Ellis slid behind the wheel without any hesitation.

"You didn't have to come back," Mercury said.

"Yeah, well, who else was going to save your sorry ass," he teased.

Mercury looked at him. "What I said, the things I did . . . I had no right."

Ellis shook his head. "You were right about one thing– I could have figured a way out this whole time. You aren't forcing me to be here. I'm here because you're my best friend and I've always got your back."

His words hung in the air as he peeled away from the abandoned lot, the sound of sirens piercing through the night.

Chapter 12

Growing more anxious by the minute, Mercury volunteered to drive the rest of the way to Astera. When they asked if he was sure, saying that he'd been through a lot that night, he shrugged off their concern and slid into the driver's seat. Yes, his legs ached with every step. Every moment he spent pressing down on the accelerator or the brake made his legs ache even more. But he knew he didn't have a choice. It was up to him to get them to Astera as fast and as safe as possible, so he dealt with the pain wordlessly.

Ellis toggled through the channels, bypassing hip-hop stations and top forty tunes to finally land on NPR. The show host, an elderly woman with a quaking yet soothing voice, listed the day's top headlines.

"Congress has confirmed the new Supreme Court justices who will take the seats of Melissa Carmichael and Allan Smitstra, who passed away earlier this month. Their replacements, Eddie Latham and Isaiah Moore, have drawn the ire of many for their pro-vampire views. The Supreme Court, now stacked with Vael's ideal candidates, will resume activity within the next few days."

Mercury's hand tightened on the wheel.

He'd always been aware of politics, having grown up in a household of two intellectually inclined, civic-minded people. He and Troian would watch CNN or C-SPAN with their parents, who would explain what was happening during each hearing or news report. The last time they had a mostly conservative Supreme Court, marriage equality was almost outlawed and a case about climate change almost never saw the light of day. Now, he was almost certain he'd have to start wearing those stupid dog tags because of Vael's Identity Act. He hoped The Witches' Council was pushing back, decrying the initiative for the hateful thing it is and insisting that it was vampires, not witches, who needed a caution label.

"The riots in Puerto Rico continue today as the newly added state protests its governor, Nuri Almada. Almada, President Vael's close confidant, and a former executive at Synthesis, is known for his extremist views on race relations, gun control and LGBTQ rights. Just last week he landed in hot water when he called a *New York Times* reporter a 'dyke' after she refused his advances."

"God, what a prick," Sloane said.

"We should have never added Puerto Rico as a state in the first place," Ellis chimed in.

"No one there wanted to be any more a part of the U.S. than they already were," Sloane replied. "And to elect this piece of shit knowing that his policies would be terrible for this place that's already full of misogynistic pieces of shit—"

"What do you expect? Vael's a monster but he's not dumb. He's succeeded in placing his cronies in almost every vacant seat. There's nothing we can do until the midterms next year," Joelle said.

"Bullshit nothing we can do," Sloane replied. "We've got to fight at the local level. Get people involved. If people don't turn out to vote or do anything, it'll be just like the 2020 election all over again."

There was silence for several moments as the host read several more news stories—the latest draft pick for the Knicks, stock exchange, an impending hurricane off the gulf coast; another serial killer apprehended by familial DNA, this time from a relative's employee drug test. Compared to their current situation, to the past week they've had, it all felt so mundane to Mercury.

"What happens to us if they pass the Identity Act?" Griffin said. "Will we be forced to wear those god awful dog tags since we've got a taste of magic?"

"I don't know," Mercury said because he didn't know. He didn't know whether humans who've gotten magic injected into their systems were considered humans or witches. Would his father even know?

They arrived at the mountain much sooner than Mercury thought they would. Each of them jumped out of the car and stretched, walked around, knowing that the plan was to sleep in the car that night and make the trek into the park early in the morning.

"How are you feeling?" Joelle asked. Mercury leaned against the car, fearful that if he tried to walk just then that he might fall. He smiled at her, trying to assuage her fear.

"I'm just fine," he said. She lifted a brow and Mercury knew he'd have to try much harder to convince her. "Really, I am. Just tired."

She leaned into him and rested a head on his shoulder. She smelled like coconut oil and sweat; Mercury's heart almost leapt from his chest.

When everyone had circled back to the car, Mercury ventured off alone to use the bathroom. He didn't want anyone to see the grimace on his face as he attempted each step.

He surveyed the darkened forest and took in the sounds. There were no cars here, no helicopters or airplanes, no motorcycles and no honking horns. The air felt different, not just pure but magical. He heard the sound of an owl, and of cicadas in the breeze. The distant sound of laughter and music wafted across the wind.

The smell of the forest was intoxicating—notes of flowers and pine made him want to venture farther into the copse of trees.

Instead, he turned toward the group and trudged back to the car. When he returned, Ellis and Sloane were already coiled up together in the first row of back seats. Griffin was stretched out uncomfortably in the rear, his long legs extended over the seat and into the trunk space. Joelle was curled up in the fetal position in the driver's seat, leaving him with the passenger.

After reflecting on their journey for a few moments, Mercury slid in and adjusted the seat back.

Joelle reached over and grabbed his hand. She squeezed it.

"Good night, Mercury," she said.

Mercury brought her hand to his lips and kissed her palm. "Good night." He closed his eyes, hoping that the worst was behind them.

That night, Mercury dreamt he was in Paris with his mother and brother. He'd only ever been once, on a study abroad trip his freshman year of college, that just happened to coincide with Astera. While there, Mercury had only been allowed to take part in the day festivals but when the music stopped and it was time for strategy, his aunt smiled and told him to focus on his school work.

In his dream, he sat on the steps of the Sacre Coeur, sipping a latte while his mother ate gelato and Troian sipped from a bottle of wine. Mercury thought his heart would burst. He knew he was dreaming but it felt so incandescent to be in the presence of his family again. He didn't care if he ever woke up.

"I miss you," Mercury said. His mother smiled, her cheeks full and the gap between her front teeth prominent.

"I know," she said warmly.

"Why am I here?" he replied, knowing that dead relatives don't show themselves in dreams unless there's a lesson to be learned.

Troian placed a hand on his shoulder. "Always searching for the why," he said. "Why does there need to be one this time?"

Mercury scoffed. "Because you're dead and the last time Mom came to me in a dream it was her roundabout way of telling me not to worry about your powers increasing before mine."

Troian leaned across Mercury and smirked at their mother.

"Fat lot of good that did– once Merc found out I could summon the dead, he skulked around the house for a few months."

"I didn't skulk," Mercury said. "And besides, I'd rather be able to see people's memories than to have to deal with the dead. Present company excluded, of course."

Their mother sighed. "I can only advise, not change behavior or outcomes– you know that."

"So what are you advising me of now?" Mercury asked. He closed his eyes, briefly feeling a breeze blow across his skin. The air smelled like ice cream cones.

"You must be discerning of this year's Astera," she said.

"Discerning?"

"Not everyone's desires are your desires; all wants are not yours."

"Can you stop talking to me like some janky fortune teller and give me a real response?"

His mother sighed again. He knew it was against the rules for her to be anything but obtuse when visiting.

"Man, just be careful," Troian said. "You've got this idea in your head that Astera will be the end of this Mr. Toad's Wild Ride you're on but it's not. It's—"

As Mercury's eyes sprung open, he felt the pain in his legs more acutely than before. He'd had them propped up on the dashboard, and now his hamstrings ached from the position. He set them down on the ground, a different yet still uncomfortable position.

"Go back to sleep; it's too early," Joelle mumbled.

He nodded even though he knew she couldn't see him. He felt so torn between his present world and the dream one. He wanted to see his mother and brother again, to be able to hold them. Already he was forgetting the exact timber of his mother's voice, forgetting the sound of Troian's laugh. But knowing that he was mere feet away from his father made his heart ache. He wanted nothing more than to get drawn up into his father's arms. Maybe then he'd finally feel like he could relax. He closed his eyes again and tried to go back to sleep, but sleep wouldn't come. Instead, Mercury just stared out the window at the slowly lightening sky thinking about his dream.

What had she meant by "be discerning?" Of course, he knew that not everyone at Astera would be on the run from a group of frat vampires. But surely they all felt the same way he did, that witches needed a seat at the table so that they could address the inequities they historically faced? Surely they wanted to improve relations for themselves with humans and especially vampires?

He didn't want to think about Troian's warning, that their journey was not the end. Though he woke up before hearing the full length of Troian's warning, he hoped he hadn't meant that it was the beginning of more shit to come.

Mercury opened his eyes and noticed the first hint of pink on the horizon.

He looked over into the driver's seat and noticed Joelle's eyes on him. A slow smile spread across Mercury's face.

"Good morning," he said.

She smiled. "Good morning."

He gestured to her and she leaned across the center console and placed her head on his shoulder.

"Did you sleep well?"

"As well as I could given the circumstances," Mercury said. He rubbed his legs.

"Are your legs feeling any better?"

Mercury shook his head.

"Is there anyone who can heal you when we get there?"

"Yes."

"You don't sound too thrilled. Aren't you excited to get to Astera?"

"It just feels so weird that we're here. This past week has been one of the most difficult times in my life. I want to see my father, but I don't know what to expect otherwise."

Joelle sighed. "I can't wait to see what Astera is like. I've heard about it for years, and I follow a few witches who openly talk about it on Twitter. And I've wanted to meet Oliana for a long time."

"I guess we better start making our way there," Ellis interjected.

Mercury turned to find Ellis and Sloane awake in the backseat. Sloane was sitting cross-legged, wiping the sleep from her eyes. Ellis slipped his beanie over his messy hair and stretched.

"Are you ready, Griffin?" Joelle called out to her brother.

Griffin grunted and sat up, his glasses hanging crookedly on his face.

"Ready as I'll ever be," Griffin said.

They stepped out of the car and followed Mercury as he trailed the sounds of music and the pull of magic. Once they reached a clearing, Mercury's eyes welled at the sight. Small tents had been set up for people–witches and humans alike–to peddle their crafts and potions and spell books.

At the end of the clearing stood a white tent in front of a great house. Mercury knew that the home was reserved for The Witches' Council and their families only. He wondered vaguely if his father's position on the council would guarantee a room for him and perhaps his friends.

"Hey, you're Mercury, aren't you?" Mercury looked up to see a trio of women standing by a tent advertising magic-laced brownies. Humans, he could tell, whose brownies were probably laced with nothing more than cocaine. Mercury nodded as they hurried over to him and the group, their cargo capri pants swishing as they did so.

"I've been following your story in the news for days. I even caught the interview of the parents," one of the women said. "You all are so brave."

She placed an arm on Mercury's shoulder. In a flash, Mercury could see that her name was Carrie and that she always fancied herself a pagan and was thrown out of her home as a teenager when her Evangelical parents caught her setting up a circle of crystals.

"Thank you, Carrie," Mercury said. He smiled at her as she gave him a confused, then knowing glance.

"Can we take a picture with you?" Carrie asked. Her two friends, both brunettes with mousy brown hair and tie-dye shirts, nodded and smiled.

Mercury glanced at his friends, who were already checking out of the conversation. Ellis had his burner phone out and was scrolling up on the screen. Griffin was coiling his dreads into a large bun, and Sloane and Joelle stood arm in arm, pointing at different tents and questioning the contents.

"Uh, I don't think it's a good idea. We can't have anything posted online, and besides, witches aren't allowed to take photos at Astera."

Carrie's mouth formed in a wide O and she nodded vigorously.

"Right, yes, okay. Of course. So sorry," Carrie said. They stood awkwardly until one of her friends grabbed a handful of brownies and thrust them into Mercury's hand.

"Here, take these. We hope you like them."

"Yes, we blessed them with calming magic. Goddess knows we need that right now," Carrie said. She chuckled and so did Mercury, though it was all he could do not to roll his eyes.

Mercury continued his walk.

Each tent he passed felt like more and more eyes followed them. Several more people gestured to them and shouted their names. There were a few who even tried to take video. Mercury knew that Oliana and The Witches' Council had set up several charms throughout the area to prevent photos and videos from taking. She did so after they allowed humans to take part in some of the Astera festivities, and after photos leaked of the Council meeting. Once these people left the park, they'd be disheartened to find that their photos and videos didn't take.

"Hey, it's those kids," someone else yelled out. Several more people approached them, and Mercury clutched the drug brownies to his chest as the crowd of humans surged toward them. He tried to run toward his friends but the surge of onlookers blocked him in. There were so many people in his face, asking about his brother, about the night of the frat party, asking if he'd been the one to start riots in the first place.

He couldn't get a word in edgewise.

He wasn't able to explain to them the magnitude of what had happened, and how he'd lost his best friend in the world because of it. Just as his anxiety threatened to overtake him, the group in front of him parted. He found his cousin, Faegan, gesturing for him to come to her.

"Hurry up, this spell won't last forever," she said.

Mercury ran toward her, hoping his friends got the hint to do the same. They followed his cousin across the field and into a white tent. Mercury paused for a moment, grateful for the silence.

"Well, I didn't know your arrival would be so interesting," Faegan said.

Mercury shook his head. "Yeah, we did all of this just so we can show up to Astera in style."

Faegan laughed and grabbed Mercury into a hug, her strength belying her Rubenesque frame. When she let Mercury go, she turned to face the group.

"What's good, Faegan?" Ellis said. Faegan rolled her eyes and smiled.

"Still getting my cousin into trouble I see," Faegan said.

Ellis clucked his tongue and brought a hand to his chest.

"Who, moi?" he said.

Faegan shook her head and patted him on the shoulder. "No need to lie to yourself." She shifted her attention to the rest of the group. "So, who do we have here?"

"This is Sloane, Griffin and Joelle." Mercury pointed to each person as he said their names.

"Guys, this is my cousin Faegan. She's a Water Hand, Communications Director for The Witches' Council, and the best dancer in Atlanta," Mercury said. Faegan scoffed and hit Mercury's shoulder, a smile on her face the whole time.

"Hello," Joelle said.

"Nice to meet you," said Griffin.

Sloane flashed a peace sign then grabbed a brownie from Mercury.

"I don't think that's a good idea," Mercury said.

"Why?" Sloane replied. "If I'm gonna meet all these new people and see some magic, I might as well be flying high while I do it."

She broke off a piece and handed it to Ellis, who shoved it in his mouth. Griffin and Joelle both shook their heads as Sloane offered the brownie to them.

"Glad you all made it in one piece," Faegan said. "I know Uncle Atlas is looking forward to seeing you."

"Can we see him?" Mercury asked.

"Well, they're in a meeting and normally don't accept visitors, but . . . I suppose we can make an exception since I know Uncle is dying to see you, and my mom is, too."

"Really? I imagine our saga has been a headache for her."

"Oh, it has." Faegan turned to walk into the great house. "But thankfully she's got an amazing Comms Director to diffuse the heat."

Faegan winked and opened the door.

The home was spartan but well-appointed. Mercury would say it looked like something out of an Ikea catalog, but he knew that even the bookend was more expensive than anything at Ikea.

They strolled through a parlor and into a long hallway, where they passed a kitchen, sitting room and bathroom before stopping at the end in front of a closed door.

"You ready for this?" Faegan said.

Mercury sighed, his emotions surging through him. He nodded and Faegan opened the door.

He expected the meeting room to be different from the rest of the home. He thought it would be where the magic happened but when Faegan opened the door, he was surprised to see that it looked just like any other meeting room he'd seen. A long marble table sat horizontally at the far end of the room. Rows of chairs were situated in front of the marble table where the main council members sat, each with a tablet or screen in front of them. Behind them a large television mounted the wall.

There were, however, more people in the room than Mercury had expected. He knew that the main council was made up of five duly appointed people—four of them represented each element and the head, or pinnacle, of the council could be any of the four elements. Each council member had a staffer or two to help them. The Council itself had several people employed to manage finances, employment, communications, and the like. All told, there were about forty people in the room.

Each person looked up from their screens as the door opened, and Mercury immediately spotted his aunt sitting in the center of the table, with his father to her right side.

"Hey, Dad," Mercury said, his voice almost trembling.

His father sat still for a moment, his chestnut-colored eyes assessing. He looked to Oliana who nodded. Atlas stood up and rounded the table, then strode down the center aisle.

What will he do? Mercury thought. *Will he hug me or slug me?* Mercury knew his father was distraught over Troian's death. He braced himself for the worst as he felt his father's strong arms sweep him up. Mercury let out a breath he didn't know he'd been holding. He whimpered, and the tears he'd been holding back flooded him.

"It's okay; you're safe now," Atlas said. He ran a hand over Mercury's hair.

Atlas pulled back and held Mercury by the arms. "You look good, despite everything," he said.

Mercury smiled. "I haven't worn a wave cap in days. It's a disaster area up there."

Atlas laughed. "I've always thought you should grow your hair out anyway."

"I told him that, too, Mr. A," Sloane said. Atlas smiled and moved over to the diminutive brunette and grabbed her into a hug.

"I'm glad you've been here to keep my son on the straight and narrow." He turned to Ellis. "And I'm glad you were there to keep him safe."

"If I hadn't taken him to that party–" Ellis said.

Atlas lifted a hand. "No point in trying to change the past. Even witches with the ability to time travel often find it a waste. What matters is you were able to save him, especially in Cape Elizabeth."

"How did you?"

Atlas nodded his head at Mercury and a look of understanding passed over Ellis' face.

"Gave Dad the highlight reel already," Mercury said.

"You must be the Whittaker twins. Griffin and Joelle, I presume?" Atlas said smiling. He grabbed Griffin's hand first then Joelle's.

"It's so nice to meet you, sir," Joelle said.

"Sir?" Atlas looked back at Mercury and winked.

Mercury blushed and looked away from Joelle.

He smelled his Aunt Oliana before she even appeared before him.

She smelled sweet, like vanilla and cinnamon. Her thick curly hair was coiled into a large bun at the nape of her neck, and she had curly tendrils of hair hanging near her face.

"Mistress Oliana," Mercury said, keeping up with Council tradition.

She clucked her tongue at him then swept him into her strong arms.

"I've been spending more time speaking to the Gods to aid in your safe travels, nephew," she said. When she released him from her embrace, she smiled at him, her teeth impossibly white.

"You've been through quite the journey, you all have. Come, let us show you your rooms where you can shower and relax for a time. Then we'll give you a tour of the grounds."

She gestured for Faegan, who stopped typing on her phone and hurried over.

"Fae, why don't you show your cousin and his friends to their rooms. We can house them on the third floor."

Faegan nodded. "Okay, Mom. C'mon, Merc, I'll get you situated."

"Oliana," Atlas said. "Would it not be prudent to introduce the group to the rest of the council?"

Oliana seemed to consider this for a moment then nodded.

"Council members," Atlas began. "I apologize for the interruption of our meeting. I'm sure some of you may remember my son, Mercury. These are his friends, who he traveled with after he escaped the recent riots in Los Angeles that unfortunately claimed the life of my other son, Troian."

Atlas' voice broke at the mention of Troian's name, and Mercury felt a hard lump form in his throat. He smiled and looked up at the other three members of the council, none of whom he recognized. They each stood and walked over to them in a line.

"I'm Effie Hyunh, an Air Hand, just like yourself," said Effie, a petite Asian woman who looked to be in her late forties. Her accented voice was low, belying her short stature. She had short salt and pepper hair and wore

166

a green floor-length dress that seemed to swallow her whole. Mercury said it was nice to meet her, hoping that his palm wasn't sweaty as he shook her hand.

"Honore Arceneaux, Earth Hand." Honore was a tall man with caramel skin, Creole features, and short curly hair parted at the side. "It's been thrilling to see your story on the news each night."

Mercury offered a tight smile, wondering why on earth he chose the word thrilling. To Mercury, the proper adjective would have been hellish.

"Encantado," said the final council member, a woman with long black hair and a prominent nose. "I'm Paloma Vasquez, Fire Hand."

"It's nice to meet you," Mercury said. Of course, he'd heard of Paloma before—she and his father had an on again off again romance, and Mercury was glad to put a face to the name.

"Encantada," Mercury replied.

Once everyone had been introduced, the group followed Faegan out of the room and back into the hallway. They took another turn and ended up at a spiral stairwell. They climbed and climbed until they reached the top staircase.

Faegan gestured to a group of rooms on the right side of the building.

"Bathroom's down the hall." She glanced at her watch. "Why don't you all freshen up and meet back downstairs in an hour?"

"Okay," said Joelle.

After Faegan trekked down the stairs, they turned toward each other.

"Who gets first shower?" Ellis said.

"Rock, paper, scissors?" Joelle proposed. Ellis nodded. They each stuck their hands in the circle and waved their hand up and down.

After three rounds, Ellis won. He grabbed Sloane's hand and rushed toward the bathroom.

"What're you—" Joelle started.

"We're saving water this way," Ellis called over his shoulder.

"Can you believe those two?" Joelle asked.

Mercury shook his head and chuckled. *This is still going to take a lot of getting used to*, he thought as he watched his two good friends walk away together.

The Freddie Karr Effect

By Cordelia Edwards

Here at *Vanguard*, we mourn the loss of a fellow journalist. *Jonquil* writer Freddie Karr was found dead in an abandoned Oakland loft Tuesday evening. He had been severely beaten, waterboarded, and had the symbol of a hexe burned into the flesh of his stomach.

Karr's co-workers at *Jonquil*, a liberal digital newspaper focusing mostly on POC culture and all things witch, first reported him missing last Thursday when Karr did not show up for work.

"Freddie was always working, even when he was sick. If he couldn't come into the office, or even if he was out chasing a lead, he always communicated," said Heidi Fields, *Jonquil*'s managing editor.

Karr's body was discovered by a local homeless man who was searching for a warm place to sleep. Eye witnesses say the homeless man walked into the building and ran out screaming. A pair of Oakland police officers were in the area handling traffic control when they were alerted of the incident.

"My partner and I approached the building skeptically because most of our homeless population suffers from mental issues or has a severe drug habit," said Deputy Sharon Barnes. "But all we had to do was peek through a window and we could see a body on the ground. That's when we called for backup."

After Karr's body was transported to the local hospital, his family was notified. Karr, who has a daughter with his husband, Marquis Jacobson, is also survived by his parents, Walter and Anna May Karr, both professors at Cornell University.

Karr's death is a shock to many in the liberal community, but we at *The Vanguard* are unfortunately not surprised.

Even before president Vael announced his candidacy, tensions between witches, vampires and the rest of us were high. And statistics show that it has only gotten worse since Vael took office, with witch-on-vampire crime rising 23%.

After the St. Basil's church massacre, which saw seventeen God-fearing vampires lose their lives that day, two other assaults occurred—one in Fort Wayne, Indiana, where a group of witches targeted a vampire exercising his free speech and wearing a "Vael Forever President" shirt. They kicked him and punched him so hard that his lung was punctured. And in Sulphurdale, a group of young witches running late for their coven meeting burned down the house of local resident Santo Manriquez.

Could Karr's death be the result of some tragic misunderstanding, or could his death have been caused by a group of witches with a vendetta? Karr was in the business of telling the secrets of witchkind for money. Could his capitalist ideals have caught up with him? Could members of his own race have killed him because he wrote too much?

Chapter 13

Two hours later, Mercury sat on the top stairs, reading the latest article from *Jonquil,* announcing the death of Freddie Karr. When Mercury saw the headline, he paused. Freddie had been his favorite writer at the online magazine, someone intellectual and witty and most importantly, a black, male witch. Though his aunt was in the spotlight and Astera had become part-tourist trap, there weren't very many known witches in the media or in entertainment, or even in sports. Freddie was someone who spoke candidly about what it meant to be black, gay and a witch in America, and how the intersection of the three things made life doubly hard.

"Damn," Mercury said. He clicked over to the Go Fund Me page that had been set up by Freddie's family, wishing he could donate. He searched for Freddie's husband, Marquis, on Facebook. He began typing a message for him when he heard footsteps.

He turned to see Ellis and Sloane emerge from the bedroom they'd claimed as their own, both smiling and holding hands. Mercury rolled his eyes in spite of himself.

"Took you two long enough," Mercury said. They'd been in the shower together for half an hour. After they exited the bathroom, Mercury took a quick shower and realized it was the first time he'd actually felt clean in a week. He dressed in the same jeans and jacket he'd had on, but he was thankful that he had a clean t-shirt and a pair of underwear in his backpack.

"Where are the twins?" Sloane asked.

Mercury gestured toward the other end of the hall, where Griffin was in the last of the spare bedrooms and Joelle was in the bathroom. They emerged minutes later and after a brief moment of silence, communicating only with their eyes, they all walked down the stairs to the ground floor.

His cousin Faegan sat at a long table, one hand on her computer and the other typing on her phone. She looked up at them and smiled.

"Oh good, you're ready. That only took you two and a half hours."

"Oh, did we really take that long? I'm sorry," Joelle said.

Faegan smirked and shook her head. "Got a goody two-shoes on our hands."

"You should see her when she's angry. She shoots fire out of her hands," Sloane smirked. There was an edge to her voice that Faegan did not pick up on.

"You a Fire Hand as well?"

Joelle shook her head. She made the move to slip the sleeve of her jacket up but Mercury stopped her.

"Where's Oliana?" he said.

Faegan looked from Mercury to Joelle then stood. "She's outside doing PR. She's got another ten minutes on this speech before the plebs, no offense . . ." Faegan said, looking at the group. ". . . get kicked off site and we can all finally let our magic hang out and get active."

She moved toward the foyer and Mercury followed.

His aunt stood in front of a semi-circle of people, many of them journalists.

"Ms. Murtaza, do you have any comment on the recent death of journalist Freddie Karr?" asked a short black woman with Senegalese twists.

"As you know, The Witches' Council has always prided itself on maintaining a mutually respectful relationship with the press, something I'm not sure all of this nation's leaders can say." Several people laughed. "And Freddie was honestly one of my favorite journos to talk to; he was so easygoing, so knowledgeable about the world. I can say that his death is a travesty and he will truly be missed. I know that myself and all the witches here send love and light to Marquis and their daughter, Imani."

Oliana gestured toward another journalist, a tall white woman with glasses half the size of her face.

"I just want to say, you're so inspirational. You should run for president or something."

The crowd cheered and whistled. Though Mercury could not see Oliana's face, he knew his aunt well enough to know her expressions.

"Can't become president if you've committed a crime."

The voice was so low that Mercury had to look around to see if anyone else heard it. He looked to his right and spotted Honore, a member of The Witches' Council, standing just far enough away from the crowd. When he saw Mercury, he lifted a hand. Mercury looked back at the group, who were still transfixed by Oliana. He walked over to Honore and stood beside him.

"Does this happen at every Astera?"

Honore scoffed. "It's a daily occurrence, especially since Oliana began opening up a few hours during the day for the plebs to come. The journalists took full advantage."

"Let me guess—you're not a fan of this tactic?"

Honore shook his head.

"I think we deserve to have something that belongs to us. I know your mother agreed."

Mercury started at the mention of his mother. "You knew my mom?"

Honore nodded, smiled. "Man, Kessia was the queen. Everyone loved everything about her—her beauty, talent; she had such sound ideals when it came to a way forward for us. She would have made a great Head of Council if—"

Honore stopped. Mercury turned back toward the crowd, trying not to look as though he and Honore were conspiring. If he'd been able to, though, Mercury would have grabbed the tall Creole by his arms and shook him.

"If?"

"Well, you know that your mother was the prime candidate to assume the position as head of the council, right?"

Mercury shook his head. He didn't know that. In fact, he had no idea that his mother had any political aspirations at all.

"So, why didn't they elect her?" he said.

Honore lifted his hand slightly and gestured toward his aunt.

"She campaigned for the position?"

"That's what some people think. Either people believe that Oliana was picked by the Gods to be the Head of Council and that no amount of politicking would have changed that. Or," Honore looked around. ". . . some people think she fought dirty, and your mother was just collateral damage on Oliana's way to the chair."

Mercury's heartbeat quickened. Was Honore suggesting that his aunt had something to do with his mother's death? Did other people feel the same way?

Just as he opened his mouth to respond, Mercury noticed Faegan standing next to his aunt. She whispered something in her ear and looked back at the group.

Oliana followed Faegan's eyes and then she looked back to the crowd. She nodded and waved her hand; Faegan didn't need another hint for her to step back.

"I'm afraid that's all the time I have today." Oliana turned as the crowd clamored for her. Several security guards served as a barrier between her and the crowd.

"Atlas, would you and your son mind joining me on the veranda?" Oliana said. Mercury's father nodded. She walked past them then turned. "Oh, and if you wouldn't mind, please bring your little friends. I hear they have quite a lot to offer."

Oliana turned on her heel without another word. His father closed the gap between them.

"Weird for Oliana to want to meet a group of plebs," Atlas said. "No offense."

Mercury swallowed hard. "I think I know why she wants to meet them."

"Oh?" Atlas asked. "Why's that?"

"Because of the ink."

They trickled back into the meeting room, and Mercury now felt dwarfed by its size. His heart beat so loud that he could barely hear anything anyone said. He looked at the group, each one looking more worried than the last.

"Did we do something wrong?" Joelle asked. Her eyes were wide and glassy.

"No, you didn't," Mercury said. *But I screwed up royally, as usual,* he thought.

"What's on your mind, Oliana?" Atlas said. He sat in the front row and draped his arms over the backs of the chairs on either side of him.

Oliana stood and crossed her hands in front of her burgundy organza dress. "It's come to my attention that these humans might be more than they seem."

Mercury stood with his arms crossed, thrumming his fingers against his forearm.

"Oh? And how is that?" Atlas asked. Mercury didn't look at his father as he tried to feign his ignorance. He wasn't good at bluffing and as Oliana raised an eyebrow, Mercury could tell she felt the same way.

"Atlas, give it a rest. You've never been good at lying, even when we were kids."

She dragged a chair and set it between the two aisles. She gestured for everyone to sit. Once they did, Oliana crossed a leg and tucked her hands into her lap.

"Now, a not-so-little birdie told me that these lovely boys and girls before me have some extra juice in their tank."

Mercury looked at each of his friends; they all eyed the ground.

Mercury shrugged. Oliana sighed.

"Look, I know you're thinking of me as the bad bitch in charge right now, and I am. But at the moment, I am just Mercury's Auntie Oliana, who just wants to get to know the friends who protected my nephew across several state lines."

As Mercury became lost in his thoughts, fearing the worst, he heard Ellis' voice break through the silence.

"I'm Ellis. And when we were in LA, we needed something to protect ourselves—so Troian suggested some modifications." Ellis lifted his sleeve and showed off the tangled branches on his wrist. Oliana's eyes widened and she smiled. She leaned forward and placed her head in her hands.

"And what about you, little mouse?" Oliana said, looking at Joelle.

Joelle smiled tightly and held out her hand, exposing the flames on her wrist.

Griffin followed suit, showing off the intricate pattern that had been etched up his forearm. When Oliana got to Sloane, she frowned.

Sloane sat with her arms crossed and mouth set in a hard line.

"Well?" Oliana said.

"I'm not showing you shit," she snapped.

Mercury gasped. From the corner of his eye, Mercury saw his father lean forward and rub his temples.

"And why is that?"

"Because this is a shake down. You're big mad because Mercury and Troian made a game-time decision to give us some power and you're trying to fake us all out. I ain't with it."

"Want me to force her?" Faegan asked.

Mercury looked up at his cousin, who leaned against the table, hands moving furiously over her iPhone.

Oliana laughed. "Well, I suppose that's it then."

She stood and rounded her chair. When she turned she extended a hand toward Sloane. Sloane yelped in pain and uncrossed her arms. Oliana closed the gap between them and lifted Sloane's sleeve. Once she saw the dagger, she looked at Mercury and clucked her tongue.

"Well, I'm afraid this puts me in quite the precarious situation."

"Oliana, please. Mercury and Troian would never have done this if they didn't think it was necessary. They know the rules of my shop very well," Atlas pleaded.

"I'm sure they do. But you see, it's always been against the rules to grant magic to humans. And given the fact that Mercury is my nephew, if I don't do anything, some people might think I'm playing favorites."

"But aren't you doing that with Faegan?" Mercury questioned. "I mean, she's got the highest pay, best insurance, PTO and amenities out of all The Witches' Council staff."

Faegan looked at Mercury and scowled.

"Nepotism toward your children is seen as your motherly duty, dear. Everyone else? Not so much."

Mercury felt his stomach churn. He didn't know what the punishment was for granting magic to humans but he knew it would be harsh.

"Well, if you're going to make an example of my son, you may as well add me to the mix," Atlas said as he stood. Oliana smiled.

"Oh, don't worry, brother. I intend to. You'll have my decision tomorrow at first meeting." She began to exit the room then turned. "But please, don't let our conversation stop you from enjoying the night's festivities. You especially, Atlas. I know Paloma is looking forward to your annual tryst."

She exited the room without another word. Mercury let out yet another breath he didn't realize he'd been holding. When Faegan passed him, Mercury grabbed her arm.

"Faegan, what the fuck? Why did you say something to her?"

Faegan jerked her arm away. "Sorry, cuzzo. Must be all that nepotism getting to my head."

She walked out of the room, her head bent and staring at her phone screen.

Mercury turned toward his father. "Dad, I'm so sorry I–"

Atlas held up a hand. "It's okay. We'll get through this."

"But this could jeopardize your position on the Council."

Atlas scoffed. "Your aunt has been gunning for my position since before she became Head. If they take me off, she'll have to deal with a lot of opposition when she announces she'll be replacing a seasoned vet with that vacuous daughter of hers. But don't let this color your evening. It's your first Astera, and you're legal now." He faced the rest of the group. "C'mon, let's go to the fete. You haven't lived until you've partied with witches."

The woods around the property had been transformed from a provincial festival to a lavish soiree. The trees were draped with silk, rich reds and oranges and golds, representing Oliana's element. Tables lined the back wall and were piled high with food and drinks.

Atlas had insisted that they all dress more presentably than they had been. He somehow managed to procure each of them a more formal outfit, and Mercury was surprised that the clothing was an almost perfect fit.

He now stood by a table lined with glasses of champagne. As Mercury lifted his arm to grab a drink, a shimmery sparkle caught his eye. He turned to see Joelle and Sloane descending the steps. They were arm in arm, and Joelle was laughing. Her long hair had been coiled into a bun on the top of her head. Her gold dress shimmered in the light of the streetlamps. Sloane's fiery red dress trailed behind her and when she reached the bottom of the steps, she wrapped the edge of the dress around her wrist.

Mercury turned to face them, straightening his black velvet smoking jacket.

"You both look beautiful," he said. Joelle smiled. Sloane rolled her eyes then smirked.

"We know," she teased. "You don't look half bad yourself."

Mercury brought a hand to the back of his head.

"Thanks, this jacket is my dad's."

"Mr. A has good taste," Sloane said. She looked from Mercury to Joelle then back to Mercury. "Well, I guess I'll leave you two alone to enjoy your meet-cute." She pulled her arm away and turned to leave. "Don't do anything I wouldn't do."

Joelle giggled as Sloane winked. She looked up at Mercury with so much care in her eyes that it brought him to tears. He leaned in and kissed her cheek.

"You look beautiful," he said.

She smiled and patted his shoulder. "You already said that."

"That's because it's true," he replied. He gestured toward the table and she nodded. He grabbed two glasses of champagne and handed her one.

"Cheers to your first Astera," he said.

She scoffed. "First and only," Joelle replied. "It seems like if your aunt has her way, we'll all be put under some jailhouse somewhere."

Mercury took another sip, his stomach twisting at the thought of what Oliana might decide. He wondered if they'd get something simple, like a fine, or if she'd do something more extreme, like stripping their powers. The thought pained him.

He shook his head, trying to rid his mind of such thoughts.

"Well, if this is to be our last Astera, let's make the most of it." He gulped down his champagne and held out his arm.

Joelle followed suit, throwing back her head so quickly that he thought her bun might collapse. She set her empty glass on the table and slipped her arm in his.

"Let's do this," she said.

They walked through the crowd. Several people were clustered in groups, some of them talking, others dancing to the music played over a loudspeaker. They passed a trio of witches who stood gazing into a ball of ice held in place by the woman in the center.

"What are they doing?" Joelle whispered after they'd walked far enough away from her.

"Divination," he said. "A witch can choose to view a certain event from the past, present or future. All it takes really is a reflective surface."

"So why ice?"

Mercury shrugged. "Because it looks badass."

They approached the edge of the clearing where there were lamps set up along the perimeter of the clearing. Couches and armchairs and side tables graced the landscape and a group of witches camped out on them. One of them was Honore, who sat in a wingback armchair. He ditched his prior baggy Hlz Blz sweater and skinny jeans for a tailored three-piece suit. His curly hair had been finger waved, giving him a more elegant appearance. On the couch beside him sat Paloma, and a woman Mercury didn't know. In the arm chair on Honore's other side sat Griffin, who held a glass of wine in one hand and looked at Honore's palm with the other.

"Griffin, you're here," Joelle said. Her twin looked up at her and smiled, his glasses catching the glare of the fire lamp.

"That I am," he said. His voice was languid, similar to how it had been when they were at the bar in Van Meter–when they were drunk. Joelle picked up on her brother's demeanor right away and approached him. She leaned down and peered directly into his face.

"Are you drunk?" she asked.

Griffin pushed her away.

"Oh, Joelle, don't be such a buzzkill."

"Griffin–"

"Jo, we're at a party! We just spent the last five days on the run and in fear of our lives. You can relax now."

Joelle stood and smoothed her dress. She looked over at Mercury, who walked closer to the group.

"Evening," he said.

"Buenas tardes, Mercury," said Paloma. "I see you clean up just as well as your father."

Mercury smiled, tight-lipped. Her eyes scrutinized him in a way that made him uncomfortable.

"Yes, well. They may say a lot about the Amell men, but at least we are snappy dressers."

Paloma laughed. "This is Shay," she said, gesturing to the woman who sat beside her. Mercury stepped forward and shook Shay's hand.

"Nice to meet you."

"You as well," Shay said, coiling a strand of blonde hair around her finger.

"Why don't you join us, Mercury?" Honore said. "I was just teaching Griffin here the art of palm reading."

Mercury tried not to groan. Palm reading was a parlor trick, typically done by Air Hands with the ability to read people's minds or memories. Countless people have fallen for the stunt, but Mercury would be lying if he said he hadn't tried to pick up a girl with the trick once.

"I think we're okay," Mercury replied. He glanced at Joelle, who was trying not to parent her brother. "We're going to grab a cocktail."

"Well, you don't know what you're missing, Merc. Griffin's life and future are fascinating. He's got success, friendship and good fortune on the map as well as, dare I say, something tugging at his heart line," Honore replied. Joelle pursed her lips and stepped toward the council member. Mercury put his arm around her waist.

"Glad to hear big things will be poppin' for ol' Griffin here. C'mon, Joelle, let's grab a drink."

Without another word he lightly pushed her to the right, where a bar stood halfway across the clearing.

As they stood in line, Mercury could feel Joelle's unease.

"You good?" he asked.

She huffed and shook her head. "Who does that man think he is? Coming on to my brother like that."

Mercury looked to the ground and crossed his arms. "Someone who has a crush on your twenty-year-old brother."

"Yeah, some man interested in some creepy May/December romance."

They stepped in line at the bar and faced each other as they waited. Mercury shook his head.

"Honore isn't old; he's only thirty-two," Mercury said. He remembered when Honore had been elected to the council and Mercury's father had commented on how good it was that they had elected a younger witch.

"We need that fresh perspective," he said.

Joelle gave him a sidelong glance. "What would a thirty-two year old want with someone that much younger?"

"I don't know." Mercury inched closer to the bar. "Sex? Someone to talk to? Love?"

Joelle scoffed, frantically shaking her head. "I don't want to think of my brother having sex," she said.

"Me neither, but as long as he's safe, shouldn't it be okay?"

"Don't tell me how to treat my brother and I won't tell you how to treat yours," Joelle's eyes widened. "I mean. Oh, fuck. Mercury, I'm sorry."

Mercury winced. For just a moment, he'd forgotten his brother's death. Even though he wasn't actively thinking about him, Mercury felt in the back of his mind that his brother was okay, that he was back in Los Angeles, kicking vampire ass, smoking weed and scarfing down burritos from La Victoria.

"That's okay," Mercury said. "I'm getting used to the fact that my brother is gone. After this is all over, I suppose Dad and I will have to figure out his funeral."

"After this is all over," Joelle said, lowering her head. "I hadn't thought about that."

"About what?"

"What to do when this is all over, and we're no longer on the run," she said. She grabbed his hand and looked into his eyes.

Suddenly, Mercury's heart began to race. What would he do when they inevitably got back to Los Angeles? Would he go back to school? Would his father rebuild his business and the only home Mercury had ever known? And what about his friends—would his relationship with Ellis, who he'd known all his life, be strained? Would he still sneak out to the beach at midnight with Sloane? Would Griffin, who still looked dazed despite all they'd been through, still want to be in Mercury's life? More importantly, would Joelle? The thought of parting ways with her made his knees weak.

"I imagine you'll probably go back to class. You're nearly done with your degree for . . ." Mercury realized he didn't know what she'd been studying.

She smirked, realizing the same thing. "Music," she said. "I play piano, guitar, bass. I'd love to find or start a band, but I've also met some people who could get me into doing session work."

"Wow, that's cool as shit," Mercury replied. He smiled on the inside at the thought of their shared love for music.

They were finally at the front of the line. He ordered himself a Sazerac and ordered Joelle a mint julep. The drinks were free, so they grabbed their glasses and walked along the grassy knoll. As they strolled they saw more magic battles, people transforming themselves into animals, others teleporting themselves to different parts of the party.

Sloane and Ellis had emerged from the woods. Now they were on the dance floor, grinding as 'Another One Bites The Dust' played. They passed Faegan and her friends, who stood at the base of the stairs, huddled next to each other. Mercury nodded at her as they passed.

"Traitor," someone called. It hadn't been his cousin, but he knew from the sound of her laugh that she endorsed the comment. Mercury refused to turn around.

"What's the matter, Merc? Couldn't find a magical honey so you had to break the law and give a human some magic?"

He felt Joelle stiffen beside him. His cousin laughed again and his anger swelled.

"'Least I'm not a coward, towing the party line," Mercury replied as he turned.

Faegan crossed her arms and rolled her eyes.

"Well, you're probably going to get your magic stripped for this, so I hope that piece was worth it," said a tall man with bright blue hair and dark skin. He draped himself against the banister, his black catsuit sparkling in the dim light.

Mercury clenched his fists, wanting nothing more than to punch him in the face, or to say a spell that would do the job even better. But he knew that it wouldn't help his cause—being violent would only make his aunt more likely to strip him and his friends of their powers.

Mercury stepped toward the man, who flinched slightly but still luxuriated on the banister. Another three steps closed the gap between them. This time the man stood, his posture tense.

"You know, my powers haven't been stripped yet and despite your bravado, I'm sure you know how much more powerful I am than you."

The man scoffed, but Mercury could see uncertainty still lingered in his eyes.

"It's true. You know it; you all know it," Mercury said, looking around the tiny group before his eyes landed on his cousin. She looked away. "I fought my way out of a vampire mob, went toe to toe with one of the most powerful witches on the West Coast, who'd also been turned into a vampire. I got the best of vampire cops, killed a few dhampirs, and was almost burned at the stake. So tell me, bro, what you got?"

The man stared at Mercury for a minute before pursing his lips and looking down at his manicured nails.

"That's what the fuck I thought." Mercury took one last look at his cousin, who was doing everything she could to avoid his gaze. He turned and grabbed Joelle's hand, leading her away from the group, away from the party and into the house.

"I'm sorry you had to see that," he said as they entered his room.

"It's okay," she replied. She sat on his bed, still clutching her half-finished drink.

Mercury sat beside her. He leaned forward and placed his head in his hands.

"Are you nervous about tomorrow?" she asked.

Mercury nodded. "I'm so sorry I dragged you all into this."

Joelle placed a hand on his back. "It's okay, truly. If it wasn't for you, I'd be slogging through classes that don't really count toward my degree. But I'm at the most magical party wearing a fancy dress, with the man I really like."

Mercury's heart stopped. He straightened his posture and looked into her eyes. "Really?"

Joelle nodded. He reached over and brushed a lock of hair from her cheek. She placed her drink down on the nightstand and pulled him into her. As their lips met, everything seemed to fall perfectly into place, even if just for the moment.

Chapter 14

Mercury was lying on his stomach, clinging to his sheets and the last bit of a wet dream when a knock sounded on his door. His eyes snapped open. He quickly sat up and instantly regretted it, his head pounding like a jackhammer. He turned to his right and looked at Joelle. She was still lying down but her eyes were open.

"Tell them to go away," she said, groggily.

Mercury lied back down, hoping that whoever was at their door would just go away if he ignored the knock. Seconds later, the knock sounded again. Mercury groaned and turned away, facing Joelle.

"Go away," he shouted. He snaked an arm around her waist and buried his face in her neck. She smelled like coconut and bourbon and Mercury never wanted to leave this place.

"Bro, c'mon we're starving," Ellis said.

Mercury didn't reply.

"C'mon, you two," Sloane urged. "We're all headed down to the front of the house. Griffin said Honore told him there'd be brunch."

Mercury shook his head and pulled the blanket up around his shoulders. Mercury groaned again when the door opened.

"Dude, c'mon. It's time you ate something other than Joelle," Ellis said. He immediately began giggling.

Mercury could hear Griffin groan, and he could sense all three of them standing in his bedroom.

"Sorry, Griff. I know she's your sister and all."

"We're all adults here. And besides, she's not the only one who was kept warm last night," Griffin replied.

Sloane let out an exaggerated gasp. Griffin scoffed and crossed his arms over his chest.

Mercury felt Joelle tense. She sat up and Mercury's head flopped on her pillow.

"You do know you could go get food on your own, right? You don't need us there," Joelle said.

"Ya, but these witches are all intimidating as fuck. I don't want to go anywhere below this floor without, Merc," Sloane said. Mercury sighed into the pillow and sat up.

"Alright, give us a few minutes to get ready," Mercury said. He gestured toward the door and the three of them left. Sloane and Ellis giggled as they walked out of the room. Griffin gave one last look over his shoulder before closing the door behind him.

"What does he mean, I'm not the only one being kept warm at night?" Joelle said.

Mercury chuckled then grabbed her hand. "Come on; let's go get dressed."

Twenty minutes later, they were ascending the stairs. The ground floor buzzed with activity. People stood clustered in tight groups, laughing and recalling the events from the night before. The front door was open, and Mercury could see his father speaking with Honore, Effie and Paloma.

"Good morning," Mercury said as he joined them. His father smiled at him, mimosa in one hand and his cell phone in the other.

"Morning, Merc," his father replied.

"Hello," Honore said.

Effie and Paloma nodded at him and while Effie looked out into the crowd, Paloma's gaze lingered on him.

"What have you and your friends been up to?" his father asked.

"We all like just woke up and got ready," Mercury replied.

His father scoffed. "I remember those days. Sleeping in 'til ten. Now, I'm lucky if I can keep my eyes closed past eight."

Paloma and Honore chuckled. Effie remained still, her arms in her jeans pockets.

"Well, I didn't want to interrupt. We were just–"

His father gestured with his mimosa, as if to say "nonsense."

"There are a lot of people here; I wasn't expecting it to be so active this morning after last night."

"Yes, well, the witches that come to Astera are already used to the lack of sleep they'll get this week, between the parties and meetings and festivals."

"And orgies," Honore said. Mercury's father looked from Honore to Paloma and smiled.

"Yes, those, too."

Mercury forced a smile. He didn't want to think about his father's predilections, even though he'd seen the string of women and men he'd brought back to their home when he first started dating after Mercury's mother passed away.

"We're going to go get food so . . ."

"I'll walk you over," his father said. He nodded at Honore and Effie, then kissed Paloma on the cheek. He knocked back his drink and set the glass down on a small high top table. "Come."

Mercury's father wrapped an arm around his left shoulder. Mercury glanced behind him, making sure his friends were following him.

"So, I hear you met some of Faegan's friends," his father said.

"Yeah. They're a colorful bunch," Mercury replied.

His father scoffed and shook his head. "Just a bunch of petty, over-sexed twerps who think they run something because of who Faegan is."

"Way harsh, Dad," Mercury said. He didn't mean it–he'd only spent a few minutes with Faegan's friends and that was enough for him.

They strolled along the exterior of the house, his father pointing to different tables set up with food.

"Have you heard anything from Oliana about our powers?" Mercury said, suddenly remembering the conversation they'd had the day before. His father moved his arm and stroked the beard growing at his chin.

"I've been schmoozing with the other council members, hoping to ensure they are all on our side."

He stood off to the side with his father as Ellis, Joelle, Griffin and Sloane stood in line at an omelet station. Mercury's eyes scanned the crowd, suddenly taking in the simplicity of the situation. He'd always dreamed of what Astera would be like—the parties, the use of magic, the decisions made that shaped witchkind. He hadn't expected omelet stations and a meat carving bar. Despite this realization, his stomach groaned. He grabbed a plate and wandered over to the waffle makers, his eyes widening as he took in more than three different cake batters and nearly twenty toppings.

He opted for the cinnamon batter. He poured the batter into the griddle then closed it and flipped it. Beside the waffle maker was a small coffee area, where a petite redhead stood, crafting lattes and speaking Portuguese.

Mercury waited until the man at the counter walked away before requesting a latte.

"I've never seen you before," the woman said.

Mercury smiled. "It's my first time here."

"Ah, a virgin," She blushed at the word.

Mercury laughed. She handed him his drink in a tall glass cup. He nodded a thank you and shifted his attention to his waffle.

As he lifted the top of the waffle maker and speared his waffle with a fork, he hesitated, feeling that all too familiar feeling. He then looked up, and that's when he saw them.

The vampires stood at the edge of the clearing. Many of them had signs; some of them had weapons. They stood in a line looking every inch the group ready for battle. Several steps in front of them stood Conner, hat backwards, sunglasses on, that same shit-eating grin on his face from the first night Mercury saw him. Was he really seeing this right now?

Mercury searched for his father, for Ellis and the rest of the group. They were on the other side of the porch, their vision of the impending mob scene blocked by a large pillar and a group of people.

He didn't know what to do. Should he grab his father and the rest of the council? Should he run and try to dispatch of Conner himself? He knew that he'd never survive the entire mob, but at least he could cut the proverbial head off the snake.

"What's going on out there?"

Mercury turned and noticed the barista staring at the group of vampires, her hand on her hip.

"Are they really coming here to protest?" said another woman to Mercury's left. As more and more people began to notice the growing crowd of vampires in the clearing, Mercury's heartbeat quickened.

He dropped his coffee and rushed over to the table where his father was telling his friends a story about the time Mercury flushed his glasses down the toilet.

"I mean, the look on his face when he came in to tell me and his mother what happened . . . I couldn't stay mad at him after that." His father looked at Mercury, his eyes glazed over from the champagne. He smiled and tried to put an arm around him. Mercury swatted it away. "Hey, Merc, what–"

"Dad–"

"Now c'mon, I know that you're probably not a fan of me telling your friends about what happened when you were young, but–"

"No, Dad, we have a problem," Mercury said as he tried to pull his father toward the awning and the group of people. He stayed rooted in place, telling Mercury not to be so rough with his suit, didn't he know it was Versace?

"Dad, shut the fuck up. There's–"

A scream rang out through the clearing. Everyone went silent. Mercury spotted Conner gripping onto a woman. He had one hand around her waist and the other at her neck. His fangs dug deep into her neck, blood spurting from the wound.

"They fucking followed us?" Sloane said as she stepped beside Mercury.

"There are so many of them," Joelle said, a hint of worry in her voice.

"I thought this place was warded against them?" Griffin asked.

They all looked at Mercury's father, whose joviality had faded. Now, Mercury could see the warrior his father had always been. He removed his suit jacket and rolled up his sleeves, preparing for battle.

"One of you, go inside and find the other council members. Tell them the West has been breached. They'll know what that means."

Griffin rushed inside without a word. Mercury looked toward his father who had already ascended the steps. Mercury turned toward Ellis, Sloane and Joelle.

"You all stay here. I'll handle this."

"Bullshit, Mercury," Ellis said. "There are too many of them. No way you and Atlas can kill them all."

"This is my mess—"

"No. This is ours," Joelle said. She clenched a fist and fire weaved its way up her arm. Sloane ejected her knives, the silver blades glinting in the sunlight. As Mercury approached the mob, he began to see other witches joining him— the barista, the blue-haired man from last night, the security guards who'd been at the house and so many more.

Somehow, Honore, Paloma and Effie had caught up to them with Faegan trailing behind them. His aunt was nowhere in sight.

They met the mob halfway across the field, each side lining up like every war movie in antiquity.

"If it isn't my friend Mercury," Conner said. His mouth was still covered in blood. His eyes were dilated and his pale skin was flush, though it would only last for a moment.

"I thought you'd take the hint back in Cape Elizabeth," Mercury said.

"Oh? And what hint is that?"

"That we'll kick your ass." Mercury prayed that his voice wouldn't sound as nervous as he felt. He hoped he sounded strong, but the sight of the vampires before him made him feel faint.

Conner laughed. "Kick my ass? The only reason why you didn't get burned alive is because your human friends came to your rescue, witch."

Mercury's mouth went dry. He looked around, wondering where Oliana, the Head of The Witches' Council, the head bitch in charge, could possibly be.

"You know you're not welcome here," Mercury's father said. "I suggest you leave this place before you lead this group of yours to their deaths."

"I highly doubt that. And maybe you should think twice about me not being welcome here." Conner took several steps, attempting to close the gap between himself and Mercury's father.

Mercury looked from his father to Conner. His father seemed unbothered, bored at the audacity of this young vampire. He gestured toward Conner and said a spell, rooting the vampire in place.

Conner growled and looked up at Mercury's father. "You'd better let me out of this spell or—"

Mercury's father laughed. "Or what? You'll bore me to death with your broitude?"

Conner narrowed his eyes, a low growl emanating from his throat.

"I said let me out of this spell, or I'll–"

Conner was knocked to the ground as a vampire dressed in a three-piece suit with slicked back hair rushed toward the witches gathered before them. He lunged at Honore, who waved his hand in an arc. The vampire crumbled to its knees as thick vines snaked their way up his body.

Mercury glanced back at the fray, at the vampires eyeing each other and seemingly getting bolder. Another vampire rushed toward them, and another.

The mob of vampires sprinted across the field until their bodies connected with the witches on the front line.

Mercury barely had time to move before he was tackled by two vampires, a pair of snarling blonde college girls. He grunted as he pushed one of them onto the ground beside him. She was on him again, quicker than he realized she would be.

"Beholmbe," he whispered. The spell sent the vampire to the ground again, seizing and sputtering.

Now that only one remained, it was easy for him to dispatch her. He lifted both hands and pushed her far enough away from him that he was able to grip her neck with both hands. He twisted his wrists and let his power add the force he needed to snap the vampire's neck.

He tossed her aside and stood, his head spinning as he did so.

He then looked to see Sloane on the back of a vampire, bringing one of her blades in and out of the vampire's neck. At their feet lied Effie, clutching at the bite on her cheek and moaning.

Mercury didn't bother trying to help–the vampire infection spread fast and by the time he'd get to her, it was likely she'd either be dead or close to turning.

Mercury turned his attention to the twins, who were battling the other frat boys who'd traveled across the country with Conner.

He rushed toward the group and pulled a vampire off of Griffin just as it was about to sink its teeth into his neck.

Griffin grunted and stretched out a hand. He let out a scream as he used his power, turning the vampire's teeth into paste. The vampire wailed and clutched its jaw.

"And what, motherfucker?" Griffin said, taking a step toward the vampire. The man sprinted toward the woods, wailing over his missing teeth.

Joelle tossed a fireball over Mercury's shoulder. He turned just as the creature burst into flames.

"Thanks," Mercury said. Joelle blew him a kiss and faced the other UGN bros.

Amongst the magic and the blood and the chaos, Mercury spotted Faegan. She'd been cornered against a pillar by a trio of vampires.

Mercury ran, quickly closing the distance between himself and the vampires before he waved them away. They fell away from Faegan just enough for her to shift and have an opening. She grabbed one by the neck, injecting it with silver. The vampire shuddered and fell to the ground, lifeless.

She conjured balls of ice and hurled them at the vampires before Mercury used his power again, sending the vampires flying into the battle.

Before Faegan could say anything, another vampire was upon her. Mercury was about to interject when he looked across the field and spotted his father fighting Conner. The two were besting each other, each one having drawn blood.

This one is mine, Mercury thought. He rushed toward them, stepping between his father and Conner just as the vampire attempted to land an uppercut.

"Mercury," his father said.

"This one's mine," Mercury said, not bothering to apologize for the edge in his voice. He punched Conner in the nose, breaking the bone instantly. By now the vampire was more creature than human, unfazed by the wound. Mercury landed another blow, this time splitting the skin above Conner's left eye. In the distance he heard his father fighting, heard his friends fighting.

He looked up to see Sloane on the ground, using all her strength to keep a vampire away from her. Beside her, Ellis punched another vampire trying to inch toward her. Just as the vampire that had pinned Sloane was about to dig its fangs into her neck, Mercury felt a sharp pain in his own.

Conner had bitten him, and now he grinned as his blood mixed with Mercury's.

"Mercury!" He heard his father cry. But his voice was distant.

Mercury's ears rang. His head swam. Black spots danced across his vision and his heartbeat raced. He groaned as his stomach was wracked with cramps. His legs buckled beneath him.

Conner punched Mercury again, sending him to the ground.

"I've been looking forward to this moment all week. I guess it really is Sunday Funday," Conner said.

"Douche," Mercury whispered. The vampire punched him again, the ringing sound in Mercury's ears growing louder. As Conner went in for the kill, Mercury screamed.

He brought his hands up over his face and turned away.

Suddenly, he felt warm.

Suddenly, he heard Conner scream.

Mercury looked over and saw the flames emanating from his own hands. Conner jumped back, desperately trying to pat out the fire that licked at his torso and arms.

Mercury stood.

He ignored the aching in his body, the nausea, the feeling of being so hot that he could claw his skin off, and breathed deeply.

He looked Conner in the eye and repeated the spell he'd used only once.

"I call upon Wadet, I call upon Oya," Mercury began, his voice quivering. His throat tightened and Mercury coughed. "I call upon the souls of my ancestors burned. Salt in the wounds, lead in the belly, fire burn bright. Let the fire burn away the hate, leaving only what is pure."

Conner dropped to the ground, his skin blistering and blood spilling from his eyes and ears and mouth. He wailed in pain and convulsed.

As his skin blackened, his cries grew quieter until they ceased.

Feeling what little remained of his energy draining from his body, Mercury fell face first on the ground, his vision going black.

"Is he going to be okay?"

"He will if we can get this on him fast enough."

"Oh my God, he's burning up."

"Get that towel on him. Ellis, can't you heal him?"

"It doesn't work like that, Sloane. Not for this disease."

Mercury heard bits of a conversation, his eyes still closed. A sharp pain pulsated behind his right eye, and he felt simultaneously hot and cold. He wanted to curl into a ball, his nausea so intense that it was almost worse than the actual headache and body aches he felt.

He opened his eyes but didn't recognize his surroundings.

He was in a dimly lit room, lying down, his shirt off and his lower half covered.

His father leaned over a black doctor's bag, his glasses on and his lips pursed.

In the corner of the room, Ellis, Sloane and the twins stood. They all looked scared, and Joelle was crying.

What happened? Mercury thought. Suddenly his thoughts rushed back to the present.

"Did we win?" Mercury said, his voice croaking.

His father looked up at him and smiled. "We did, because of you," he said. He lifted his tattoo gun from the kit.

Mercury's heartbeat quickened.

"Will this work?" Ellis asked, his arms around Sloane.

"It should. But I'll need the time and space to work."

"But we can't leave him," Joelle said.

"This particular tattoo can be . . . dangerous. I don't want you here in case it fails. Now go. Go!"

Mercury's head flopped to the side and he watched as his friends walked out of the door, Ellis casting one last look before closing the door.

"Okay, pup. Just relax." He shifted his gaze to his father.

Mercury then heard the sound of the tattoo gun buzzing before he lost consciousness again.

Chapter 15

Mercury's eyes snapped open.

Where am I? He thought. The room was quiet, dark. He didn't know what day it was or how long he'd been out. *What happened?*

He remembered fighting the vampires–remembered saving Faegan and watching as Sloane struggled against a vampire while Ellis fought to get to her side.

He remembered stepping in between his father and Conner.

Then there was the bite. The pain, acute and burning, in his neck. He jumped up. A sharp pain in his chest made him gasp. He set his feet down on the ground slowly, trying to determine where he was by the texture of the ground.

It was carpet–and he'd been lying on a bed.

Was he in his bedroom? Was he there by himself?

He stood.

His legs were sore but he no longer felt like he'd topple over. A pain lingered behind his left shoulder blade. It even hurt to let his hand rest by his side. He wrapped his arm around his stomach and shuffled around the bed, one hand out feeling for the curtains.

When his hand touched the textured fabric, he gripped the curtain then pulled.

Sunlight poured into the room, and he brought his other hand up to shield his eyes. The light seemed too bright for it to be the same as before. Had he really been asleep for a whole day?

Mercury tried to recall if he had any dreams, but all he could see in his mind was darkness.

Still, he felt that sharp pain in his chest.

He looked down and discovered the source of the pain, an intricate design in green ink. He couldn't recognize the symbol completely–it looked like the healing rune he'd used on Ellis, but there was another element that he didn't recognize.

He had to find his father, find his friends.

His breath hitched when he thought of his friends–had Sloane survived? Had the rest of the vampires killed the other witches? How many witches died in the fight?

Mercury grabbed a shirt and slid his feet into his Reeboks, the fabric stained and worn.

He opened the door and listened for any activity.

He then walked down the stairs and paused on the second floor. There was silence.

After a few moments passed, he continued to the first floor where he found the group sitting outside the council room.

"Mercury!" Joelle shouted. She ran toward him and leapt into his arms.

He grunted then brought her closer to him. He caught her lips in his and kissed her deeply.

"I was worried about you–we all were," she said.

Mercury looked at the group, each of them standing and wearing matching expressions of relief.

His gaze settled on Sloane and his heart swelled. Joelle followed his gaze and stepped back.

Mercury closed the gap between them and pulled Sloane into a hug.

"I thought you had been killed," he said, relieved.

"Well I wasn't, but you're about to choke the life out of me."

"I'm sorry," he said. He stepped back and looked from her to Ellis and Griffin.

He hugged each of them.

"Glad you didn't get dead," Ellis said.

Mercury shook his head. "What happened?"

"Well," Sloane started. ". . . you got bit by that bitch ass Conner, and then you flamed him and you passed out. We grabbed you and brought you to the house, where your dad gave you the coolest tattoo ever, and then you passed the fuck out, again."

"I flamed him?"

"Yeah, it was so cool. I've never seen you use fire before," Ellis said, clearly in awe.

Mercury didn't respond but his pulse raced. He hadn't used fire before because he'd never had the ability. No Air Hand did—fire was not his element, yet somehow he'd manifested it.

"What happened with the other vampires?"

"We killed so many of them, the rest just turned tail and ran," Griffin said.

"We killed them," Joelle exclaimed. "We did it! We're free."

Mercury smiled but he didn't feel relieved. He turned his attention to the door behind them. He could hear the sound of people speaking but couldn't make out the words.

"What's happening in there?" He nodded toward the door.

Joelle shrugged. "They said we aren't allowed in there, since we're humans."

Mercury rolled his eyes. "For fucks sake." He pulled the door open and the room went silent.

Oliana, Faegan, Paloma and Honore sat at the long Council table. His father sat in one of the chairs across from them, his arms crossed. He glanced back when Mercury walked in and balked.

He stood and walked toward him, sweeping him into a hug. Mercury breathed in his father's scent, amber, sandalwood and peppercorn.

"I knew you'd survive this," his father said.

"What did you—"

His father shook his head. "Later. We can catch up later and I'll regale you with tales of your friends' bravery."

He spoke the last part louder. Oliana rolled her eyes.

"Mercury, I'm so happy that you're okay," she said.

"I'm sure you are," Mercury replied. He turned to face his friends, who stood at the entrance. He waved them in.

"Mercury, this is official Council business."

"Since I'm sure you're talking about stripping our powers, they should be here to defend themselves."

Oliana sighed.

"Very well. The council was just about to vote."

"Well then, I hope the council takes into consideration our bravery and the fact that we kept Astera safe."

Oliana scoffed then stood. She walked to the front of the table and leaned against it, her long legs seeming endless in the black jumpsuit and black pumps she wore.

"I hate to be a bitch here—"

Mercury's father laughed. "You never hate being the bitch, Oliana."

She narrowed her eyes and smirked at him. "You're right, Atlas. I don't hate it. I also don't hate to say that while your fantasy of yesterday's events is that you kept us 'safe,' the reality is that you were simply cleaning up your mess."

The fire in Mercury's belly roared to life. He clenched his hand, suppressing the urge to send a fire blast in his aunt's direction.

"Is that what you were doing when you had my mom cremated before she could have an autopsy? Cleaning up your mess?"

Oliana's eyes narrowed.

"Asshole," Faegan called.

From the corner of his eye, Mercury noticed Faegan stand and stride toward him. As she did, an ice ball formed in her hand. She lobbed it at Mercury, but he dodged it. He flung his hand to the side, pushing his cousin back against the Council table.

"Looks like the girls are fighting," Honore said as he glanced at Paloma. She giggled and learned forward in her chair, resting her head in her hand.

Faegan stepped forward and lifted a hand.

Mercury planted his feet and stood at the ready.

"Enough of this," Oliana called. "I won't have you turn this meeting into a brawl. Mercury, despite what you might think, I am on your side. I do love you. But rules are rules—witches are not supposed to bestow magic on

196

humans, even if the application would save lives. We must now take a vote to see if your powers will be stripped."

Oliana seated herself behind the table in the center. Faegan settled in beside her, huffing about her hair and fussing with her top.

"Mercury, would you please join your father? Your friends, I guess, should also be seated."

The group shuffled in behind Mercury, each one filling in the front row.

Another witch that Mercury didn't recognize entered the room. He was a tall, lithe man with pale skin and ice-blonde hair. He wore a three-piece grey suit despite the warmth outside.

"All, this is Bati. He's filling in for Atlas, who cannot vote in matters that pertain to himself and his kin."

Bati nodded and sat beside Paloma.

"The Council will now come to order. Each member is allowed a brief statement as to why we should strip the powers of the group before us," Oliana said.

Mercury bristled at his aunt's statement, noticing she failed to acknowledge the option for them to keep their powers.

"I acknowledge that you, Mercury, felt a deep need to save your friends from a vampiric attack. After all, it was your decision to harm Delanie Sanders that put them in their precarious position in the first place." Oliana looked at Mercury pointedly, smirking. "But one of the rules that have kept witches safe and our kind pure is that we are not to bestow magic on any human. You and your father have broken this rule, and as such I vote to strip your powers immediately. Honore?"

Mercury's heartbeat was so rapid that he could hear it reverberating in his ears.

Honore cleared his throat. "Merc, I know that you know you fucked up. Right?"

Mercury nodded.

"Can you please state your answer?"

"Yes."

"Good. You used a spell too powerful for your young self to comprehend the weight of, which resulted in a gaggle of vampires coming to collect. If this were any other situation, I would agree with Oliana and insist that you all lose your powers. But," Honore looked from Mercury to Oliana and back. ". . . I've seen what you can do. I know that your powers are unique and deserve to be fostered. I think you're designed for great things, Mercury Amell, and your clique should be there to support you. I vote against stripping your powers."

"That was surprising, Honore. But this is a democratic process, after all. Paloma?" Oliana motioned for her to speak.

"Well, I would be lying if I said I was not partial to Atlas and the others before me. I know that as council members it is our job to uphold the rules. However, I've always felt that we should not be working to hold fast to the old ways and to try and keep our magic from humans. For so many years–"

"Paloma, does this rambling have a point?" Oliana interjected. Paloma pursed her lips and looked down. Honore looked from Paloma to Oliana and raised a brow, but said nothing.

"It does, Oliana, and that is that this rule is bullshit. The original intent behind the rule was to prevent witches from being identified. And guess what? That's happening already. Perhaps having more people with magic would help tip the odds in our favor so that our people can stop being killed by vampires. I say let them keep their powers."

Oliana scoffed and rolled her eyes.

"Fine, Paloma. That's two for allowing the group to keep their powers. Faegan, darling?" Oliana grabbed her daughter's hand and held it.

"I don't have much to say, so I'll make this brief. I think there's been a blatant abuse of power and disrespect for this council by the group before us."

Mercury's father scoffed.

"Is that funny to you, Atlas?" Faegan said, her voice rising.

"What's funny to me, my dear niece, is your sudden self-assuredness."

"Oh, yeah?"

"Yes," Atlas said. Mercury placed a hand on his father's shoulder, trying to get him to calm down. He pushed Mercury's hand away. "You don't know shit about shit, you sheltered brat. The fact that you're on this council now is what's disrespectful, as it's blatant–"

"Brother," Honore said. He tilted his head and lifted a brow. "Let us not create more issues for this council to deal with. We are here to address powers, not our leader's questionable decision to add her daughter to our non-partial council."

Oliana narrowed her eyes at Honore. He returned her glance, his face blank, and shrugged.

"Well, that's two against two. Bati, please bring some sense back to this room."

Bati chuckled. "Well, Oliana, I've not had the pleasure of meeting the group before us, aside from dear Atlas, of course," Bati said, his accent clipped. "But from what I've observed, they seem to be people who genuinely care about each other and those around them. I think Mercury's decision was foolish—and I truly believe he will have to live with the consequences of his actions for the rest of his life."

"Thank you, Bati, I'm so glad you agree—"

"Oliana, I was not finished. I believe that Paloma and Honore are right. We are living in troubled times—just the other day, a group of witches were accosted in Reykjavik. Vael's influence is bleeding into the countries around us. Now is not the time to lose valuable members of our community. And I feel that, especially Mercury and Atlas, they are valuable and will be essential in shaping our future. So, Councilwoman Murtaza, I do not support stripping the powers of the group before us."

Mercury gasped, despite himself. He looked at his father, who seemed just as relieved as he was.

Mercury opened his mouth to speak but his father put a hand on his shoulder. Mercury looked at him and shook his head. They both turned to Oliana.

Her lips were pursed and her eyes were narrowed. She had her hands steepled beneath her chin, her long, black nails mirroring ink spills. Silence filled the room. Everyone looked at Oliana with baited breath. Would she accept the decision? Would she pull rank and decide to override them all?

Finally, she spoke.

"Well, the Council has spoken and decided that Atlas Amell, Mercury Amell, Ellis Hall, Sloane Salvanera, Griffin Whittaker and Joelle Whittaker will not be stripped of their powers. A foolish decision, to be sure, but one I must honor nonetheless." She gazed at Mercury, her dark eyes boring into him. "I hope you enjoy the rest of your time at Astera and that you have a safe trip back to LA. This meeting is adjourned."

They all stood and Mercury received a hug from each member of the group. When he finished, he grabbed Joelle's hand and they strolled up the aisle.

"Mercury," Oliana called. Mercury stopped and sighed. He faced the front of the room, where Oliana stood.

"I would hate for you to take this decision as permission to continue to break Council rules. I hope that your father is able to better guide you now."

"Oh, Oliana," Atlas said. "Your concern is so heartwarming. I'm sure my son and his friends will be paragons of goodness henceforth."

"Good. I'd hate to have to call another vote. The next one might not end in your favor."

Her gaze shifted from Atlas to Mercury before she hurried off, leaving Mercury wondering if the next time might be much sooner than expected.

The next day they were on a plane flying back to Los Angeles. They were in first class, paid for by the Council. The plane was full of west coast witches who had attended the event. Most were sleeping, trying to rid themselves of their hangovers before returning to normal life.

They all were more quiet than normal. It forced Mercury into his thoughts, which made him all the more anxious. The last thing he remembered on the news about Los Angeles was another riot, almost as big as the Rodney King riots in the early 90's. His father's shop was ruined, not to mention they had no idea where Troian's body was.

His father sat beside him, glasses on, reading a book about Nicolas Copernicus.

Joelle sat to his left, leaning against the window. She slept, her mouth open and her hair wild. Mercury's heart swelled, and he couldn't help but feel lucky that she chose him.

He peered across the aisle, where Griffin, Sloane and Ellis sat. Ellis was asleep and Griffin had his headphones on. Sloane, ever the media maven, scrolled up and down on her phone.

Mercury had barely turned back in his seat when she called out: "What the fuck?"

Mercury stared at her. She looked from him to the aisle behind him and mouthed sorry. She undid her seatbelt and crawled over Ellis who groaned as she moved over him.

"Sorry Mr. A, Merc. Have you guys seen this?"

Mercury's father closed his book and set it in his lap. Mercury read the headline and his heart sank.

"Witches' Council Head Oliana Murtaza Strikes Peace Deal with President Vael–American Witches to Receive Their Own Land."

"What does that even mean?" Mercury said.

His father sighed. "I suspected she might do this. She plans to take all the witches in America and move them to a larger area, like Alaska or Montana, or something."

"Why?"

"She wants witches to be their own governing body. Believe it or not, a lot of people agree with her."

"What's up with this separate but equal bullshit? We should be fighting for equality, true equality, not trying to hide ourselves away."

His father studied him, one eyebrow up.

"Mercury, I completely agree. But I'm not the head of The Witches' Council. To be honest, I'm not even sure I'm still on the Council."

Mercury was silent. Inside he was seething. What sense did it make to run away, to tuck tail in isolation? Mercury knew there was also no way Vael would properly honor their agreement. He knew he needed a scapegoat and without witches, vampires would soon be the targets. *This can't happen,* Mercury thought. *I won't let this happen.*

"We've got to do something."

"What do you have in mind?" Atlas asked.

Joelle, Griffin and Ellis stirred, staring at them in bleary-eyed wonder.

"We're going to fight this," he said. "Are you all with me?"

"I'm sorry–what are we doing?" Ellis asked.

Mercury rolled his eyes.

"God, don't you ever pay attention?" Sloane said. "Oliana wants to send all the witches to like a reservation, where only the laws of the Council apply."

"I'm confused as to why this is a bad thing?" Ellis replied.

Griffin sighed. "It's a bad thing because she's a tyrant, and because we shouldn't be fighting for separation; we should be fighting for equality."

"I mean, but this won't happen for years, though, right?" Ellis asked.

"Didn't you see how quickly the Council house came down at the end of Astera? With all the witches channeling their energy, something like this could happen sooner than you think," Mercury's father said.

"So what are you going to do about it?"

Sloane gave Ellis a sidelong glance.

"I'm sorry, what are 'we' going to do about it?"

Mercury didn't know the answer. His friends all eyed him, as well as his father, and even some of the other passengers who'd overheard.

"I say we protest." Mercury raised his voice. "Take to the streets, take the fight to them. There shouldn't be any separate but equal bullshit. I thought Oliana was going to be the one to bring equality to us, but it looks like we're going to have to do it ourselves."

The first class section erupted in applause. Someone had a phone out, no doubt planning to post the video on an Instagram story.

"What about what you said to Oliana, Mr. A? About Mercury and us abiding by the rules?" Joelle said.

Mercury's father shrugged. "Honey, I only said that so she'd shut up. She's been disliked by the community for years; even half the Council is fed up with her. It's time she's knocked down off her Swarovski-crystal studded pedestal anyway."

Once the plane landed, Mercury dreaded facing the backlash that would surely follow his return to LA. Much to his surprise, several people rushed up to Mercury as they exited the plane and as he made his way out of the terminal. Some of them wanted pictures, others wanted to add him on Twitter so that they could help plan the protest. *I guess I should get used to this, too.*

As they walked out of LAX and into the California sunshine, Mercury pulled out his phone and opened his notes app.

"Too many people are happy with the status quo. Too many people are happy with the idea that witches are separate yet equal to humans. The recent peace deal brokered by Vael and Councilwoman Murtaza is just another way for vampires to discriminate and continue their hate. But we're tired of being killed, of being silenced, and of being told to be okay with the bare minimum. The revolution is coming–and like Gil Scott-Heron said, "the revolution will not be televised."

He uploaded the note to Twitter with the hashtags revolution, all you protest kids and separate is not equal.

Then he slipped his phone into his pocket and grabbed Joelle's hand feeling something he had never felt before– fearless.

IOS Press Relase

America, we love you. We love your blue skies and your purple mountains majesty. We love your cities, glimmering metropolis' that put Babylon to shame. We love the people who you've born and the revolutions you have sparked.

It is because of this love that we must say: girl, you're in danger.

You elected a man with a smart mouth and tongue slick with the blood of his victims. This man and his ilk have not only uncovered the hatred for witches that had been tamped down since the Salem Witch Trials but also nurtured it and fed its snarling and snapping mouth with the blood and tears of so many. He has elected two Supreme Court justices who not only see his vitriol as justified but also as patriotic. In the span of five months, not only have they passed the Identity Act, but they've stripped funding for colleges with a majority magical student body. They have insisted that witches are unfit for the military, for the C-suite, for the very world we live in.

There once was a woman, thought to be a savior. She was special, a graceful black woman who'd assumed the highest office in all of witchkind. "There she is," witches would say. "She's the one who will lead us to equality." But when she had the chance to meet with the undead man in the White House, she decided that the solution was not equality but separation. That witches need not worry about fitting into modern society because we'd make our own. Not only does this decision mean that those who choose to stay outside of her bubble will still be persecuted, but it means she will create a village in her own image, with laws and rules that are easily broken.

America, we must save you. We must break these chains and help you rise up against these evils. Too many people are comfortable with the status quo. Too many people would rather be comfortable and oppressed than uncomfortable and free. Will you join us, America? The revolution is now, and it "will not be televised."

Sloane Salvanera

The revolution begins in a city near you on May 15th. #revolution #allyouprotestkids #separateisnotequal

CPSIA information can be obtained
at www.ICGtesting.com
Printed in the USA
LVHW090118090421
683868LV00005B/1122